You can return this item to any library but please
note that not all libraries are open every day.
Items must be returned on or before the due date.
Failure to do so will result in overdue charges.
Items may be renewed unless requested by
another customer, in person or by telephone, on
two occasions only. Your membership card number
will be required.
Please look after this item – you may be charged
for any damage.

Headquarters:
Education, Culture & Community Learning,
Town Hall, Bournemouth BH2 6DY

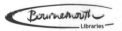

Sword of Darkness

Sherrilyn Kenyon
writing as
Kinley MacGregor

PIATKUS

PIATKUS

First published in Great Britain in 2008 by Piatkus Books
This paperback edition published in 2008 by Piatkus Books
First published in the US in 2006 by Avon,
An imprint of HarperCollins*Publishers*, New York

A CIP catalogue record for this book is available from the British Library

ISBN 978-0-7499-3872-7

Typeset in Times by Action Publishing Technology Ltd.
Printed and bound in Great Britain by Clays Ltd, St Ives plc

Papers used by Piatkus Books are natural, renewable and recyclable
products made from wood grown in sustainable forests and certified
in accordance with the rules of the Forest Stewardship Council.

Mixed Sources
Product group from well-managed
forests and other controlled sources
www.fsc.org Cert no. SGS-COC-004081
© 1996 Forest Stewardship Council

Piatkus Books
An imprint of
Little, Brown Book Group
100 Victoria Embankment
London EC4Y 0DY

An Hachette Livre UK Company
www.hachettelivre.co.uk

www.piatkus.co.uk

Dear Reader,

The Lords of Avalon started while I was in college, working on a paper about the Celtic origins of the Arthurian legends and how they were woven into the Courtly Love movement. Later, that paper became a thesis of how Celtic lore was the basis of the entire Courtly Love movement and not Arabic poetry as has been suggested.

Those years of research set fire to my imagination. As I continued my work, I began to wonder what happened after Arthur's death. Surely such magic didn't just die . . . Surely such evil didn't die. No, it had to have lived, and with that seed of an idea, their world exploded.

Not since I started my Dark-Hunter series have I been so captivated by the vibrancy of my characters. They have completely seized my imagination, and I hope they enthrall you as well.

Thanks for taking this journey with me.

Sherrilyn Kenyon

Prologue

Long ago in a land that was lost in anarchy, there was an enchanted sword that had been forged by the hands of the fey. Imbued with their power and nurtured by the soul of the goddess Britannia, the sword was said to grant immortality and superhuman strength to any who wielded it. Even the scabbard that protected the sword was special. So long as a man wore it strapped to his hips, he would never bleed.

It was a sword that could not be broken. Nor could it be defeated.

But as with all things of great power, there were those who feared it. Those who sought to destroy this sword, only to learn that nothing forged by the fey could be destroyed by mere mortal hands. Fearful of who would one day command its magic, its owner sent it out into the world with a sole guardian who imbedded it deep into a boulder. For years it lay fallow in the heart of the darkest forest of Britannia, unseen and unknown, and protected by a spell that would allow only one person of special birth to draw it forth from its resting place.

They hid it well, hoping that it would be lost to the world of man forever.

And so it was until the day when a young man happened upon it.

Born to a peasant mother who was known to despise and resent him, he was nothing remarkable. He was just a lad in the height of his youth, trying to survive the harshness of his life. One in need of a sword to protect himself from those out to harm him, and lo and behold, there in the deep, dark, overgrown forest was a sword he might use.

Grasping the rusted hilt of it, he gave a yank, praying with all his heart that it would come free so that he could fight those who sought him.

The sword refused to move.

He could hear the thundering hooves crashing through the brush as his enemies came closer and closer still. They would be upon him at any moment, and he would be beaten or worse.

They would kill him.

Terrified, the sweaty, breathless boy, dressed only in filthy rags, wrapped both of his grimy hands around the rough hilt and heaved with all his might. Suddenly a surge of painful power went through him. It felt as if his hands were now melded and forged to the rusted hilt that turned to gold underneath his hands. The sword's power crept through his body, invading him, hurting him.

The gold on the pommel parted slowly to reveal a red dragon's eye. It stared at him for a full heartbeat as if measuring his worthlessness.

Then with a resounding scrape of metal that echoed through the dark, cursed forest, the sword came free. The boy cried out as the bittersweet pain seized his heart.

The blade of the sword glowed red, then turned to fire. It cast its fey light on those in pursuit of the boy, striking them down instantly where they stood. Men before the light touched them, they became nothing more than smoldering piles of ash.

The fire vanished from the blade that still glowed as if it were a living creature. With its red light shining brightly in the dim foliage, the sword seemed to sing like a dragon cooing to its young. The boy held the sword aloft in his sweaty palm as he felt the power of it running through him like hot wine. It was warm and heady and intoxicating. Seductive. Consuming.

And he knew he would never be the same again.

'You are the one ...' the breezy, haunting voice whispered ominously through the trees, scaring the boy even more than the light had.

But this is not the tale of King Arthur.

And this is not the sword Excalibur.

This is the story of the Kerrigan, the champion of all things evil.

Like the Arthur of legend, his destiny was to rule over Camelot, only his Camelot was unlike any you have ever seen or heard before ...

Chapter One

Seren stood before the aged guild masters with all her hopes showing brightly on her face as they examined the workmanship of her precious scarlet cloth. They reminded her of a group of crows, swathed in black, gathered over their latest victim. But not even that thought could dampen her hopes that they each held in their gnarled hands.

For the whole of the last year, she had worked diligently on the scarlet cloth they examined, using every spare coin, every spare moment to prepare it. Like a woman possessed, she had dragged out her mother's old wooden loom at night and worked with only the firelight to guide her.

With every brush of her comb, every thread, she had felt the power of her creation.

It was perfect. There were no discrepancies in the dye or stitches.

Truly, it was a masterpiece.

And if they accepted it, then she would finally be a journeywoman and a guild member. At long last, she would be her own person! All her dreams of freedom and of being paid coin for her hard work would come true. There would be no more days of working from sunup to sundown for room and board from Master Rufus, of having to scrub clothes late at night for Mistress Maude to pay for her supplies.

She could sell her own cloth . . .

She could—

'Not good enough.'

Seren blinked at the harsh pronouncement as she stared at the four men before her. 'P-pardon?'

'Not good enough,' the master craftsman said with a curl to his lips as he looked at her work. 'I wouldn't use it for a horse blanket.'

Seren couldn't breathe as her heart shrank. Nay! He was wrong. He had to be. 'But I—'

'Take it,' he said, tossing the cloth at her. 'Come back to us when you're worthy of the trade.'

The red cloth stung her face from the force of his throw. Unable to move, she stood there with it falling from her head to her arms. Instinctively, she held it to her even though she didn't know why she bothered to protect it since it was now worthless to her.

Her soul cried out in disappointment as all her dreams withered and died in the cold room.

How could they say such a thing about her work? It was a lie. She knew it. Her cloth was perfect.

Perfect!

She wanted to scream that word, but all the bitter disappointment gathered in her throat to tighten it and choke her until she could no longer speak. This couldn't be happening. It couldn't be real.

Someone came forward and pulled her away from the masters, toward the door in the back. Tears fell uncontrollably from her face as the harsh words echoed repeatedly in her head.

How could her cloth not be worthy?

'I spent all my time on this,' she whispered, her

heart breaking. 'All my precious coin.' She'd worn rags so she could buy the materials she'd needed to produce the cloth. She'd gone all winter with holes in her shoes, only to be told that all her sacrifices had been in vain.

How could this be?

' 'Tis not your cloth,' the man whispered as he pulled her from the hall. 'There are too many weavers here. They will admit no more to the guild until one leaves or dies.'

Was that supposed to comfort her? To feed her? Nay, it did nothing but make her angry.

Damn them all for this.

'Take my word for it, child, you are better off without being in the guild.'

'How so?'

He placed her hand on her cloth and gave her a peculiar look of warning. 'You have much larger matters to concern yourself with than being an apprentice. Believe me.'

Before she could ask him what he meant, the man pushed her out into the street. She heard him bolt the door behind her.

Seren stood there on the stoop of the guildhall with all her dreams shattered. She was an apprentice still, and so long as she bore that title, she couldn't charge a fee for her work. Couldn't marry. Couldn't do anything more than what Master Rufus or Mistress Maude told her to do.

She had no life to call her own. And from the looks of it, she never would.

Bitter anger washed through her as she stared at her perfect, useless cloth.

'What good are you?' she sobbed. By law, she couldn't even use the cloth to make a gown for herself.

Only those of noble birth could wear the bright color. It was fit for naught but burning.

All was lost.

'Excuse me?'

Seren wiped at the tears on her face as she turned to see a tall, well-dressed knight nearing her. His golden blond hair brushed his incredibly wide shoulders. He was dressed in mail armor covered by a deep green surcoat that bore a rampant silver stag ... The weave of said garment was not nearly so fine as her scarlet cloth, and yet she held no doubt it had been made by someone those beasts had granted guild status to while denying it to her.

Stop it, Seren.

The cloth he wore wasn't important. The fact that a man of his class spoke to her was. She couldn't imagine what he might want with her.

Making sure that she didn't offend him by meeting his gaze, she spoke in an even, calm tone. 'Is there something I can do for you, my lord?'

He glanced behind him toward another handsome knight who looked close enough in features to be a relation of some sort. Only that knight had his blond hair cut shorter and wore a well-trimmed beard.

'Are you Seren of York, the weaver's apprentice?'

She cocked her head suspiciously, wondering how noblemen had learned her name and why they would know it. 'Why do you ask me such, my lord?'

'I am Gawain,' he said with an eager, gentle smile, 'and this is my brother Agravain.'

The names surprised her. She'd only heard of them in one place. 'As in the tales of King Arthur?'

His face lightened instantly. 'You know us?'

'Nay, my lord, I do not. I only know of the stories the old men and minstrels tell at night for food and shelter, or in the street when they seek coin.'

He frowned at her. 'But you do know of the knights of Arthur's Round Table?'

'Aye, my lord. Is there any who does not?'

His smile returned. 'Then you know us. We are the same. My brother and I have been sent here to find you. You are to be mother of the next Merlin, and you must come with us so that we can protect you.'

Seren went cold at his words. Mother to the next Merlin? What was this game they played?

But then she feared that she knew. It was more than common for a nobleman to set his sights on a peasant girl for his pleasure. There was nothing she could do to stop it. Peasants had no rights before their noble masters.

Yet if she went with them and Master Rufus learned of it, he'd throw her out. Both he and his wife required chastity of all their apprentices. Gilda had been turned out just last year when they had learned she'd done nothing more than walk home from Mass with a young man.

They hadn't even held hands, and now Gilda was ruined and working in the local stew with no hope of anything better.

'Please, my lord,' she said, her voice shaking with sincerity, 'do not ask this of me. I am a good and decent woman. I have nothing in this world except my untarnished reputation. I am sure there is goodness in you that you would not see an innocent woman suffer for your lust.'

He looked confused by her words.

'You're blowing it, Wain,' the other knight said in an aggravated tone.

What strange words to use. She'd never heard such before, and they most certainly didn't apply to their situation since the knight he addressed held nothing to his lips.

He moved past Gawain and bowed low before her. 'My lady, please. We mean you no harm. We are only here to protect you.'

It was a struggle not to look up at them. 'Protect me from what, my lord?'

The only thing she needed protection from was men such as these.

It was the one called Gawain who answered. 'Morgen's clutches. You belong with us and are to be a bride of Avalon and as such we need you to come with us now before the mods find you and take you to Camelot.'

She couldn't help looking up at them after all that. What odd words they used. 'Mods? What the devil is a mod?'

'Minions of death. Mods. They are a race that was created by the Celtic god Balor before he died. Now they are controlled by Morgen and she will send them for you. Mark my words.'

They were mad! Both of them. Seren took a step back, her heart hammering. What could she do? If she called out for help, they could claim her as one of their serfs. She wasn't even sure if Master Rufus would help her. He wouldn't dare contradict a nobleman.

God save her.

There was nothing to be done about it. She'd have to run and pray she escaped them.

Holding tight to her cloth, she dodged into the street, away from them, and ran with all her might. She heard the men shouting at her to stop. But there was no way she would allow them to catch her and have their pleasure with her.

Darting down an alleyway, she stumbled over a piece

of broken cobblestone, then caught herself. She looked about for an escape.

There was a small, narrow pass between two buildings that would only just let her through. The men should be too large to follow.

Seren ran to the opening and pressed herself against the wall before she inched her way down it. There was an awful smell here, and it was a struggle not to breathe through her nose. Even so, smelly or not, it was infinitely better than the alternative. Better her nose be assaulted than her body.

She heard the men enter the alley behind her and curse.

'Where is she?'

'Merlin will kill us if we don't return with her.'

'You and your bright ideas. I swear, Gawain, I should have strangled you at birth.' He changed his tone to a high-pitched, mocking one. 'We'll just tell her who we are and she'll come with us willingly. No problem.' His voice then returned to its deep, accusing tone. 'Damn you for the stupidity. I should have left your rank ass in the twentieth century instead of bringing you home.'

'I wish you had. I certainly prefer it to this. Not that it matters. What was your bright idea to get her away from Morgen? Huh? You didn't have one at all, did you, Brother Intellect?'

While they argued and berated each other with nonsensical phrases, she continued on her way toward the end.

'There she is!'

She turned her head to see the knights at the opening behind her. They tried to follow and couldn't, so then they pulled back to run around the building.

Seren popped out of the alley, then ran headlong

down the narrow, cobblestone street. There were people everywhere, going to market and to businesses. With any luck, the knights would lose sight of her in the crowd.

Or at least she thought so until she rounded a corner and found herself face to face with Gawain again.

How had he gotten here so quickly?

'You can't hide from us, Seren.' He took her arm.

Seren twisted away from him and bolted again into the thronging mass. People cursed and pushed at her as she collided with them in her haste. Her heart felt as though it would explode from her fear and panic.

What was she going to do?

Looking behind her to see them still in pursuit, she darted into the street, then skidded to a stop as she heard a horse shrieking.

Seren glanced up to see a large black destrier rearing before her. Its shiny hooves pawed the air as if it wanted nothing more than to pummel her with them. She held her arm up to protect herself and prayed the animal stopped before it savaged her.

The knight spoke to the horse in a language she didn't understand as he brought the beast under control. 'Are you trying to kill yourself, woman,' he snarled at her.

But the anger on his fair face faded as he looked at her, and his features softened to something less than severe. 'Forgive me for my rudeness, good woman. I hope that I didn't frighten you overmuch. It was only the surprise of my horse rearing that caused me to snap.'

Seren could only gape at the handsomeness of the man on horseback. His raven black hair fell in waves around the perfect features of his clean-shaven face. Eyes so black that they didn't even appear to have a pupil stared at her with an intensity that left her even more breathless than her run through the streets.

She heard the men behind her curse.

The knight on horseback looked past her to see the men running toward them. 'Have you need of assistance, good woman?'

'Aye, my lord,' she said breathlessly. 'I need to escape them before they catch me.'

'Then as a knight and champion, I offer my most humble services to you. Come, and I shall see you home without harm.' He extended his hand.

'Nay!' the knight called Gawain shouted as they ran toward her.

Before she could think better of it, Seren placed her hand into his.

The knight pulled her astride his saddle to ride before him, then set his heels to the horse's flanks. They tore through the crowd at a speed that amazed her. It was as if his great black steed had wings.

For the first time since she had arisen that morning, Seren took a deep breath as relief coursed through her.

'Thank you, my lord,' she said to the knight holding her. 'You have truly saved my life this day. I can never repay you for your kindness.'

The chase didn't seem to concern him at all as he guided his horse with expert hand through the town. 'And how is it I have saved your life?'

'Those men who were after me. They were mad.'

'How so?'

'They claimed that I was to be the mother of the wizard Merlin. Mayhap they were only drunk, but . . .' She shivered as she considered what had almost befallen her. 'Thank the Lord and all His saints that you came when you did. I shudder to think what they would have done to me had I gone with them.'

12

He gave her a knowing look. 'Aye, there was a higher power that brought me to you this day. Of that I have no doubt.'

Seren had just started to relax when she heard the sound of hooves behind them.

The knight turned to look.

'It's them,' she breathed, her panic returning as she saw the two knights again in pursuit. 'Why won't they let me go?'

'Have no fear. I won't let them take you.'

His words thrilled her. Who would have believed that such a handsome knight would defend a simple peasant maid? 'You are truly a kind and noble knight, sir.'

But as he looked down at her, Seren would have sworn that his eyes flashed red before he spurred his horse to an even greater speed. The other two knights continued to give chase. They raced through town until they flew over the bridge that took them out into the countryside.

Seren cringed. 'I'm not to leave the town,' she told the knight. 'My master will have me beaten for leaving without his permission.'

'There is nothing I can do. Should we return, they will take you. Is that what you want?'

'Nay.'

'Then hold tight until we lose them.'

Seren did as he said. She turned to face him in the saddle and wrapped her arms about his waist and inhaled the scent of leather, man, and beast. His horse flew over the open meadow, racing toward the dense woods that lay before them.

All of a sudden, something exploded by their side.

'Accero, accero domini doyan,' the knight said in his deep, resonant voice.

Seren gasped in terror as the gargoyle decorations on the horse's bridle lifted themselves off and took flight. They screeched like banshees before they headed toward the men pursuing them.

'What is this?' she asked.

'You're lost in a dream.' His voice was inside her head. 'Sleep, little one. Sleep.' Seren blinked her eyes as exhaustion overtook her. She tried desperately to remain awake, but couldn't.

Before she knew what was happening, darkness consumed her.

Kerrigan pulled the woman closer to him as he felt her go limp from his spell. She was completely soft and pliant in his arms. Satisfied that she couldn't fight him, he slowed his horse so that he could turn around to see Gawain and Agravain fighting his gargoyles.

He let his malevolent laughter ring out. 'She is ours,' he called to them.

Gawain launched a sorcerer's fire blast in his direction. Kerrigan dissolved it before it came near him.

'You know what I want, Gawain. Tell Merlin to give it over or see this woman die.' With his orders issued, Kerrigan spoke the sacred words that took him away from the world of man, into the nether realm of Camelot.

In an eerie black mist, the visible world faded into darkness. The veil that separated the two realms mingled until he found himself once more on the black soil of Camelot.

Here Kerrigan was more than a knight. Here he was king and champion. Laughing in triumph, Kerrigan rode over the black drawbridge, into the outer, then inner bailey. As he reined his horse before the donjon, a misshapen grayling male came forward to take his horse.

Theirs was a cursed elfin race that had once been tall and graceful. But they had run amok of a Celtic god who had made their exterior as abhorrent as their hearts. Now they were damned to serve here at Morgen's behest.

Giving no thought to the haggard creature, Kerrigan gripped the woman tightly in his arms before he slid to the ground with his precious bundle. She was the key he needed that would open up the world and make it his.

'Give him extra oats,' he told the fey grayling.

'Aye, my lord.'

Kerrigan shifted the woman's slight weight before he headed toward the blackened doors of the once-famed castle. They parted of their own volition as he approached, allowing him to enter. With every step he took, his heels and spurs clicked eerily against the stone floor.

As he walked through the hallway that was scented with nutmeg and mace, torches lit themselves to illuminate the way to the turret stairs. He was headed to a bedchamber on the uppermost floor. One that would guarantee this woman had no choice except to stay here until they killed her.

It was a room that was segregated in the northern-most tower where no one could hear her screams. Not that it would matter. There was none here, including he, who would ever render aid to another. It was merely a courtesy to the others that their ears wouldn't be abused by her wretched cries and pleas for mercy.

Like the rest of the castle, the room was decorated in black and gray. The only color in this land was found in Morgen's direct domain. The fey queen wanted nothing to detract from her beauty or her presence. So all color had been banished.

Kerrigan laid the woman down upon the black bed and pulled back the covers for her. She was pale and fragile against the darkness. Her long, straight hair was so fair as to be almost white.

To his surprise, she wasn't a beautiful woman. In truth, her features leaned toward plain, except for her eyes. A clear, crystal green, they were large and almond-shaped like a cat's. Her nose was of average shape and form, and her lips were full. Her body was undernourished and thin, with next to no feminine curves to cushion a man who might take her.

There was nothing remarkable about her. Nothing that marked her as the future mother of a Merlin.

She reminded him of a simple mouse.

And even unconscious, she still clung to the vibrant red cloth in her hands. He frowned at her actions, wondering why she bothered. He started to take it away from her, then paused for reasons unknown.

'You trusting fool,' he snarled at her. He couldn't imagine ever reaching out his hand to someone for help.

And what had it gotten her? Nothing but her own doom.

A shadow slithered into the room from the keyhole of the door. 'Mistress Morgen wants word with you, my lord.'

'Tell her I will come in my own good time.' It never boded well to keep her waiting. Morgen possessed a nasty temperament that was matched only by his own. But then Kerrigan refused to let anyone, even Morgen, command him.

Besides, there was nothing more the fey queen could do to him. He was already damned by his own actions, and no one, not even she, could kill him.

The sharoc, or shadow fey, continued to hover beside him as if it were trying to rush him.

'Leave me,' Kerrigan snarled.

The sharoc retreated immediately.

Again alone with the unknown woman, Kerrigan found himself studying her curiously. She was unlike the women who lived here in Camelot. Granted they, due to their magic, were all beautiful to behold, but none of them possessed the spark that seemed to glow from within her.

Her skin appeared somehow softer, more appealing. Inviting.

You are being a fool. She is nothing but an insignificant mortal.

Aye. And she most certainly wasn't worth his time.

'Anir!' he called for his gargoyle servant.

The beast flew through the open window and hovered over the bed where the woman rested. Anir's stark yellow eyes glowed against his dark gray, stone-like skin. 'Aye, my lord?'

'Guard her and let me know the instant she wakes.'

The gargoyle nodded, then came to rest on the foot of the bed. He crouched there in a small, watchful pose, then hardened back into his true form of stone.

Kerrigan paused as he took one last look at the woman who beguiled him. He still didn't understand her appeal. Not that it mattered. The time she had left to live was extremely finite. Even if those at Avalon gave over the table he sought, she would still be killed.

She was to be the mother of a Merlin. That alone carried with it a death sentence.

'What do you mean she got away?'

Gawain cringed at Merlin's question. He looked to Agravain for some reprieve, but none was forthcoming.

'Lord Smooth,' Agravain said snidely, 'told her she was going to be the mother of the next Merlin, so she panicked and ran.'

Merlin pressed her hand to her head as if she had a fierce ache above her brow. A tall, slender woman, Merlin was the epitome of beauty. She had long, golden hair that flowed around her lithe body, which was covered by a white gown trimmed in gold. Truly, there was no woman more fair.

Or more angry than she was at present.

She glared at them as a book appeared before her and hovered there, suspended by nothing. The pages of the book turned to a passage. 'Let me see if I have this right.'

She read from the book. *Gawain, the noble and chivalrous knight of Arthur, a king's champion. His prowess with women was unsurpassed.* She looked up from the book to pin Gawain with a most unhappy glare. 'This is you, is it not?'

Gawain chafed under her angry scrutiny. The pages of the book then turned to another passage so that he could read from it. 'And according to that book, Merlin, you're an old, bald man.'

Merlin's eyes widened as the book burst into flames. 'Have you a wish to die?'

'I can't. I'm immortal.'

Agravain sucked his breath in sharply between his teeth. 'Caution, brother. The last man to anger Merlin now sits locked in a cage underneath our precious home.'

That was true. Merlin had vowed to never forgive Sir Thomas Malory for what he'd told of them.

'I'm sorry, Merlin,' Gawain said, trying to calm them all down. 'Believe me, you are no angrier over this than I am. How did the Kerrigan know to be there?'

Merlin sighed. 'His powers have grown much over the centuries. If we do not stop him soon, they will be stronger than even mine.'

Gawain exchanged a nervous look with his brother. No one needed to tell them what would happen should that occur. The Kerrigan held no heart, no compassion. He was the male counterpart to Morgen, and he was her champion. If he grew stronger than Merlin, there would be no stopping them from taking over the world and enslaving them all.

Gawain narrowed his eyes thoughtfully. 'I shall have Percival research him. Maybe there is something written that can expose a weakness—'

'Nay,' Merlin said. 'Morgen is more intelligent than that. Unlike us, she seems to be able to keep her minions out of written legends.'

Agravain snorted. 'Not our fault Thom got drunk and started talking. I still think we should have killed him.'

'It wasn't the talking that was bad,' Gawain said snidely. 'It was the writing.'

Merlin stiffened. 'Thank you for that reminder.'

'Sorry, Merlin,' they said in unison.

'So what do we do now?' Agravain asked Merlin.

Merlin sighed. 'We wait to see what Kerrigan does. We can't give over the table to him ... at least not without a wheelbarrow and a bucket. And even if we do, I am sure he will kill Seren and end her bloodline for us.' Merlin took up pacing the hall. 'Somehow we must find a way to get Seren out of Camelot.'

Gawain looked up to the seal of the Pendragon that hung on the wall above them. A brightly colored fresco, it held the image of a dragon with a lion sleeping at its feet. Fire curled around the beast that stood with its wings spread wide. The dragon was alert and ready to defend its power and territory.

Behind that seal, lying asleep in a tomb, wasn't the king of legend.

It was one of his true sons that he'd sired with Queen Guinevere.

'Should we wake Draig for this?'

'Nay,' Merlin said. 'His time to rise isn't now. Summon the others. Whatever we do, we cannot allow evil to win. If they do . . .'

Everything good would die and the world would seriously reek.

Chapter Two

Kerrigan entered Morgen's room with his arms folded over his chest. Her receiving room was open and light, decorated in pale yellows and gold. Her blond hair was striking against her darker skin. She looked like an angel, but Kerrigan knew from experience that those looks were definitely deceiving.

Her gown was a vivid, unnatural red that moved like blood on her body. She was dancing in the room with her Adoni. Unlike the graylings, they were tall, fair of form, and agile. Humans oft called them elves, but they should never be confused with their Germanic cousins. The Adoni were a separate, vicious race that preyed on mankind whenever they could. It was what endeared them so to Morgen.

She paused in her dancing as she saw him. 'So you've come to me finally.'

He shrugged nonchalantly. 'Why did you send for me?'

'I want you to keep a very close eye on our guest. If I know that bitchtress Merlin, and I do, she will set loose her dogs to come here and liberate her.'

He scoffed at the witch. 'I don't make such mistakes. Neither Merlin nor her bastard minions will ever be able to breach these walls.'

Morgen smiled at that as she crossed the room to stand beside him. She reached out to brush his hair back from his face. Her touch was as icy as her heart. 'Why do you never come to my bed anymore, Kerrigan?'

He cut a glare to the handsome Adoni male who watched them with jealousy and interest. 'I find your bed too crowded for my tastes.'

She laughed coldly at that. 'There was a time when you didn't mind crowds. But you are very daring, my evil heart. I'm not sure why I allow you to speak to me thus.'

'Then kill me, Morgen,' he said without fear or passion. Honestly, he couldn't care less at this point.

She sighed at that as she continued to toy with his hair. 'We both know I can't so long as you carry the sword Caliburn and its scabbard.' She gave him a pretty, seductive pout. 'You have been with me all these centuries past, Kerrigan. Always serving my needs. Always killing and torturing others for my whims. You remind me so much of my son.'

Hardly. Mordred was a weakling milksop compared to Kerrigan, and they both knew it. True, Mordred had been cruel, but he was nowhere near as inventive or zealous as Kerrigan. 'But I am not Mordred.'

Her eyes sparked at the reminder of her son who lay in stasis, awaiting the time when he would awaken again to torture the world of man. 'Nay, you are not.' She pulled his head down to hers so that she could kiss him.

Kerrigan didn't respond. He'd long ago grown tired of her cold, demanding touch.

She pulled away from his lips with a curse, then shoved him back. 'Begone from me.'

He inclined his head to her and for once, obeyed.

*

22

Seren rubbed her eyes as she felt herself waking up. What a terrible dream she'd had. First she'd thought the guild had turned her down, then she'd been chased by strange knights who had battled gargoyles.

'I shall have to tell . . .' Her voice trailed off as she opened her eyes and saw the eerie room. She lay on a bed that was completely black. The covers, the wood, even the curtains. The windows were open to show her a dark, overcast sky that held gray clouds and no trace of sunshine.

'Where am I?' She sat up slowly, trying to remember how she could have come to such a place.

A sudden movement drew her attention to the foot of her bed. She shrieked as she saw the gargoyle statue come alive. Its eerie yellow eyes focused on her as its forked, stone tail whipped around it.

'Fear not, human,' it said in a deep, ragged voice. 'I won't eat your heart from you. At least not yet.'

'I'm dreaming.'

'Nay,' it said in a sinister tone as it eyed her with malice. 'No dreams here, bobbin. Only nightmares.'

The gargoyle launched itself into the air to fly about as it watched her. 'Kerrigan, Kerrigan,' it called. 'My Lord Darkness, 'tis time for you to return.'

A wispy smoke appeared beside her bed.

Dropping her cloth, Seren scooted to the opposite side of the bed and watched as the smoke took the form of a man with glowing red eyes. The smoke solidified into the knight who had rescued her. The cinders of his eyes flared to flames, then turned as dark and cold as coal.

As soon as he appeared, the gargoyle flew from the window and vanished into the eerie sky.

She whispered a prayer as she crossed herself. 'What are you?'

The edges of his lips twisted up ever so slightly. 'Evil incarnate.'

She didn't want to believe that. And yet, how could she not? 'But you helped me to escape the others.'

His gaze was cold, blank. 'Nay, I helped myself.'

'I don't understand. Why am I here? Why is this happening to me?'

He watched her without mercy or compassion. 'Why should it happen to someone else? What is so special about you that you should be immune to the callous machinations of Damé Fortune?'

She swallowed at his harsh tone. 'I never said I should be immune to anything. I want only to know why this is happening. Where am I?'

'You are in Camelot.'

She looked around at the cold, sinister walls that bore no resemblance to the place of legend. Camelot was said to be a jewel, a warm place with gold walls and brilliant tapestries. There was none of that here. 'Camelot?'

'Aye,' he said. 'Can you not see the beauty of it? The magic? Here is where Arthur united a kingdom and saw his whole world crumble before his own nephew brutally killed him at Camlann.'

She knew the famed legend well, but she'd never imagined Camelot looking like this. 'Are you one of his knights of the Round Table?'

He laughed coldly at that. 'Do I look like such? Nay, woman, I am their scourge. You ran from your blessed knights of the Round Table in town when they would have saved you.'

'Saved me from what?'

'Me.'

Seren bolted from the bed and ran for the door. Before she could reach it, the knight was before her, blocking her way. 'There is no way out of here, little mouse.'

'Please,' she begged, terrified of what was happening to her. 'Please, let me go. I am just a peasant. I am nothing special, nothing out of the ordinary. I want only to go home and become a journeywoman.'

A faraway look came into his cold eyes. 'And I, too, was once just a peasant. A liar and a thief, I spent my entire youth running from those who would beat me. Now I am king of Camelot. The wheel of fate is ever on the move. Today you are a simple apprentice without prospects, but in the days to come your destiny was to marry and breed with one of Arthur's famed knights.'

But that didn't make sense to her. It wasn't possible. 'I don't understand. I cannot marry a knight. I am a peasant.'

His eyes flashed red as he skimmed his evil gaze over her body.

Kerrigan felt himself growing hard as he watched her standing so courageously before him. She was terrified, he could smell it, and yet she continued to fight even though she knew it was hopeless.

She wasn't anything special and yet . . .

His body reacted to her nearness in a way it had never reacted to anyone before. He found himself curious over why Damé Fortune had chosen this meek little mouse to birth one of the greatest powers on earth. What a strange vessel to nurture and breed a Merlin.

'Have you ever taken a man into your body, little mouse?'

Her face flushed instantly as she sputtered.

'So you are a virgin.'

His little mouse straightened her spine as she stared

25

defiantly at him. 'And I intend to stay one until the day I marry.'

One corner of his mouth turned up at her challenge. 'You could hardly stop me if I decided to take you.'

And still she gave him no fear, only an unfounded courage met his taunts. 'There is no satisfaction in stealing someone's property, my lord. True value only lies when you earn it or the owner gives it to you of her own free will.'

Her bold words gave him pause as he considered them. 'I know nothing of gifts.'

'Then that is a shame. Perhaps if you were to ask instead of take, then you might have knowledge of them.'

She was a quick little mouse. Surprisingly intelligent, point of fact, and he found himself intrigued by her argument. 'Would you give me your virginity if I asked it?'

'Nay!'

'Then what is the point of asking when the only way to have something is to take it?'

'Then take it if you must,' she said bravely, her eyes flashing a vivid shade of green. 'but know that by doing so, you are stealing away the only thing I have that is truly mine alone to give. I hope it gives you great satisfaction to leave me with absolutely nothing.' She lifted her chin as if readying herself to take his blow.

Take her.

The voice in his head was overwhelming, and normally when it issued a command, he followed it regardless of consequence, and yet he couldn't quite muster the desire to do so now. There was a rare fire in her green eyes that burned away the coldness inside him.

It was her dignity, he realized.

He remembered a time once when he had held such. But those days were past him. His dignity, like his humanity, had been stripped from him, layer by layer, until it left him a hollow, angry shell.

Before he could think better of it, he lifted his hand up to touch her soft, delicate cheek. Her skin was warm, soothing. Sweet.

He lowered his gaze down to her small breasts that would barely fill his palm, then lower to the rest of her body. She was a scrawny woman in need of food and care. He could snap her neck with barely more than a thought.

Even if she tried to fight him, she would have no strength for it. And still he was amazingly curious over her.

'What is your name, girl?'

She hesitated before she answered. 'Seren.'

Seren. In his language that had meant star. 'And what would you give me, Seren, to preserve your virginity?'

'I don't understand.'

He let his hand fall from her face while he watched her curiously as she shivered from his nearness. 'You speak of gifts that are so valuable. Show me one that is more special than the gratification I can have with your body, and I shall sate my desire with another.'

She cast her gaze around the room as if seeking something to give him. Her eyes widened as her gaze fell to the bed where her red cloth rested. 'All I have is my scarlet cloth.'

He sneered at that. 'I have no need of fabric.'

He saw the panic on her face, and for once he felt no satisfaction from having caused it.

'I have nothing else,' she said.

'Then give me a kiss.'

Her eyes widened as if he shocked her. 'A kiss?'

'Aye,' he said, enjoying this strange game of teasing her without malice. 'Let me see the benefit of having something that is freely given and not taken. Kiss me, Seren, and let me judge the value of your gift.'

Seren swallowed at his words, petrified and yet oddly intrigued. There was something about the knight that appealed to her even though he scared her beyond reason.

Why would he be pacified by a single kiss?

'I have never kissed a man before.'

He scowled at her. 'You've never kissed. Never tasted a man's body? How old are you?'

'A score and four.'

He tsked. 'A woman full-grown. How is it you have remained so chaste in a world of hungry men?'

'By choice, my lord. By *my* choice.'

He snorted at that. 'And now I give you another choice, little mouse. A kiss or your body. So what's it to be?'

Seren shivered as she wondered if a kiss would truly sate this powerful man. 'And what if I don't kiss you correctly? Will my actions be for naught?'

His gaze was blank, cold. 'You ask a liar for the truth? Are you that trusting or that foolish?'

'Then how do I know you won't take my body after my kiss?'

'You don't.'

Seren breathed deeply at his dispassionate words. At least he was being honest. But then she had no real choice in this situation. No matter how much she hated the thought of it, she was at his utter mercy and they both knew it. 'Then I shall trust you to be a man of your word. I pray you, don't disappoint me, my lord. I have had quite enough of disappointments this day.'

Before Kerrigan could ask her anything more, she laid a chaste kiss to his lips. His body fired at the innocence he tasted, at the knowledge that no other man had ever tread upon this mouth before him.

His heart pounding, he nudged her lips apart with his and swept his tongue deep inside her sweet, decadent mouth to taste the first innocent kiss he'd ever known. It washed over him in waves of desire, making his groin hard and aching. Aye, she was much more than she'd seemed at first. An odd surprise of innocent hunger.

Seren moaned at the taste of her dark knight. His skin was cold as ice, as his tongue danced through her mouth, licking and teasing her. She'd never experienced anything like it before.

He pulled her roughly into his arms and held her close as he deepened his kiss even more. She felt him bulging against her hip and knew exactly how much he wanted to take her.

He left her mouth to trail his kisses over her cheek, then down to her neck where he buried his cold lips against her throat. Her breasts tightened as desire pooled itself to the center of her body. Chills swept the full length of her body.

She'd never known desire before, but she felt the heat of it stinging her now. A foreign, frightening part of her wouldn't even mind if he pressed her for more . . .

'Aye, Seren,' he breathed against her ear in a ragged tone that sent chills the length of her body. 'A kiss freely given is most sweet indeed.'

Seren felt his hand against her back lift the hem of

her gown. She went ramrod stiff in fear of what he was about to do.

Kerrigan's body was molten. All he could think of was tasting more of her virgin flesh. Of spreading her creamy thighs wide and driving himself deep inside her wet heat over and over again until he was fully spent.

But she had trusted him.

No one had ever given him trust before. No one.

And she had kissed him of her own free will.

His body screaming out in protest, he let loose her dress and forced himself to step away from her. Even so, his cold lips still burned from the taste of hers.

And he wanted more. He craved it with a ferocity that stunned him.

Seren watched him carefully, half afraid that he would rape her after all.

He didn't. But there was something painful in his eyes. Something so deeply tormented that it made her chest ache for him, and she didn't understand why.

He cleared his throat. 'Are you hungry, little mouse?'

She nodded.

'I shall have food prepared for you.' He paused at the door and looked back at her.

'Aye,' he said quietly as he swept her from head to toe with his gaze. 'That's much better. I could never abide a woman in rags.'

It wasn't until after he left that she realized her tattered dress was no longer on her body. Instead she wore a shimmering gown of pale blue samite with a gold girdle and soft leather shoes that matched it.

Seren's legs went weak. It was all she could do to keep standing. Surely this was all a vivid dream. How could it be real?

'Wake up, Seren.' But it wasn't a dream. Somehow this place was real.

The black knight was real. And something inside her warned that if she didn't find a way to escape this place, she would be doomed and damned here forever.

Chapter Three

'So you're the Penmerlin's mother.''

Seren turned away from the window where she'd been watching an angry black sea crash upon the castle's stones far below, to see an old crone entering her room. The crone was dressed in black, which seemed to be the color du jour here in the castle, with her gray hair pulled back into a gnarled braid. 'I am no one's mother.'

'But you will be, God willing.'

There was something in the old woman's hopeful tone that gave Seren pause. A slither of instinct that begged her to listen to it.

The old woman drew close to her and looked about nervously as if afraid someone might be able to overhear them. When she spoke, her tone was barely more than a whisper. 'There isn't much time, child. You have to leave here before it's too late.'

'Too late for what?'

'To save you. Right now the Kerrigan is focused on using you to barter with Merlin, but once that fails, he will take your head and drink your blood.'

That was something Seren would most definitely like to avoid. 'Then how do I escape this place?'

The old woman sighed as if the answer troubled her greatly. 'Unfortunately, you have only one choice.'

Seren waited expectantly, but the woman appeared to lose her train of thought as she trudged about the room, examining the stones. 'And that is?' she prompted.

The crone stopped and looked at her. 'The Kerrigan.'

Seren frowned at the unfamiliar name the crone kept using. 'The Kerrigan?'

'The black knight who captured you and brought you here. You have to seduce him so that he will drop his guard and let you escape this damned place.'

How easy the crone made it sound to drag a man to her bed, but it wasn't easy and she knew it. Not to mention the small matter that she was a virgin who rather liked her innocent state. The last thing she wanted was to barter her maidenhead to a professed demon in exchange for a freedom she was certain would be only temporary. If she were to run, the black knight would most likely come after her, and then what would she have to barter with?

'I can't do that. I know nothing of seducing men.'

'You have no choice, child,' the crone insisted in that low, commanding tone. 'There are only two people who can come and go freely in and out of this realm. Morgen, who, no offense, will never help you, and the Kerrigan.'

Still, she refused to believe it. 'There has to be another way to escape.'

'There isn't. Trust me, men are susceptible to their lust. He is already attracted to you. Use his lust to gain your freedom.'

Seren rebelled at that idea. ' 'Tis wrong to use people in such a manner.'

The old woman snorted. 'It is wrong to kill them as well, and they will kill you. Do you not understand me, chit? The Kerrigan is evil to the marrow of his bones.'

'He has been kind to me.'

She scoffed at that. 'He knows nothing of kindness. Trust me. I have seen him cut the throat of his own men for nothing more than looking askance at him. He feels for no one, and it is by his own hand you will be slain when the time comes for it.'

Seren's heart pounded at her dire prediction. 'And why should I trust you?'

'Because I am the only hope you have. I have been here since the time when Arthur was king. I was here when this mighty castle fell to Morgen and I was here when they brought the Kerrigan in. Barely more than a boy, he had a good soul in the beginning and they destroyed it, piece by piece, until he learned to be one of them. And they will destroy yours, too. Mark my words. I tried to warn him as I am warning you, and he failed to listen. He allowed Morgen to seduce him to her cause, and now he is eternally damned.' Her gaze was sad and frail until she looked back at Seren. 'Please, don't be so foolish. I beg you.'

Seren nodded in agreement. She didn't want to lose her soul or her life. Honestly, she was attached to both with equal amounts of fervor. 'Very well then. What do I do?'

'Be nice to him. Seduce him so that you can take the star amulet from around his neck. It bears the sign of a dragon. Take it from him and run for the bailey, toward the drawbridge. If you cross the drawbridge with it, you will arrive in the world of man at the same place and time where he whisked you away from it.'

'And if I leave without the amulet?'

'You will be lost forever in the Val Sans Retour.'

Seren's eyes widened. The Valley of No Return. 'That is the valley where Morgen banishes her lovers who cease to please her,' she breathed.

'You know of it?'

She nodded. Over the years, she had heard many bards and minstrels tell tales of Morgen le Fey and her evil Val Sans Retour. It was said to be the most horrible place in existence. Worse than even hell itself.

If that was a real place, it made her wonder what else might be true.

'Do you have a name?' she asked the old woman.

'Magda.'

'Tell me, Magda, how many of the stories I know of Arthur and Camelot are true and how many are false?'

Magda patted her hand comfortingly. 'There's not enough time for all that, child. But know this. Camelot has fallen into evil hands, and the evil that lives here wants nothing more than to make the world a copy of it. In this *terre derrière le voile* there are two great powers. Morgen, who is queen of the fey people, and the Kerrigan, who is king of Camelot. On the side of good are the Lords of Avalon. They are the knights who survived the fall of Camelot. With the help of the Penmerlin's successor, they retreated after the battle of Camlann to Avalon, where they continue to fight for all that is good. We must get you to them so that they can protect you. You are far too important in this battle to stay here.'

'But why was I chosen? I am only a peasant.'

'Why is the sky above us . . . well, here it is always gray or black, never blue, and I actually know why. However, the fact is this, you were chosen by Damé Fortune to be an instrument of good. Accept your fate, child.' Her eyes flared with a life that belied her years as she held her hands up in fists to illustrate her impassioned words. 'Embrace it.'

Magda patted her on her arm as she lowered her voice to scarce more than a whisper. 'There are thirteen Merlins who are important to Avalon. But the most important of all is the Penmerlin – the one who rules them all. The Penmerlin is the most powerful instrument for good. For two hundred years, the Penmerlin watches over and guides the Lords of Avalon. Then he or she is allowed to retire and to live out his or her life in peace and comfort. The child you are to bear will be the next Penmerlin. Because of her dark magic, Morgen knows this, and it is why she will ultimately kill you after Kerrigan gets what he wants. If you die, there will be no replacement, and when the current Merlin's reign ends, the Lords of Avalon will be without leadership.'

Her eyes narrowed on Seren. 'You hold in your hands the future of all that is good and decent. You and your child are the only ones who stand between Morgen and the Kerrigan, and the world of man.'

Seren still didn't understand why she was chosen for this. She wasn't up to such a challenge. She was only a young woman of insignificant birth. 'I only want to have my own loom. My own shop. I don't want to live in a fabled place and be broodmare to some man I have yet to meet.'

Magda gave her a sympathetic pat. 'Life is seldom what we want it to be, child. But think of it this way. The mother of the Penmerlin lives in a place of honor at Avalon. Your husband won't be a peasant or merchant, he will be a noble knight who adores you. You will have a life of unimaginable riches and happiness. You'll never again know want or hunger.'

It was too good to be true. Seren looked down at her

work-worn hands. There were places on her fingers that were broken open from using the comb on her loom. Her nails were ragged and unkempt, her skin raw and chafed. There had seldom been a night in her life when she hadn't collapsed on her small pallet on the floor from sheer exhaustion, her hands throbbing and bleeding, her back and shoulders aching.

Even with her eyes open, she could clearly see Mistress Maude sitting at her table that was laden with succulent food. Seren and the other apprentices ate modest meals. They had never been allowed to partake of guild banquets.

To eat until they were full . . .

'Aye,' Magda said in her ear. 'I can see the lust for it in your eyes. Seduce the Kerrigan and you will have all that and more. Think of the softness of the gown you wear now. Imagine an entire wardrobe of them.'

Seren ran her hand over the delicate fabric that didn't chafe or scratch. It settled against her skin like the coolness of water. 'It is not for a peasant to reach for better. Our lot—'

'You were born for greater things, child. Accept it.'

But that was easier said than done. How could she accept something that completely contradicted everything she'd ever been told?

A knock sounded on the door. Magda jumped away from her as the black portal opened to show her the sight of a misshapen gray creature dressed in a robe that matched its skin tone. It glared at Magda, who quickly scooted away, then shifted its cold gaze back to her.

'The master bids you to join him in the hall.'

Seren glanced to Magda, who patted her own neck to remind Seren of the amulet. Taking a deep breath for courage, Seren nodded, then headed for the creature.

It led her down a dismally black corridor. She gasped as she realized that the torches only lit as they approached them. The instant they walked past, the light was extinguished. Amazed by it, Seren stopped to examine one. It was a peculiar sconce. It looked as if a black human hand held the small torch. Her heart hammering, she reached out to touch it.

The hand moved.

Seren screamed in startled alarm, jumping away from it. The creature laughed at her, then pushed her closer to the sconce.

'Go on, bobbin, let it feel you again.'

She screamed once more, trying to pull back.

'Drystan!' the powerful voice echoed like thunder in the hallway.

The creature let her go immediately.

She turned to see Kerrigan taking long, quick strides toward them.

He grabbed the creature and backhanded him so hard that the creature rebounded off the wall. 'You do not scare her,' he growled.

He moved to strike it again, but Seren caught his hand to stop the blow. 'Please, it was only a jest. No harm was done to me.'

The anger on his handsome face dissipated. The creature, whose lips were now bloodied, looked up at her with a disbelieving frown.

Kerrigan glared at the creature as his eyes glowed red. 'Out of my sight, worm.'

It scurried away from them and ran until it vanished around the bend in the corridor.

Seren was appalled by the Kerrigan's behavior. 'Why did you attack him?'

Rage filled every part of his body. 'You do not understand the rules here.'

'Nay, not if they include punishing people for small matters. Your reaction was overly harsh and unnecessary for his slight offense.'

He scoffed at her. 'And if you allow him to get away with that, he will become bolder and more harmful. Trust me, I know. Unless it is immediately quelled, malice only grows.'

'I didn't feel his malice.'

'Then you are a fool.'

She stiffened at his insult. 'So you keep telling me. Fine then, I shall take my foolish self back to my room where it cannot offend you any further.' She started away from him.

'I thought you were hungry.'

'I have lost my appetite.'

She continued down the hallway, without looking back. As she neared the bend that would return her to her room, Kerrigan appeared before her. 'You need to eat.'

She stamped down the fear she felt at his unholy powers. It would do her no good to break off into a fit of terror. Her mother had raised her to be strong in the face of any challenge – though to be honest, she doubted if her mother had ever conceived of a challenge such as this. 'If I refuse, will you beat me, too?'

He looked confounded by her. 'Why are you so angry over how I treated a grayling? He would just as soon eat your heart as look at you. The only thing they respect is someone more powerful and more sinister than they.'

'Might should never make right.'

He looked even more baffled. 'What?'

' 'Tis something a bard said about the king of Camelot. The purpose of this castle was to be a protection against evil. The goal of the knights of the Round

Table was to protect those who couldn't protect—'

'There are no knights here, Seren. Only demons.'

His words gave her pause. 'Does that include you?'

'Aye, it does.'

'Then I am sorry for you, my lord. Everyone should know kindness and compassion.'

Her words seemed to anger him again. 'Bah, go, return to your room. I couldn't care less whether or not you starve.' He stepped around her and headed away.

'My lord?'

He paused to look back at her.

'Have you a name, sir?'

He glanced away before he answered. 'Nay, I do not. I am only known by the fey title that they give to all who command demons. You may call me Kerrigan.'

Kerrigan. It was a strong name and seemed somehow suited to the role it was chosen for. However, it wasn't the name she wanted. 'But the name you had before you came here? What was it?'

His eyes blazed red fire at her. 'They called me boy, bastard, or maggot. I now only answer to those with the blade of my sword.'

Her heart clenched at his words. How horrible for him to not even have something so simple as a name to call his own. 'I am sorry for that, my lord. No man should be without a name.'

He cocked his head as he studied her curiously. 'You're not afraid of me, are you, little mouse?'

'Should I be?'

'Everyone else is.' His tone was cold and matter-of-fact.

'But should *I* be afraid of you?'

Kerrigan reached out to brush his hand through the softness of her hair. Aye, she should be terrified of him. He held no regard for anyone or anything. Life, whether his own or someone else's, held no meaning or value whatsoever where he was concerned.

Yet he didn't want this tiny woman to fear him.

'Nay, Seren. You have nothing to fear from me.' He brought the lock of hair to his lips so that he could feel it against his lips, smell the faint, sweet rose scent of her.

Seren trembled at the sight of a man so dark, so fierce, being so tender. It was incongruous and puzzling.

He released her hair, then smoothed it down. 'Come and eat, girl. You need to keep up your strength.'

She started to remind him what he had just said about not caring, but decided to hold her tongue. She was, in fact, starving.

He held his arm out to her. Seren took it, then withdrew with a hiss. His black armor was so cold that it burned her skin. 'Forgive me,' he said, moving away from her. 'I forgot about that.'

'Why are you so cold?'

' 'Tis the nature of my existence. My armor only knows heat when it's beneath the human sun, otherwise it's the same temperature as my skin.'

She frowned as she balled her hand into a fist to warm it. 'Are you always so cold?'

A tic started in his jaw. 'Aye, little mouse. Always.'

Without another word, he led her back down the hallway to the end where two doors opened into what must have been a grand hall at one time. It was clean, but dark gray like the rest of the castle. A large, shiny, black round table was set in the center of the room, where it held precedence. Intricately carved black chairs were placed around it every few inches.

Like Kerrigan, it was both beautiful and sinister.

Staring at it, she wondered if it was the table of legend. 'Is that—'

'Nay,' Kerrigan interrupted quickly. 'This is *le cercle du damné*. It is similar to Arthur's Round Table, but very different.'

'How so?'

He pulled a chair out for her where one of the places at the table was set with trencher, food, and a golden goblet. 'Have a seat, Seren.'

She did as he bade.

'Drink.'

'But my goblet is empty.' The words had barely left her lips before wine appeared in it. She looked at it suspiciously.

An amused light seemed to dance in Kerrigan's midnight eyes. 'There is no spell in your food, mouse. You may eat and drink in peace.'

Still, she hesitated as she sniffed at the scented wine. 'Can I trust you to be honest with me?'

'Nay, you cannot. Ever. But in this, I do not lie. Eat without fear.'

There was far too much food for one person to consume. 'Would you care to join me?'

Kerrigan looked longingly at the food before he shook his head. How he wished he could sample that fare, but he hadn't tasted food in countless centuries.

He moved to the other side of the table while she began to eat.

She was strangely beautiful as she gracefully cut her roasted lamb and brought it to her lips. She closed her eyes as if to savor the flavor of it. Her manners, unlike his, were flawless. When he'd first come here, he had eaten with his hands like a savage. Morgen had been repulsed by him. It was why food could no longer sustain him.

'We shall have to find something to nourish you that you can ingest without disgusting me.'

Morgen had done much to change him from the man he had once been. Indeed, he didn't even recall being human anymore. At least he hadn't until he saw the trusting fool before him. She touched something inside him, and he wasn't sure what it was.

She paused in her eating to look up at him. 'Am I doing something wrong?'

'Nay, why do you ask?'

'You watch me so intently that it makes me nervous.'

He shook his head at her guileless words. 'You should never tell someone when they make you nervous, little mouse.'

'Whyever not?'

'It gives them leverage against you since they know how to make you uncomfortable.'

'Or it gets them to cease the behavior that causes the discomfort.'

He scoffed at that. 'You are terminally naive, aren't you?'

'I wouldn't think so. I only believe that most people will do the right thing whenever they can.'

Aye, she was a naive little chit. 'I am of a differing opinion. I only have faith in people taking advantage of any situation to serve their own purposes.'

'And what advantage do you have with me here, eating your food and dressed in your gown?'

'You are my prisoner. My advantage is your presence here. I am using you to get what I want.'

'And what is it you seek?'

'Arthur's Round Table.'

Seren frowned at him and his quest. 'Why do you want it?'

He had no business answering her question, but

43

what harm could there be? It wasn't as if she could do anything to stop him and it wasn't as if Merlin didn't know exactly why the table was important to them. 'It holds at its center a great magic. One that when combined with other sacred objects is capable of rendering its wielder invincible. With it here, there would be no one who could stop us from ruling the earth.'

He could tell by her innocent face that the very concept baffled her. 'Why would you wish to rule the earth, my lord? What point could there possibly be in it?'

'If you have to ask that question, then you cannot possibly wrap your tiny little mind around the concept to understand the answer. I am a selfish and self-centered bastard. I only want to play by my rules. As a great man once said, it is good to be king.'

Her eyes snapped at him. 'Thank you, my lord, for the insult to my intellect. But I would return to say that it is indeed a small-minded man who cannot allow others to have their own share of the world. It is a surprisingly large place with room in it for all of us.'

Kerrigan was taken back by her angry retort. 'Are you a fool to insult me?'

She lifted her chin to pierce him with a malicious glare. 'You insulted me first.'

Kerrigan felt something he hadn't felt in centuries. Humor. He actually laughed at her audacity. It amazed him. Anyone else who dared insult him would now be lying dead at his feet. But this woman . . .

She amused him.

'You are a brave woman.'

'Not especially. I'm merely a frank one.'

'Well, I find your frankness refreshing.'

Seren returned to eating, but she was still uneasy with the way Kerrigan stared at her as if he were a starving man and she his feast.

As she finished her food, she started to rise. Kerrigan vanished from his seat to appear directly behind her chair so that he could pull it back from the table.

She jumped at his sudden appearance.

'Forgive me for startling you.'

'How do you do that?'

He shrugged as he moved the chair back for her. 'I think it and it happens.'

She crossed herself. 'You are a devil, aren't you?'

'Aye, my lady *souris*. Damned and cursed.'

And yet there was something about him that reminded her of a lost soul that wanted to find itself again. It was a stupid thing to think. She had no idea why she even thought it when he seemed to take such pleasure in being evil.

He leaned toward her ever so slightly, his presence overwhelming as he seemed to smell the air around her. The corners of his mouth lifted. It softened the harshness of his features and the chill in his gaze. 'You had best return to your room now.'

'Why?'

'I am a man of very finite patience, my Seren. I am not used to denying myself what small pleasures I can have. And you . . . you test the limits of what little self-control I possess.' He reached out one cold hand to lightly brush against her cheek.

Seren could feel the warmth leave her skin at his touch. As she stood before him, her gaze dropped down to his neck, and there she saw the star amulet Magda had mentioned.

Her heart hammering, she reached to touch it.

Kerrigan immediately captured her hand. 'What is it you do?'

'It . . . it is lovely.'

He moved her hand away from it and stepped back. 'Go, Seren. Before it's too late for you.'

One moment she was before him, in the next she was back in her room. Only now it no longer had a door in it.

She swallowed as true fear took root inside her. Whatever was she going to do? Kerrigan was so powerful, so dark. How could she ever escape someone like him?

You have no choice.

Nay, she didn't. Somehow, someway she must find her way out of this land of the damned, back to her own home.

Chapter Four

Kerrigan reclined against the cushioned seat of his large, black throne as he watched Morgen 'entertain' the other members of her *cercle du damné*.

Like him, most of the other one hundred and forty-nine men and women of their brotherhood had once been human. Some of them had even sat at the Round Table with Arthur and pledged their swords to goodness.

But there was no goodness or humanity left here in Camelot. Much like its famed king, it was long gone and would most likely never be seen again.

With one hand resting on the dragon head carved into the arm of his throne, Kerrigan tipped his goblet back to drink deep of a wine that could never nourish him.

Nor could it make him drunk.

'Come, my king,' a beautiful Adoni female begged as she approached his dais. Her long black gown plunged all the way past her navel, baring to his gaze most of her abdomen and breasts – the tips of which had been painted a vivid red to stand out as they puckered invitingly against the sheer material of her dress. She was an amply endowed woman who would most likely please him for a moment or two. 'Will you not join us for a dance?'

Kerrigan slid his black gaze to the gathering where his demon knights danced with the fey. Some of them were already sprawling half naked in corners, uncaring of who watched them as they sought to sate their bodies. The loud dance music that played through the room came from CDs that Morgen had brought back from her journeys into the future – like many of the residents here, she loved the grace and style of the medieval, but preferred the conveniences and toys of future societies. And one of her penchants was for a style of early twenty-first-century music known as Dark Wave. Rather fitting, all things considered.

Personally, he could take or leave the music. For that matter, he could take or leave the inhabitants of Camelot.

He'd long grown weary of this place and of the creatures who called it home. He wanted more than the cold passion of the fey who gave their kisses and bodies without care. One cock was as good to them as any other.

'Begone from me,' he snapped at her.

The Adoni's eyes flashed red. She would attack except she knew the folly of such an action. Curling her lip, she left him to seek out another of the knights.

'What say you, my lord? Are you ill?'

Kerrigan tensed at the voice that came from behind his throne. 'Don't stand behind me, Blaise. Not if you wish to continue living in your current state.'

The tall, lithe mandrake moved forward to stand to the left of Kerrigan's throne. Born with albinism, Blaise had been cast out by his superstitious people when he'd been barely more than a babe.

His eyes were a pale, unforgiving shade of violet.

He wore his snow white hair in a long braid that fell over one shoulder, to his waist. His skin was a deep, golden tan that belied what most expected from one with his condition. It was a common misconception that all of those with albinism were completely lacking color. If not for the fact that he knew the mandrake took pride in his physical differences, Kerrigan would have suspected the darkness of Blaise's skin to be from his magic.

In human form, Blaise could barely see at all. He used his magic to sense where others and objects were around him. But as a dragon . . . his vision was sharp and clear.

He was without a doubt one of the most powerful mandrakes in service to Kerrigan and the closest thing to a friend he'd ever known. Though to be honest, Kerrigan didn't understand why the mandrake chose his company.

If he didn't know better, he might actually think the mandrake liked him.

Kerrigan took another sip of his drink.

'Why do you not participate in the orgy, my king?' Blaise asked quietly.

'Why do you not?'

Blaise shrugged. 'I sensed your discomfort. Your restlessness. I was hoping to find a way to amuse you, my lord. Do you wish me to take dragon form?'

'Nay. A ride will do nothing to improve my mood.' Not even bloodshed would ease the fire that currently simmered deep in his loins.

Only Seren could sate his mood.

But she had trusted him, and for some insane reason he couldn't name, he didn't want to violate that trust.

Suddenly the music in the hall changed. Kerrigan grimaced as he heard Morgen's favorite song from a century far ahead of the one in which he'd been born. Moments such as this, he hated that they could travel through time.

Morgen danced to the beat of it as her male Adoni consorts circled her.

He groaned.

Blaise's expression remained stoic. 'Does my king not like INXS?'

'I did until your lady decided to play it to the point of nausea.' If he never heard 'Need You Tonight' again, it would be too soon.

Morgen swayed to the music. She turned around, looked at him, and crooked her finger for him to join her.

Kerrigan shook his head.

He felt her powers invading him, pulling at him. But he refused to let her control him. Those days were long past.

Closing his eyes, he summoned his own song. Papa Roach's 'Do or Die.'

Morgen's eyes blazed at him as he gave her a taunting smile. The music immediately returned to INXS with 'Devil Inside.'

'You are either the bravest man ever born, my king, or the most foolish,' Blaise whispered beside him.

'Perhaps I am both,' he said before drinking.

'It appears our king is possessed of malaise,' Morgen said to the group as she approached his throne. 'What do you think we should do to cheer him?'

One of her Adoni males moved forward to whisper in her ear.

Morgen smiled evilly. 'Aye, my pet. I think that would be a wonderful idea.'

Kerrigan yawned at her. Knowing the Adoni, whatever the idea, it was guaranteed to only bore him more.

Two heartbeats later, Seren appeared before Morgen.

He sat up instantly and handed his cup to Blaise. 'What are you doing, Morgen?' he demanded.

Seren looked around with panic in her heart. She'd been alone in her room, trying to find a way to escape. The next thing she'd known, she was here in a gilded hall with horrible music playing that thumped like a frantic heartbeat.

The voice of the singer was wickedly smooth, but the words were unintelligible to her.

There were beautiful men and women all around her, mixed with the twisted graylings and other things that appeared to be demons of some sort.

But the woman who caught her attention most was the one beside her who wore a dress so red, it didn't look natural. It looked as though the material itself were bleeding.

The woman's long blond hair was worn in tiny braids that were held in an intricate design around the crown of her head with jewel-tipped pins. She approached Seren with a sinister twist to her lips. The woman grabbed Seren's long blue manche sleeve and pulled at it angrily. 'Who put her in this?'

Kerrigan came instantly to his feet as his eyes turned a vibrant red that matched the woman's dress. 'I did.'

The woman hissed at him. 'You know the laws here, Kerrigan. I am queen of the fey, and no one wears such a color in my world. No one!'

'And I *am* the law here, Morgen. It goes with my crown. That is, unless you wish to challenge me for it.'

Seren swallowed at his words as she stared anew at the woman who held her sleeve. Could this truly be the famed Morgen le Fey? Sister to Arthur and mother to Mordred?

If she was, then this sorceress held wicked powers that could enable her to take the form of beasts and enchant anyone she chose. There was no telling what she could do to them.

It was a sobering thought.

'I will challenge him for you, my lady,' one of the handsome knights offered as he moved forward in the crowd.

Morgen arched a brow at that as a slow, evil smile curved her seductive lips. 'A challenger. Why, Kerrigan, it appears your reign may be over.' She grabbed Seren roughly and pulled her toward a door.

Kerrigan moved toward them with deep, angry strides. 'Release her, Morgen. Now!'

Seren fought against the woman's hold. When Morgen refused to let her loose, Seren bit her.

Morgen screamed and released her instantly.

With nowhere else to go, Seren ran toward Kerrigan. He met her and placed himself between her and the other woman. The sound of steel scraping steel rang out as he drew his sword forth to confront them.

Seren trembled as she looked about for somewhere else to flee to, but the crowd of people wasn't conducive to such. They completely encircled her and Kerrigan. No doubt they would fling her back toward Morgen if she dared to run. Therefore, her safest course of action would be to stand with Kerrigan.

Morgen arched a brow at Kerrigan's raised sword. 'Well, isn't this interesting? I haven't seen fire in your cheeks in centuries, Kerrigan. Tell me what it is about this pathetic little human that you would dare raise your sword against me in protection of her?'

'You gave her to me, Morgen. Remember? You said

she was mine to do with as I please until she ceases to be of use to us. And I protect what is mine, whether it is this throne, my sword . . . or her.'

'That's far from comforting,' Seren said in a tone she was sure Morgen and the others couldn't hear.

Kerrigan passed her an irritated glare.

She stared her own ire back at him. 'Well, I'm not your shoes,' she whispered. 'I am a person . . . with value.'

The withering look on his face said he might not share her view.

'Are you rebelling?' Morgen asked him.

He turned his heated stare at the fey queen. 'Are you?'

Her insidious laughter rang out over the music and echoed in the hall. Morgen crossed the distance between them. With an unparalleled daring, she brushed his sword aside with her hand so that she stood toe to toe with him.

'Careful, my lord,' she said in an almost sweet tone. 'Remember who it is who gave you your power. Damé Fortune is fickle. One day a peasant, the next a king, and the day after, a peasant again.'

He didn't flinch. 'One day a sorceress, the next a bad memory.'

Seren gasped as the Morgen's eyes slithered between yellow and orange.

'Tostig,' she snapped at the knight who had agreed to fight Kerrigan. 'Don your armor. Kill the king and you shall replace him.'

Seren sucked her breath in sharply at those words. She was quite certain that if the black knight was dethroned, she wouldn't fare very well.

Kerrigan shook his head. 'Stand down, Tostig. I've no wish to thin my army needlessly.'

Black armor, the likes of which Seren had never seen before, appeared on the knight's body before he drew a black sword with the strangest blade she'd ever beheld. Instead of a straight blade, it was rippled and shone with an eerie green light.

Kerrigan gave a heavy sigh as if the matter of the fight merely bored him. He turned toward her. 'Seren, stay with Blaise until I kill him.' He pushed her gently into the arms of a man who was every bit as eerie as Morgen. 'Guard her, mandrake.'

Blaise nodded grimly as he pulled her to the side.

Kerrigan, unlike his opponent, didn't bother with a helm as he stood ready to fight. Indeed, he appeared as nonchalant as a man waiting for a friend to join him. There was nothing in his stance or countenance to say that he was about to fight to the death.

Seren frowned as she saw Tostig whisper to another knight. Unlike Kerrigan, he appeared nervous and uncertain.

'What is he doing?' she asked Blaise. 'Is it some spell against Kerrigan?'

'Nay,' he said in a flat tone. 'He's not strong enough for that. Tostig is new to our company. He is asking the men around him for Kerrigan's weakness.'

'And that is?'

One corner of his mouth lifted into a knowing smirk. 'None.'

She scoffed at that. 'All men have a weakness.'

'Men do, but Kerrigan is no longer human.' As if to prove his words, a large, black shield appeared on Kerrigan's arm out of nowhere. 'There is no way to defeat him, and Tostig is being told that by the others. It's why no one, not even Morgen, dares to challenge him for power.'

She watched as Tostig went from knight to knight.

There was no pity on their faces, nor was there any help as one by one they shook their heads at him.

'I grow weary of waiting, Tostig,' Kerrigan said in a bored voice. 'Either fight me or cede your challenge.'

Morgen faced the knight with a condescending sneer. 'Have you grown craven, Tostig? Where is my new champion and future king?'

The knight let out an unholy bellow as he raised his sword and ran at Kerrigan, who deflected him with ease. The crowd fanned out, giving them a large circle in the center to fight.

Seren went weak as she watched the two powerful warriors encircling each other. In spite of what Blaise had said, she was nervous. Should something happen to Kerrigan, there was no telling what Morgen or the victor would do to her.

Kerrigan might be frightening, but he was the devil she knew. She sensed heat in him, even wickedness; however, there was no true malice there. Not like she felt whenever Morgen or the others looked at her.

Tostig attacked again, striking Kerrigan's sword with a powerful blow that caused sparks to fly from it. Kerrigan raised his round shield that held what appeared to be a dragon devouring a castle and used it to drive the other knight back.

Tostig twisted and swung for Kerrigan's waist. Kerrigan deflected the blow, then shoved the knight away with his shield. Tostig staggered a bit before he returned with a swing that barely missed Kerrigan's neck. Only Kerrigan's speed and agility kept it from making contact. He immediately parried with a thrust that cut across Tostig's arm.

The knight cried out, but didn't falter as he attacked, and again Kerrigan parried.

While the men fought, Morgen approached Seren

with a wicked and delighted smile on her beautiful face.

Blaise pulled Seren back from the fey queen.

'Don't worry, mandrake,' Morgen all but purred, 'I mean your charge no harm.'

Blaise scoffed. 'You mean everyone harm, Morgen.'

Morgen laughed.

A chill went down Seren's spine as Morgen moved closer ... so close that she couldn't move without making contact with the woman. She tried to step nearer to Blaise, only to find her body unwilling to obey. It was as if someone else was controlling her.

'Kerrigan is incredible, isn't he?' Morgen asked her as she moved to stand just at her back.

Seren agreed, but couldn't answer. It felt as if her vocal cords were frozen.

'Look at the way he moves,' Morgen whispered softly in her ear, her voice strangely echoing through her head. 'He twirls, he parries, and then he thrusts and thrusts again. Look at the power of him. The strength. The masculine beauty. In all the world there are only a few who can match him in fairness of form. None who could touch him for savagery or mercilessness.' Morgen breathed in her ear. 'It makes you lust for him, doesn't it?'

A strange, foreign heat went through Seren at the words. It was as if her body were pierced by a bittersweet pleasure.

'Mor—' Blaise's words were cut short as Morgen waved her hand.

Seren glanced to see the mandrake every bit as frozen as she was. Morgen stepped even closer to her until their bodies were touching.

'Watch him, Seren,' she commanded.

Seren had no choice except to obey.

'Look at the way his muscles strain as he fights,' Morgen breathed in her ear, causing chills to run the length of her body. 'The way his beautiful black hair flies in the wind with every advance, every studied movement. The beauty of his face as he grimaces in fearsome combat.'

Morgen brushed the hair back from Seren's shoulder as she leaned even closer to whisper directly into her ear. She snaked her arm around Seren's waist in what could only be called a lover's embrace.

'Now imagine all the power of him sliding deep inside you, Seren.' Something wickedly warm and erotic flicked deep at the core of her body to emphasize those words. The pleasure of it actually made her gasp. 'Imagine him stretching your virgin's flesh until he fills you completely. Think of the sensation of his hands caressing your naked skin . . . your breasts.' It felt as if he were already touching her. 'The sensation of his body sliding in and out of yours, pleasing you while you beg him for more . . .'

Seren couldn't breathe as her entire body burned with a lustful ache she'd never before experienced. Her breasts were heavy, full. It was almost as if she could feel the very things that Morgen described.

'Imagine his lips on yours. His tongue flicking over your virgin's flesh while you're spread out naked and bare for his pleasure. His heavy, muscled body covering you completely . . . His breath mingling with yours as he whispers tender words for only you . . .'

Her body was on fire at the things Morgen described. Some alien part of her was crying out for Kerrigan. Hungry and needful, it scared her senseless.

'Beg for me, Seren.' It wasn't Morgen's voice she heard in her ear. It was Kerrigan's. 'Beg for me to take you.'

'Morgen!' The fierce shout echoed through the silent crowd as Kerrigan ran his sword through Tostig's poor body, causing Seren to blink for the first time since Morgen had approached her.

Without feeling or compassion for the life he'd just taken, Kerrigan jerked his sword free of Tostig's chest and paid no heed to the man who fell dead at his feet as he turned to face them.

An instant later, he was before her, his sword and hand coated in bright red blood that matched the vibrancy of Morgen's dress.

Seren stared up at Kerrigan's merciless face as Morgen's images still played through her mind. She could already feel his weight against her body. Feel his touch on her breasts. Feel his cold kiss again.

He looked down at her, and something hot flickered in his black eyes.

She felt his desire for her with the same intensity as she felt her own. He didn't move, didn't speak as those eyes penetrated her. Pierced her. It was as if they were the only two people in this room.

Morgen laughed cruelly an instant before she literally ripped the pale blue dress from Seren and exposed her nude body to everyone there. Seren cringed at the sudden rush of cold air against her skin. Still, she was held by Morgen's spell that left her unable to move. Unable to run from the horror of this moment and escape it.

This was something from her nightmares!

Her face twisted with hatred, Morgen shoved her toward Kerrigan, who caught her against his hard chest. His unyielding armor bit into her flesh and chilled her completely. She wanted to scream at them all, but no sound would leave her throat.

'You would take this poor, haggard creature to your

bed?' Morgen asked cruelly. 'Are you truly so desperate for a woman, Kerrigan?'

Naked and bared to them all as they laughed at her, Seren was horrified and embarrassed to the deepest part of her soul. She wished she could wither and die right on the spot. But Kerrigan didn't laugh at her humiliation.

Instead he cursed Morgen before he wrapped himself around her. An instant later, they were gone from the hall, into a room she didn't know.

Suddenly her body was back under her own control as she collapsed against the man who held her carefully.

Seren screamed as the horror of it all consumed her.

'Shh, Seren,' Kerrigan whispered in her ear as he kept her against his cold body. 'All is fine. You are safe now.'

'Nay,' she choked as she shivered. 'I have died and gone to hell. Surely, there is no other place this can be.'

She shoved him away from her as her thoughts tumbled over one another in her mind. She struggled to make sense of them all, but her emotions were too raw and exposed as she relived her horror.

'You're covered in blood,' she said as she noted the way it coated his black armor, reminding her of glaze over a blackened roast. 'You ruthlessly killed that poor man, knowing he stood no chance against you. Still you fought him. Killed him for no real reason other than for Morgen's amusement.' She shook her head as the image of Tostig's violent death replayed in her mind. 'You're the devil.'

His expression empty and blank, Kerrigan stepped back as a black fur cloak appeared over her naked body. Seren would have cast it off, but she didn't dare.

It was all that saved her dignity, such as it was at the moment.

Kerrigan said nothing as he watched her with those emotionless eyes.

'You don't deny it?' she accused.

'Nay,' he said quietly. 'You are in hell and I am the devil who keeps you here. It is the way of it.'

Her mind screamed out in denial. This couldn't be happening. 'I want to go home.'

He shook his head. 'You should have gone with Gawain when you had the chance. 'Tis too late for you now. You chose of your own free will to come with me. With me you will stay until I no longer have need of you.'

Seren swallowed the tears that she refused to cry. She'd been weak enough before them. The time for tears was past.

In that moment, she hated him and all the creatures who dwelled here. 'I can't believe that my entire life will be ruined by one thoughtless mistake.'

He gave an evil half laugh. 'We are all damned by our deeds, my lady, whether they are thought out or not.' His eyes turned back to their dull blackness. 'You may rest peacefully here. No one will disturb you.'

She looked around the cold, ebony room. Nothing here was inviting or welcoming. It reminded her of a witch's black pot. 'Where is this place that I am safe?'

'My bedchamber.'

As soon as those words were spoken, he dissolved into a cloud of smoke and vanished.

Seren looked around the dark, foreboding room. There was nothing warm here. No fire burned in the hearth. His bed was overlarge, and covered with black furs, but even so, it didn't appear comfortable. There were no chairs, no table. Nothing. It was large and empty.

Like their hearts.

Aye, they were all monsters. All of them.

'I have to escape,' she whispered. But how? The only way she knew was what Magda had told her.

Did she dare trust one of them?

Did she dare not?

Closing her eyes, Seren tried to wish herself back to her loom. She tried to convince herself that it was all a nightmare, but with each pounding beat of her heart, she realized that it wasn't a dream. This was her life, and those below fully intended to kill her.

'I won't let you,' she said aloud to the room. 'Do you hear me? I am Seren of York, apprenticed to Master Rufus of London, and I will not be bested by the likes of you. I—'

Am just a peasant.

Those words ran around her head and taunted her. Mocked her.

Aye, she was a peasant, but she was also a survivor, and she wouldn't let them best her. Ever. This matter was far from over. She would find her way home no matter what it took.

Kerrigan didn't dare head back to the throne room. In the mood he was in, he might very well kill Morgen.

Or at least try.

At the end of the day, he knew he could no more kill her than she could kill him. They were at an impasse.

Both immortal. Both powerful.

Both hateful.

But Morgen did have one advantage. She knew the source of his immortality while he knew nothing of hers. He had no clue as to what gave her her powers.

She knew his weakness. And, to borrow an expression from centuries ahead, that pissed him off.

Kerrigan gripped his sword as he materialized on the roof of Camelot. He sat at the highest point so that he could look out into the darkness of this land where he ruled. When he'd first come here, he had been ecstatic with his newfound powers and with the pleasure and riches Morgen had given him. She had taken him to her bed and had played to every desire he'd ever had.

A callow youth, he'd grown to manhood here, under her callous tutelage.

Morgen had shown him marvels the likes of which he'd never dreamed of. Dragons and gargoyles for his command. Willing whores for his every amusement. Planes that flew over skies filled with buildings that made a mockery of mountains. Magic that could turn them into any beast they chose. And sex so raw and blinding that he'd once feared it would incinerate him.

In those days, he'd been an eager pawn for her.

But those days had long since passed. Somehow he'd grown tired of this realm.

Tired of Morgen and her childishness.

'Why do you wish to rule the world?' Seren's voice taunted him from the mist of his mind.

The true answer he'd withheld from her. 'Because I am bored with this one.'

There was nothing here except a dissatisfaction that grew daily. That was why Seren was such a fascination to him. She was new. Fresh.

In time she would grow as stale to him as this world. It was the way of things.

'Get the table and kill her,' he breathed. There was no need in wasting his time with any other thought. Like everything else in life, Seren was a pawn to be used and then discarded.

Nothing more, nothing less.

And yet even as those words flitted through his mind, there was some part of him that argued it. Whatever it was that had chosen her as the mother of a Merlin, it also made her far too appealing to him.

Seren heard something scratching at the door. She sat up on the bed, clutching the fur cloak against her.

'Seren . . .'

She breathed in relief at the sound of Magda's voice. Scooting off the bed, she ran to the door, where she splayed her hand against the rough black wood. 'Magda?'

'Aye, my lady. Are you all right?'

'Aye.'

'Are you alone?'

She glanced over her shoulder to be sure. 'I am. Lord Kerrigan left sometime ago.'

'That is bad, my lady. Do you not remember what I told you about seducing him?'

'I remember.'

'Good. Now listen closely . . . If you want power over the master, while he sleeps, you must take his sword from him and hide it.'

Seren frowned. That seemed to be most dangerous for her to try. 'What say you?'

'Take his sword from him, Seren. Take it and—'

'What are you doing here, Magda?'

Seren tensed as she heard Blaise's deep, silken voice from the other side of the door.

'I am checking on the lady.'

'Begone, vermin!' Blaise snapped.

Seren struck the door with her hand. 'Don't talk to her like that. She is a good soul.'

'And you are a fool if you believe it.'

Seren tried to open the door, but it didn't budge. 'Where is Lord Kerrigan?' she asked him through the wood.

'Wherever it is he wishes to be.'

She grimaced at his bland tone. 'I want out of here. You can't keep me prisoner.'

'There's nothing to be done about that, my lady. No one enters or leaves the king's bedchamber unless he takes them in or brings them out. Not even I can venture there without his permission.'

'Are you his steward then?'

'Nay. I am his servant.'

'How so?'

'Seren?'

She jerked around at the deep familiar voice to find Kerrigan standing behind her. There was an eerie dim light that seemed to have no source that cut across the angles of his handsome face. His black armor held a ghostly glow in the darkness that only seemed to heighten his size and aura of power. Against her will, her gaze dropped to his hip, where the black scabbard held the sword Magda had told her to steal.

Her heart pounded. 'I despise the way you just appear without warning.'

He glanced past her, to the door. 'Your shift is over, Blaise. You may retire for the night.'

'Thank you, my king.'

She heard Blaise's footsteps fall away from the door.

Kerrigan spread his hand out and a fire roared to life from the dead coals in his hearth.

She blinked against the sudden brightness, and held her hand to shield her eyes.

'It is late, Seren. You should be asleep.'

Her fur cloak turned into a thick, warm woolen kirtle that was lined with fine silk to protect her skin.

She stared in amazement of the pale green color. It was beautiful.

'I will not molest you tonight, Seren. Sleep in peace.'

She lowered her hand to find him staring at her with those penetrating, soulless black eyes. His black hair fell loosely around his wide shoulders and face, tousled as if he'd been in the wind. He held his hand out, and a great black throne magically appeared before the fire.

She shivered at the sight of it and the effortless way he'd conjured it into being. He was intense and omnipotent.

Even so, she refused to cower before him. 'Have you any idea how upsetting it is to have no control over your life?'

He took a seat on the throne that was facing the fire, but he didn't look at her. 'Have you ever had control of your life, Seren?'

'I . . .' she hesitated before she finally answered. 'Yea. I did once.'

A stool appeared so that he could rest his long, mail-clad legs upon it. He crossed them at the ankles as he stared at the fire. 'And when was this?'

'Until you captured me.'

He snorted at that. 'You had no control. You told me yourself that you were forbidden to even leave that paltry town without permission from your master.'

'It's not true. I am a freewoman. I had hope for my future. I had potential.'

He scoffed at her words. 'Potential. A sad word, that. Have you any idea what it really means?'

'Of course. It means that at any moment, things could improve.'

He shook his head, but still didn't look at her. 'It is

a word used by those above you to make you tolerate your present lowly status by hoping for something that will never be. There is no such thing as potential. It is only a lie peddled to imbeciles.'

She refused to believe his words. 'You only think that because you had no potential,' she whispered angrily. Then louder she said, 'What happened to make you so cynical?'

She wasn't sure, but she thought he might actually be stifling a smile. 'Life, my lady. Sooner or later, it destroys the potential in us all. As we strive like ants dancing to the command of our queen, it passes us by while we dream of a better place and time. Then one day all too soon, you awaken to find yourself old and shriveled, still working for others while you have nothing left but memories of work and suffering. Your potential gone, it leaves nothing in its wake. Nothing but hatred and bitterness to accompany you to your grave. You may take your potential if it comforts you. But I know the truth.'

Seren had never heard anyone speak thusly, and in truth it made her heart ache for him that he had nothing to believe in. 'And what comforts you, then?'

Kerrigan grew quiet at the question. At first she didn't think he would answer, until his deep voice filled the emptiness. 'Nothing comforts me.'

'Truly nothing?'

He didn't look at her or respond as he stared into the flames.

Even though he scared her, Seren forced herself to cross the short distance between them. She stood just behind his throne so that she could watch him. He sat there quietly as if he were made of stone while the fire crackled and danced. The air was thick with the scent of wood and pine.

For some reason she couldn't even begin to understand, she felt a peculiar urge to brush at his hair. Instead, she clenched her hand into a fist and rested it against the back of his throne.

'When I was a girl, my mother used to sing to me whenever I hurt. She would hold me close and promise me that one day I would have my own little girl to love. That I would find my place in the world and be happy. To this day, I think of my mother's voice and it warms me. Surely you had a mother.'

He gave a bitter laugh. 'My mother was a drunken whore who couldn't abide the sight of me unless it was to blame me for her wretched state in the world. I assure you, I found no comfort in her mewling insults.'

Her heart ached for him. She couldn't imagine what it must be like to be hated by the woman who had birthed her. Instinctively, she reached out to touch him, only to have him grab her hand in a rough grip.

'What are you doing?' he asked angrily.

'I was offering you comfort, my lord.' She grimaced as his grip tightened. 'Please. You're hurting me.'

His black eyes bored into her. 'That is what I do, Seren. I hurt people. Never let yourself forget it.' He let go of her instantly.

Seren rubbed her wrist where she could see a perfect outline of his handprint. 'Have you ever tried being nice to anyone?'

He looked back at the fire. 'Go to bed, Seren.'

Before she could move or speak, she found herself lying in the bed. She tried to get up, but couldn't move. 'I am not your slave, Lord Kerrigan. I am my own person.'

The next thing she knew, he appeared above her out of the shadows. His armor gone, he wore a loose black tunic and hose, with his sword still firmly buckled at his hip. The firelight flashed against the star medallion as it fell free of his shirt to hang in the empty space between them.

He held himself above her as he stared down at her lips. He ran one cold finger down her cheek. 'You are at my mercy, Lady Star. You *are* my slave.'

She shivered even though a part of her found his weight strangely enticing. 'I do not toil for you and I am not your property. I am freeborn and I shall remain that way.'

One corner of his mouth curled up into a taunting expression. 'And what of your apprenticeship?'

It angered her that he threw that in her face. 'I will pay Master Rufus back . . . eventually.'

He cocked his head as he studied her. He moved his hand from her face to the satin laces that fell from the neck of her kirtle. He took one in his hand and rubbed it between his fingers. 'Why are you so defiant of me?'

'Should I not be?'

Kerrigan was completely dumbfounded by her. No one had ever stood so strong against him. Not even Morgen. She knew when she was bested and she withdrew.

Yet here was this . . . servant girl. She had no magic powers. No alliances. She had nothing to barter with. Nothing. And yet she stood strong before him even though he scared her.

It was inconceivable to him.

His gaze dipped to her small breasts that all but disappeared while she lay on her back. There was nothing about her really attractive. Nothing except those vivid green eyes that seared him with her spirit.

There was a warmth inside her that reached out to him even more than the fire in his hearth. In his mind, he could imagine her naked beneath him. Imagine her sighs of pleasure as he took her until the boiling need in his blood was fully sated.

Those green eyes of hers taunted and defied him even now.

'Kiss me, Seren.'

Still she didn't flinch or flee. 'Is that a master's order to his slave?'

One corner of his mouth quirked up into the first real smile he'd known in centuries. She was daring him. If he said aye, she would deny him. It was on the tip of his tongue to say so just to see her fire, and yet another part of him didn't want to fight with her.

It only wanted to taste her again.

'Nay, lady. It is a simple request from a man to a woman.'

'But you told me that you're not a man.'

He shook his head at her continued argument. 'Kiss me, Seren . . . please.'

Seren held her breath at that one word she was sure this man never spoke. The reason inside her said to push him away, and yet she didn't dare to truly anger him. He could have his way with her, and she was lucky that so far he found her amusing and not annoying.

What harm could come in just placating his one request?

Her heart racing, she lifted her head up ever so slightly to place her lips to his.

Kerrigan fisted his hand in the furs of his bed as her hesitant tongue swept against his. Cradling her head in his left hand, he laid his body down so that he could feel every inch of her body pressed against his.

Aye, this was what he wanted. A warm woman to hold. A virgin mouth that had been tasted only by his. A guileless woman who spoke her mind without malice, slander, or fear.

Most of all, a tender touch that didn't demand or hurt.

All it did was soothe.

Closing his eyes, he savored the rich scent of rose and woman as she sank her soft hand into his hair. She didn't pull at his hair, didn't nip painfully at his lips. She stroked him with a gentle, caring touch.

He'd never before known the like. The newness of it haunted him. Touched him.

Seren groaned at the wicked feel of Kerrigan kissing her. The swell of his groin pressed demandingly against her hip as he deepened his kiss. It was hungry and devouring, and it stole the very breath from her.

His tunic melted from his body as he moved from her mouth to bury his lips against her throat where his dark whiskers tickled her skin. The coldness of his naked flesh sent chills over her even as desire heated her body. It was such a strange sensation – hot and cold clashing inside and out of her.

He tasted so good and felt even better. She'd never had a man hold her like this. If she didn't know better, she might even think that he had feelings for her. But that was foolish. He knew nothing of her and she knew nothing of him. They were strangers and he held no feelings for anyone. He'd told her that.

Even so, Seren trembled as she ran her hands over his naked back.

At least until she felt the deep ridges on his flesh. Shocked by them, she opened her eyes to see the deep scars that bisected his back.

'Who beat you?' The words were out before she could stop them.

His eyes turning red, Kerrigan pulled back with a hiss as his black tunic reappeared to cover those scars. 'Sleep, Seren.'

'But—'

'Sleep or be raped,' he growled in rage. 'Decide!' The shout rang against the stone walls.

That was a choice? Swallowing at his untoward anger, she immediately rolled over to give him her back.

Kerrigan fought for control as he again faced the fire that did nothing to warm the coldness inside him.

Take her!

To what purpose?

Aye, he could rape her. Or use a spell to make her welcome him even. But in the end, it would be nothing more than a passing amusement that could be found with any wench in Morgen's court.

In the morning he would awaken with her blood on his sheets and body, and his loins would ache anew. He would still be restless.

Nothing would change.

Nay, that wasn't true. Seren would be changed. She would be violated, and the fire that burned so bright in her green eyes would be extinguished.

Finally, she would be defeated.

He didn't know why the thought of her being broken disturbed him so, but it did. More than anyone, he understood the pain of betrayal. The lasting sting of humiliation as others abused him while he could do nothing to stop them. There was nothing worse in this world or beyond it, and for the first time since Morgen had found him, he didn't want to lash out in anger.

He wanted . . .

Kerrigan paused as he realized he didn't even have a name for what he wanted.

Returning to his throne, he looked to where Seren lay in his bed. She was ramrod stiff.

'Relax, Seren,' he whispered softly.

She stiffened even more.

A slow smile curved his lips in humor as he whispered a spell for her. Even so, she fought it until he forced her to sleep.

Kerrigan shook his head at her as she finally relaxed and succumbed to his spell. He was beginning to see how it was that his little mouse would birth a Merlin. No doubt she would be the kind of mother she'd described to him. One who held her child to her bosom with love and not resentment.

The babe's father wouldn't be some nameless man who had paid for her body and left his seed inside her to take root and grow into a despised abomination. Most likely the father would be someone she cared for.

Someone she gave her most prized possession to.

Untoward rage gripped him.

The thought of one of the knights of Avalon inside her was enough to make his blood boil. They were mewling half-witted bastards who didn't deserve something like her.

She was . . .

She's a pawn.

Pawns didn't matter in the game. Only winning did.

Kerrigan let out a disgusted breath. What was wrong with him?

I'm too idle.

Aye, it wasn't in his nature to sit and do nothing. But he didn't dare leave her unattended. There was no telling what Morgen might do should he leave Seren alone. Growling, he rose from the throne to open the door he conjured to the side of his hearth.

He pulled up short as he found Blaise in his council room. In small dragon form, the beast was curled up on his desk, draped around the very orb he'd come seeking.

'What are you doing?'

The mandrake opened one violet eye to peer at him. 'Sleeping.'

'I told you you were excused.'

Blaise closed his eye as if unconcerned by Kerrigan's wrath. 'And I angered Morgen tonight. I thought it best I sleep elsewhere until she becomes distracted by someone else.'

The mandrake had a point.

'I want my ball, dragon.'

Yawning widely, the mandrake slid from the crystal to the desk, then crawled to one side where he again coiled up to sleep. Kerrigan ignored the mandrake as he circled his hand over the crystal and concentrated on the Lords of Avalon.

A deep, red mist cleared to show him several of them in a boat, leaving the shores of their land, no doubt to find Seren and bring her home.

He curled his lip at the sight of them. For all he knew, one of them could very well be the future father of Seren's child.

The thought singed him. Thumping the ball, he sent a wave crashing against them. Their boat overturned and sent the men scrambling. They shouted as their heavy, mail-clad bodies sank quickly to the bottom of the sea.

'Now that was real mature,' Blaise said.

Kerrigan turned to find the mandrake watching him. 'Did I ask for your opinion?'

'Nay, but I felt the need to give it.' Blaise stretched and yawned before he turned over to expose his scaly belly so that he could sleep on his back. 'At least you were kinder this time.'

'How so?'

'They'll all live. What has possessed you to such mercy?'

Kerrigan shrugged. 'Dead, they pose no challenge to me. Besides, I can't kill them while they're in Avalon and they know it. I can only make them miserable there.'

Blaise snorted a small wisp of fire.

Silence fell between them while Kerrigan opened and closed several books around him. He paused as he uncovered a portable DVD player that he'd brought back from the twenty-first century. A slight smile curved his lips as he considered Seren's reaction to something that future mankind would find trivial.

In truth, he found the future world even colder than this one. True, there were marvels to be had. But not even they could compare with the magic he commanded. In the end, even that had left him morose.

'How old are you, Blaise?'

The mandrake gave him a curious stare. Kerrigan didn't blame him. Blaise had been in service to him for more than three hundred years, and in all that time, he'd never asked anything personal about him.

'I was born three years after Arthur.'

'Over six hundred years then?'

'Give or take. I long stopped counting such events, as they are meaningless to the likes of us.'

It was true. Kerrigan could barely recall his own age. There had been a time when living forever had seemed like a good idea. But as the centuries passed and he found nothing new to explore, it had all become just another day.

'Why am I so damned bored?'

He didn't realize he'd spoken aloud until Blaise answered him. 'Simple. If you toss a stone at Magda, what does she do?'

'Nothing. She rubs the spot, curses, looks to see

that it's me, and then goes on about her work.'

'Does that ever change?'

'Nay.'

Blaise rolled to his side. 'And if you insult Morgen?'

'She insults me back.'

'And if I were to open the window, what would be outside?'

'Gray clouds or black ones.' Kerrigan felt a flash of irritation. 'Where are you going with this?'

'Simple. Your problem is that nothing here ever changes. You don't do anything different anymore. You just sit around this castle moping. It's truly boring, my king. Face it, you're in a rut.'

Kerrigan shot a blast of fire at him, but he deftly dodged it . . . as he always did.

Blaise made no comment.

Kerrigan sighed. 'I used to enjoy being evil. It wears thin, doesn't it?'

'Not really. Better than being good. At least here the people are far more entertaining. You never know when one of them is going to run at your back, trying to kill you . . . well, for me that's true. They're too damned scared of you to try it. Maybe that's part of your problem, my king. You've made them too scared of you. But either way, good guys never fight dirty. You always know what to expect from them.'

There was truth to that. Even now, he wondered what mischief Morgen planned for both him and Seren. For there was no way that she didn't have something in the works. Her mind was ever plotting new evils.

But whatever she had planned, it would turn out the same. He would attack and she would back down.

Kerrigan cocked his head as he heard a whisper of movement from his bedchamber.

Could it be Seren moving about? Nay, not likely. The spell he'd given her should have her asleep for hours.

Again he heard the faint noise.

He opened the door to his bedchamber with his thoughts, then flashed into the room.

Seren turned from the window with a gasp to face him.

Kerrigan had barely opened his mouth to castigate her when the shutters behind her shattered.

Before he could react, a talon came through, coiled around her, and snatched her from his room.

Chapter Five

Seren wanted to fight the gargoyle who held her as the vicious winds whipped around her, but she refused, since to do so would be extremely stupid. It was a long way to the ground, and she held no desire to become a splotch of color on the dismally gray landscape.

The gargoyle who held her was huge, at least ten feet tall and twenty feet in diameter, and as black as pitch, with gleaming silver eyes and horns. Truly it was a fearsome sight that she would have preferred to remain ignorant of.

Suddenly she heard the sound of more wings flapping. *Please, tell me it's not more of these.* Twisting in the gargoyle's hand as a great shadow fell over her, she saw a dragon nearing them.

It took a full heartbeat before she realized the knight in black armor astride the dragon was Kerrigan.

Fire blasted out of the dragon's nostrils, shooting dangerously close to the gargoyle who held her.

'Release her!' Kerrigan's angry voice shouted.

'Oh please don't,' Seren shouted as panic consumed her. If the gargoyle did, she would surely die.

She watched as the dragon dipped below, then shot up to rise before them.

The gargoyle darted to the left, then went tumbling through the air. Seren groaned as his grip tightened on her. It was so tight now that she swore she felt her ribs starting to break. Fire blasted at them again. The heat of it burned her skin even as the gargoyle recoiled.

The next thing she knew, he let go of her.

She screamed as she fell haphazardly through the air, toward the rocky ground below.

Just as she was sure she'd die, something grabbed her and scooped her into cold arms. She glared at Kerrigan. 'You bastard!' she shouted before she hit him on the arm, which only succeeded in hurting her hand since he was dressed in his black armor.

Kerrigan was aghast at her actions. 'What is wrong with you, wench?'

'Me? What is wrong with you? Did you not see how close I came to dying? Why would you attack something that was holding me so far above the ground?'

'Because you were in danger.'

'I was in greater danger falling toward the earth than I was being held in his talon.'

'She has a point, my king,' Blaise said in an even tone as they glided effortlessly back toward the tower.

Seren gaped at the sound of the familiar voice coming out of the dragon's mouth. Certainly. Why not? Why should that be impossible given everything else she had seen in this cursed place?

It only stood to reason that the dragon would be Blaise. The very sky could yet turn out to be Morgen. Why not?

Kerrigan kicked his spur into the side of the dragon, who dipped them sharply to the right in response to the painful prodding.

'See!' Seren snapped at him. 'There you go again. Has it never occurred to you to be kind to the very thing that is keeping you from falling to the ground?'

'Blaise would never drop us.'

'How do you know?'

'Because the fall wouldn't kill my king,' the dragon said calmly. 'It would only make him angry and then he would nail my scaly hide to his wall as a trophy.'

Kerrigan gave her a smug look.

Still she was far from appeased. 'As if that would make it right. Have you no conscience?'

'Nay, Seren.'

'No decency?'

'I think she missed the part where you are pure evil, my king.'

'Nothing is pure evil,' Seren argued. 'There is goodness in all.'

'Did she not meet Morgen?' Kerrigan asked the dragon.

'Aye. I think the woman is daft. Mayhap delusional as well.'

Seren actually growled at him. 'You are impossible. Both of you.'

Kerrigan took her angry words in stride, which surprised her, really, since he didn't seem to have much patience with others. 'And why were you not abed after I left you?'

She narrowed her eyes on him. 'Let us see ... because I wanted to escape?'

'And you see where that led you,' he said in a flat, even tone. 'Had you stayed abed, you'd be safe now.'

She wanted to choke him. She really, truly did.

As they neared the dark tower where she had been torn from the window, Blaise pulled to a stop and hovered there in the middle of the air as his great wings flapped thunderously loud.

Kerrigan looked up from Seren to see what had alarmed the dragon.

His features hardened as he saw the entire Stone Legion flying toward them. There were at least two hundred gargoyles in formation. To most, it would be a fearsome sight. To Kerrigan, it just pissed him off.

'I think Morgen wants the girl,' Blaise said simply.

'Morgen!' Kerrigan shouted into the wind. 'Call them back or lose them all.'

He was answered by a smug, disembodied voice. 'Give me the Penmerlin's mother.'

'Why?'

'Because I want her.'

'As do I.'

A shriek echoed. 'Give her over, Kerrigan. Now!'

'Nay.'

'Are you sure about that, my liege?' the dragon asked in a low tone.

'Positive.'

Seren was extremely grateful that Kerrigan wouldn't surrender her and yet at the same time, she thought him rather daft for that decision. And her belief in his foolishness only increased with Morgen's next words.

'Take his sword and scabbard and he is naught but a mortal man to be killed,' Morgen ordered the gargoyles. 'The one to bring his head to me will be my new right hand.'

Blaise let loose a blast of fire. 'We are really screwed, my king,' he said afterward. 'Any ideas?'

Kerrigan jerked the reins to turn the dragon about. 'Pull out of Camelot.'

Seren covered her eyes as the gargoyles encircled them.

The next thing she knew, the dark gray sky was blue with bright, blinding sunlight all around them. The light was harsh against her eyes as they flew through the open air. But at least they appeared to be alone.

She couldn't see a single trace of the gargoyle army they had left behind.

They approached a lonely castle set on a small island that appeared to be surrounded by the bluest water she'd ever seen. It looked strangely tranquil, especially given the near disaster they had just escaped.

Blaise landed them on the tallest tower before he took the form of a man again. Dressed now in a green tunic and brown breeches, he looked out over the water as if he half expected the gargoyles to rejoin them, too. 'They'll be coming for us.'

Kerrigan shook his head. 'Unless you've spoken to her to inform her otherwise, Morgen knows nothing of this place.'

Blaise looked less than convinced. 'Are you certain?'

He nodded. 'I have kept it from her.' Then he passed a droll look to the mandrake. 'For good reason.'

'And the Lords of Avalon?' Blaise asked.

'They won't venture here. They fear this castle and the curse placed upon it.'

Seren arched a brow at his confident words. Should she find comfort in that or just more terror? 'Where is here?' Seren asked Kerrigan.

It was Blaise who answered her. 'We are at Joyous Gard.'

Seren gaped at the name of the famous castle. 'The home of Lancelot du Lac?'

Kerrigan snorted.

'It used to be, my lady,' Blaise said quietly. 'But now Lancelot lies entombed in the chapel of this hall. Quite dead and harmless.'

Kerrigan gave the mandrake a withering stare. 'And now *I* own it.'

She wouldn't argue with that, mostly because she couldn't ever seem to win an argument with Kerrigan no matter how hard she tried. 'What curse is here?'

Blaise crossed his arms over his chest as he stepped closer to her. 'Before Lancelot died, he denounced all the knights of the Round Table for their treachery. Should any of them dare to step foot into his home, misfortune and illness will plague them until they die . . . which generally isn't too long after they leave here.'

'That's his curse,' Kerrigan added. 'Death to any of Arthur's people who venture here.'

She was offended that Lancelot would do such a thing. 'He's the one who turned on them. How dare he.'

'Nay,' Blaise said quietly. 'Lancelot never betrayed Arthur, nor did Guinevere. They loved each other, true enough. But neither one would have ever dared to cuckold Arthur, for they loved him even more than they loved each other. It was a simple lie that brought down the great King Arthur, and his willingness to believe it.'

Seren swallowed at his dire words. 'What say you?'

'It's true,' Kerrigan said from behind her. 'Morgen and Mordred concocted the lie based on a truth and let it fester inside Arthur until it infected him and he destroyed the fellowship of the Table. And now Lancelot lies yonder, a victim of jealousy and rumor. It's amazing how much power a simple false phrase repeated can have.'

Seren considered that. It was true. Harsh words were never softened by time, and hurtful rumors lingered long after the fact. But what a shame that something so innocuous could destroy such a glorious world.

Such a glorious king.

'Could I see Lancelot's grave?'

Kerrigan's eyes sparked as if her question surprised him. 'Could it be that my lady has a degree of morbidity?'

'Nay, I would just like to see the resting place of a man so revered and slandered.'

To her amazement, Kerrigan held his hand out to her. Seren took it, then instantly found herself in a darkened room with no sign of Blaise.

'Where are we?' she asked.

'As you requested, the chapel.'

'Why is it so cold here?'

'We are far below the castle's foundation, which some say is embedded in a wall of ice. No one ever ventures here.'

As Seren stepped into the small room, three torches and a fire in a wall hearth were lit. Shadows danced wickedly against the stone walls. Her own shadow mingled with Kerrigan's, joining them into one large shape that reminded her of some evil beast.

But as the light brightened to show her the sarcophagus of a handsome knight, she gasped.

Seren approached it reverently so that she could better observe the sharp angles of the knight's face. The carving was so intricate that she could see the individual strands of his hair, the veins in his neck and hands. See each link of his armor. See the leather of the gloves he had tucked into his girdle. His eyes were closed, but part of her half expected them to open the way the gargoyle had done in her room.

Whoever had made the carving had been a master artisan. Her heart hammering, she ran her hand over the inscription at his feet:

HIC JACET SEPULTUS INCLYTUS LAUNCELOT DU LAC

'Here lies interred the renowned Lancelot du Lac,' she whispered. Her gaze returned to his handsome stone face. It was hard to believe that this was the man she'd heard so many stories about. That he had once fought beside Arthur.

A chill went through her. Those stories were real. There really had been a Camelot, a Guinevere, and a great king . . .

'Did you know him?' she asked Kerrigan.

'Nay. He died long before I was born. I came to Camelot three hundred years after it had fallen to Morgen.'

'And Arthur. Is he dead, too?' she asked, looking back at Kerrigan.

His gaze turned dull. 'No one knows for sure. He was taken to Avalon, where he rested for a time. Some say he rests there still, and others say that he left after he heard of the deaths of Lancelot and Guinevere. Many of them believe that he died of a broken heart.'

Seren didn't know what to think of all this. It wasn't every day that someone learned a beloved fantasy was reality. 'And now I am caught in their struggle. 'Tis unbelievable.'

'Nay, not really. Unbelievable is that a worthless thief found a sword and used it to become a king.'

'Is that what you were?'

Kerrigan nodded, even though he wasn't sure why he spoke to her in such a manner. It wasn't like him to speak of the past, but then all in Camelot knew what he'd been . . . where he'd come from. It wasn't as if he hid it. And for some reason, Seren was easy to talk to.

'I was only seeking an escape from the soldiers who were sent to arrest me. One moment I was scared of being taken by them and in the next, I had more power than I had ever dreamed of.'

She looked up at him. 'What is to become of you now that you have betrayed Morgen?'

The concern in her tone surprised him. No one had ever given a damn in the past what happened to him, and he doubted that she truly did. Indeed, her lot would most likely improve if Morgen killed him. 'I honestly don't know. It wasn't the wisest thing to do. Most likely I should have thought it through better before I acted.'

Seren considered that. Aye, most likely. From Morgen's orders to the gargoyles, it was obvious she wanted him dead. But that made her wonder another question. 'Why does Morgen want me taken from you?'

'To corrupt you, most like. As she corrupts everyone who comes to her.'

Seren was stronger than that. Nothing would ever corrupt her. She would never be so weak. 'So what do we do now?'

His eyes were completely blank as he watched her. 'I don't know, Seren. If I were wise, I'd return you to Morgen.' He placed a surprisingly gentle hand to her face.

It was on the tip of her tongue to ask him to return her, but she already knew the answer. He wouldn't, and in truth, she was grateful for that fact. She didn't know how Morgen might try to corrupt her, but it could be most painful, and pain was something she would like to avoid if possible.

Kerrigan hesitated as he felt the softness of her skin in his palm. Her green eyes were large and bright. They tugged at the very thing inside him that he'd spurned centuries past. How could this little ragamuffin mouse entice him so?

He brushed her lips with his thumb, wanting to taste them again. But to what purpose?

He'd openly defied Morgen. If he returned to Camelot, he'd have to placate her . . .

If he could.

But he didn't want to think of that now.

He just wanted to feel the warmth of this woman. Dipping his head low, he didn't kiss her. Instead, he rubbed his roughened cheek against her smooth one just so he could feel the softness of her and inhale the sweet scent of her skin.

'Tell me, Seren,' he whispered in her ear. 'If you were with a man you loved, what would you do now?'

Seren wasn't sure what to answer to that question. 'I know not,' she answered honestly. 'I've never been around any man save Master Rufus, and he is so old and angry that I never let my fantasies loose.'

She felt him smile against her cheek.

'And at night?' he whispered raggedly. 'When you dream all alone in your bed, what man do you see in your arms?'

'I've never seen his face,' she said in a low tone. 'I only see an image of him. A quiet man with a good heart. One who is respectable and charitable to all around him.'

Kerrigan flinched inwardly at her words as she described the very things he could never be. A woman like her could never love a thief. A liar.

A beastly animal.

The sudden surge of anger made him want to lash out and hurt her. Punish her for her honesty.

But even as the thought crossed his mind, he knew he couldn't. He'd asked her for the truth and she had given it to him.

His dead heart shriveled as he pulled away from her.

'Come, Seren, and I'll show you to your chambers.'

'You're not going to just think me into my—' Her words broke off as he did just that.

He watched as her eyes grew round at the lush and beautiful room. The bed was large and gilded. It was the room for a queen, surely, and not one of her status.

'Where am I?'

'You are in Lancelot's chambers.' Kerrigan had to force himself not to smile at her gaping expression.

'What of you?' she asked. 'Where will you sleep?'

'I don't.' At least not more than a few winks at a time. He'd learned long ago that sleeping men were vulnerable to attack. As a youth, he'd been forced to sleep without a bed and be ready to fend off any who wanted to prey on him for either coin or other things best left unspoken. There had been no shelter for him. No safety. And so he'd learned to sacrifice sleep for peace of mind.

Without another word, he started to withdraw from the room, only to have her stop him by laying her hand to his arm. Kerrigan stared at the graceful, delicate touch.

'Thank you, my lord.'

'For?'

'Saving me from Morgen and giving me such a beautiful room.'

He inclined his head to her even though what he really wanted was to crush her to him, and make use of the bed behind her until the heat in his loins was completely sated. 'You should rest, Seren. You will need your strength.'

She nodded before she withdrew from him. But as she crossed the floor, he saw her tense unexpectedly as if something suddenly pained her.

'Is something amiss?'

She looked back at him with an expression so sad that he actually felt her pain. 'My scarlet cloth. I left it in my chambers . . . I can't believe it, it's lost now. Gone forever.'

He snorted at that. 'It is cloth. What good is it?'

She stiffened at his words as tears gathered in her eyes. 'It was mine, my lord. I spent much of my life this past year preparing it, and it was all I had in the world. It might seem trivial to you, but to me it meant everything.' Then under her breath she repeated the word. 'Everything.'

Kerrigan scoffed at her sentimentality. Cloth. Leave it to a woman to care so for something so minuscule.

But as he watched her wipe away a tear, he felt something inside him shatter. He wanted to comfort her.

What is the matter with you?

She's nothing.

Disgusted by his untoward thoughts, he slammed from her room. However he didn't make it any farther than the hallway as the thought of her broken heart crushed him.

Forget it, Kerrigan.

Aye, he fully intended to put it out of his mind.

Morgen smiled to herself as she returned to her chambers alone. She paused as she caught sight of a naked Brevalaer waiting unabashedly for her by her carved wooden bed. The tall, dark Adoni was beautiful as always, but then, being a trained courtesan, he knew exactly how much of his value depended on those looks.

His black hair fell just above his broad, muscled shoulders that tapered to a most succulent six-pack of abs . . . she so loved that term from the late twentieth, early twenty-first century. Dark eyebrows slashed above a set of feral eyes that were hazel green and always inviting.

He was her favorite lover above all others ... at least for the moment. And he would most likely be the successor to Kerrigan when all of this was over. If Damé Fortune willed it that way.

'How did it go, my queen?' he asked in that deeply seductive voice of his.

She laughed as she moved to stand before him so that he could remove her heavy red velvet cloak. 'The fool is playing right into my hands, just as I knew he would.'

'Are you certain?'

'Of course.' She didn't truly want the Round Table. At least not yet. The table at this point would be as worthless to her as the black one in the hall below. Without a Penmerlin here to charge the table, it would never work properly.

She'd tried right after her brother's death to access those powers herself. But she was the negative that needed a positive to charge it.

That required a new, untainted Penmerlin, but unfortunately, no Merlin would come to Camelot so long as it was in her hands. And neither she nor any of her people could force a Merlin here. The last time they had tried, it had been disastrous.

Nay, a Merlin must enter this hall of his or her own will ...

And that was what had led her to the current plan. If she couldn't bring a Merlin here, then she would birth one. Gods and goddesses, how she loved a good loophole.

She'd planned on the father of the child being Brevalaer, but as she considered it further, Kerrigan would be a much better donor. He, like the little hag he'd captured, also had the blood of their magical line within him.

If two such creatures joined . . .

The birth of the child would render Kerrigan obsolete. At long last, she would be able to kill him. But more than that, she could bring back Mordred and restore him to perfect health. Happiness poured through her at the thought of her son returning to her side. It was all she'd ever wanted.

And she knew that if she'd tried to force Kerrigan to bed the mouse, he'd have refused just to spite her. So she'd sent Magda to Seren with the directive for the chit to seduce the beast.

She should have known that Seren wouldn't be able to accomplish such a feat, and so her latest ploy had been born – put the two of them together long enough, and Kerrigan was bound to take the chit at some point. It wasn't in his nature to deny himself carnal pleasures.

Now that it was only the two of them and he no longer had any of her fey to choose from . . .

Aye, it would only be a matter of time before he slept with the wench.

Only a matter of time before she could kill the Kerrigan and the mouse, and claim their ill-begotten child for her very own. She laughed lowly in anticipation. Soon the world would be hers and there would be no one to stop her . . .

Chapter Six

Kerrigan sat idly in the window, balanced precariously on the whitewashed stones as he gazed out to the fulminant sea below. The sounds of the waves echoed in his ears, but not even they were enough to drown out the sound of Seren's heartbroken voice.

The sight of the hurt that had been in those catlike eyes. It haunted him still.

How could worthless, uncut cloth mean so much to anyone?

And yet it did.

Worse, he remembered a time when something as simple as rotting cabbage had meant everything to him. Had been worth braving the severest of beatings just so that he could have a taste of it.

Unbidden, his memories surged. Even now he could see himself as a boy in his home village . . .

He'd been starving, but then starvation had been nothing new in his world – he'd been born hungry and had stayed that way every day until Morgen had found him.

Only seven in age at that time, he'd bartered with the local baker for work. He'd spent the entire morning sweeping the floor of the baker's shop and moving flour bins while the scent of fresh baking bread had made his stomach cramp in hunger. As the morning wore on, he'd become obsessed with the thought of tasting one tiny morsel of that bread.

'Might I have a bite now, sir?'

'Finish your work, boy, and then you'll be paid. And don't get lazy or you'll get nothing from me.'

Kerrigan had tried to return to work, but as the baker peeled off the bad leaves of the cabbage he was cooking for his midmorning meal, he'd been so hungry that he feared he'd be ill where he stood. He could barely stand the pain of it.

It'd been two days since he'd last eaten . . .

The baker had tossed the discarded leaves into the refuse bin. Kerrigan had stared at them while he tried to sweep. Those wilted leaves hadn't been worth eating and yet he could already taste them. Imagine them as he chewed and swallowed until it eased the ache inside him.

When it became obvious that the baker was through with the cabbage – that he had no intention of doing anything but tossing it out, Kerrigan had reached to take a leaf.

The man had instantly backhanded him. His lips had burned like fire as he tasted his own blood from the blow.

'You thief!' the baker had growled in anger. 'Worthless son of a whore. Get out!'

Kerrigan had gone, but not before he'd shoved the man back and stolen an entire loaf of bread. He'd downed most of it before he'd been arrested, beaten, and thrown into the stocks.

His three days of humiliation had been worth the taste of the warm, sweet bread that had melted so deliciously in his mouth. The momentary satisfaction of a full stomach.

Was Seren's cloth so precious to her that she would risk her life for it?

Aye, most likely. Even unconscious, she had clasped it to her bosom with the grip of a lioness as if daring anyone to try and take it from her.

For the first time in a lifetime of cruelty, betrayal, and brutality, Kerrigan felt an odd stirring of compassion. Like him before he'd joined Morgen's army, Seren had nothing in this world to call her own. Nothing but a bit of worthless cloth.

Sighing, he closed his eyes and mentally summoned Blaise to him.

'You have need of me, my king?'

Kerrigan stepped down from his perch in the window so that the mandrake wasn't at his back. 'Aye. Watch the wench for a bit. I have something I need to do.'

Blaise frowned. 'You're leaving?'

'I'll return.'

The mandrake arched a brow at that. 'Why do I have a feeling that you are about to do something stupid?'

'Most likely because I am about to do something stupid.'

'And is there a particular reason for this act of stupidity?'

'Not really.'

Blaise's violet eyes danced with humor even though Kerrigan knew the mandrake could see nothing more than a shadowy outline of his body. 'Well in that case, I shall guard her zealously rather than join you in said stupidity, as I try my best to always avoid such moments.'

'Good.' Kerrigan stepped back as he summoned his powers to dissolve his form from this realm and take him back to Camelot.

It was always a bit disconcerting to travel this way. There was a small electrical shock that went through him, then a moment or two of nausea before everything righted itself. But even so, he much preferred it to the normal mode of traveling. It was much quicker and easier.

He shimmered himself into the tower room he had given to Seren and was prepared for an ambush. It would be like Morgen to have such a thing planned. Yet there was nothing there. The room was just as she'd left it.

Eerily so.

Kerrigan glanced about, making sure he was undetected before he saw the red cloth on her black bed. Rolling his eyes at the worthlessness of it, he grabbed it.

Something moved from the corner.

Kerrigan jerked his head to catch sight of a quick, shadowy movement. He felt his eyes grow red as his temper surged. 'Pax?'

The shadow vanished.

Kerrigan hissed as he fought himself not to pursue the cursed sharoc who was no doubt heading straight for Morgen. It wouldn't do him any good to pursue Pax. He had to get back to Seren before Morgen used her magic to locate them.

He would need to put a barrier up over Joyous Gard to keep her away. If she were to find them ...

There was only so much he could, or more to the point, *would*, do to keep Seren safe.

Seren lay on her side on the large gilded bed as she stared out the open window to the perfectly blue sky. If she were at home now, she would be working on material for a gown for the earl's daughter's wedding.

No doubt poor Wendlyn was cursing her for the extra work. Without Seren there to weave, the other hapless apprentices would have to work even harder.

She felt terrible about that. She'd told them all that she would return quickly from the guildhall.

If only she'd known then what was to befall her ...

Closing her eyes, she conjured an image of her loom that sat across from the shop's windows. She loved to glance up from her work and watch the children who sometimes played out in the street. She could also catch glimpses of ladies and their maids who drifted into various shops as they looked for items.

The earl's daughter had been particularly lovely as she visited Master Rufus and told him of the pale yellow samite she wanted for her wedding.

Seren smiled to herself as she imagined the day when the lady would marry her lord. How lovely the woman would be in the shimmering cloth ...

She felt something fall across her arm.

Opening her eyes, she saw her scarlet cloth, but no sign of anyone else.

She sat up with a gasp as she examined it. Aye, it was her cloth without a doubt. She knew every stitch, every fiber.

'Lord Kerrigan?'

There was no answer.

'Please, my lord, if you are here, show yourself to me.'

'Why?' the word whispered in the air around her like a dream.

'I should like to thank you for this, face to face.'

She heard him make a rude noise. 'Keep your thanks, woman. It's as worthless as your cloth.'

And then she sensed that she was alone in her room. Stung by his words, she looked down at her cloth. It was worthless indeed. But even so, Kerrigan must have gone to some effort to retrieve it. Indeed, to return to Camelot while Morgen was angry at him could even be construed as foolhardy.

Yet he'd done it for no other reason than to ease her mind. Mayhap, dare she think it, to make her happy. She knew firsthand that such an act wasn't normal for a man like Kerrigan.

You should thank him again for it.

But he didn't want thanks with words. It wasn't his way.

Suddenly, she was struck with an idea. She finally knew what she could do with this cloth.

Kerrigan frowned as a small strip of a plastic thermometer appeared on his forehead. 'What the . . .?'

It immediately flew across the room into Blaise's outstretched hand. The mandrake ran his fingers over it so that he could read it, then he arched both brows in surprise. 'It's forty-five degrees, which . . . well, for humans is fatal, but for you, my lord, is quite normal. Damn. I could have sworn you had a fever.'

Kerrigan leaned back in the chair where he sat and growled low in his throat. 'What madness has possession of you now?'

'The same madness that possessed you to venture to Camelot a short time ago to make an insignificant peasant happy.'

Kerrigan looked away. 'Who says I did so to make *her* happy? What I did, I did for myself so that I wouldn't have to listen to her whine and pout over paltry fabric.'

Doubt shone from the mandrake's face. 'Since when does that bother you? I thought you lived to make others miserable.'

He did normally. But for some reason, he wasn't feeling like his usual churlish self. 'Is there a point to this conversation other than you are suddenly possessed with a desire to be disemboweled?'

Blaise held his hands up in surrender. 'I only thought my king would like to know that you have made the woman extremely happy.'

He scoffed at that. 'She is simpleminded. It takes naught to thrill such people.'

'Personally, I find her quite intelligent.'

'Because you, too, are simpleminded.'

Blaise took the insult in stride as he flashed himself across the room to stand just to the right of Kerrigan's chair. The mandrake leaned down to speak softly. 'It feels good, doesn't it?'

'What?'

'To do something decent for another. You've never done that before, have you?'

Kerrigan reached up and grabbed the mandrake by his throat. He pulled him down until he was sure the creature could see him. 'You overstep your bounds, servant. Do so again and perish.'

He released Blaise, who stared at him unblinkingly. There was a perfect outline of his hand against Blaise's skin, and still there was no fear in the mandrake's expression. 'As you wish, my king.' The words were spoken with a degree of sarcasm.

Kerrigan flung his hand out and used his powers to banish the beast from him before he did something more permanent to Blaise.

He should see the creature punished for his insubordination. It would serve him right.

But as he sat there alone, the mood passed and he considered what the mandrake had said. He'd made Seren happy. In all these centuries, Kerrigan had never made anyone happy before.

Not even himself.

Seren sang quietly to herself as she sat on the floor of her room working. How she wished she knew Kerrigan's measurements. But it was too late now. The cloth was already cut. Not that it really mattered, she had an uncanny ability to always make clothing to fit. It was something Master Rufus commented on constantly.

She didn't know why. She just seemed to know when something was right and when it was wrong.

Blaise, who had been kind enough to get her the shears, needle, and thread, had warned her that Kerrigan would most likely spurn her gift.

He might at that. But it felt right to do this. He was the only one she knew who held a high enough position that he could wear the color of her cloth, and it would look good on him. The deep red would accentuate his dark coloring.

And it would match his eyes when they burned . . .

Seren!

Well, it was true. His eyes did burn almost the same exact red.

Dismissing those thoughts, she fell into what Wendlyn called her working trance. Every time she wove on her mother's loom, something strange happened to her. It was as if time stood still. She could work endlessly without tiring.

If only the same could happen while she worked Master Rufus's looms.

'Seren?'

She heard the sound of Blaise's voice as if he were a great distance away. 'Aye?'

'I've brought your supper to you.'

'Please set it aside. I'm not hungry yet.'

Blaise did as she bade while he watched her work. He could tell that she was only vaguely aware of his presence. There was an odd aura around her ... one he'd only seen a few times in the past.

It was something that only his magical sight could pick up on, not his true eyesight. He listened to the beauty of Seren's voice as she sang an ancient lullaby under her breath. Her hands worked the stitches on the tunic in an effortless beauty. There was no snarled thread, no misstitching whatsoever.

He'd never known anyone to work faster, and at the rate she was going, she would have the tunic ready in only a few more hours. He was impressed.

But more than that, he was suspicious. He'd been around enough magical beings in his life to recognize the species, and as he watched Seren working, he was beginning to understand why she was so important to Morgen.

There was much more to this 'simple' peasant than what met the eye.

'Seren?'

It took her several minutes before she realized he'd spoken. 'Aye?'

'Who were your parents?'

He could tell by her face that the question surprised her. 'My mother was a weaver and I know nothing of my father. He died shortly before I was born.'

'And your mother? Where is she now?'

Her green eyes turned dull as a deep, heartfelt sadness filled them. 'She died not long after I was apprenticed to Master Rufus.'

A chill of foreboding went through him. 'How did your parents die?'

'I know not of my father. My mother refused to

speak of it. As for her, she perished in a fire that broke out while she was sleeping.'

'Are you sure?' the question was out before he could stop it.

She frowned at him.

'Forgive me, my lady,' he said quietly. 'It was a thoughtless question.'

'Is there something you know that I do not?'

Blaise shook his head. There was no need to speak of his suspicions. Not until he had more proof, anyway. 'You should eat before it grows cold.'

Slowly, she got up and crossed to the platter, where she picked up a piece of bread to taste it.

There was something beautiful about her even though her features were rather plain. She moved with a decided grace and assuredness that was unusual for a woman of such lowly birth. She wiped at her mouth daintily with the white linen cloth. 'Am I doing something wrong?'

'Nay.'

'Then why do you stare at me so?'

Blaise laughed at her innocent question. 'I can't truly see you when I am in this form,' he explained. 'I see your shadow, and when you move, I see you much like a gray haze that is a bit blurry.'

'You're blind?'

'Only as a man. As a dragon, I have perfect vision.'

'Why?'

'I know not. 'Tis a curse of my birth.' What he didn't tell her was that with his magic, he could see a great deal even as a human (that was a secret he'd always kept to himself), but colors and such weren't true to form.

'I'm sorry, Blaise. Do you need any help?'

It was all he could do not to laugh at her question.

Imagine *her* helping him. And yet the kindness of her gesture warmed him. 'Nay, my lady. I shall leave you to your work.'

'Blaise?' she asked as he turned to leave.

'Aye?'

'Thank you so much for bringing the food. 'Tis most delicious and appreciated.'

Her sincere gratitude sent a strange warmth through him. 'My pleasure, Seren.'

Blaise took one last look at her before he used his powers to leave her. And as he dissolved into his nether form, he saw the faint white aura around her . . .

Aye, she was as he suspected, and he wondered if Kerrigan knew it.

Blaise let out a long breath as he realized that he was in a precarious position. He was caught between two Merlins.

One who had embraced evil happily and one who didn't even know she had those powers. It was actually a frightening thought because whenever you put a positive with a negative, you either got a deep attraction . . .

Or one hell of an explosion.

Blaise let out a slow breath. May God have mercy on the girl. Poor Seren had no idea what was in store for her. Especially if Morgen ever learned the truth of her birth.

Chapter Seven

It was almost dawn before Seren completed the tunic. Stretching her cramped muscles, she yawned. She was tired, but her joy at having finished her project overwhelmed her. It was truly her finest work ever. The scarlet cloth practically glowed in the candlelight.

Even her embroidery around the neck was exceptional. If only she'd possessed gold thread to stitch it, but even so, the black had turned out quite well. Surely even a man as temperamental as Kerrigan would like it.

Smiling at the thought of pleasing him, she stretched her cramped muscles once more before she rose and left the room. For once her door wasn't locked – most likely because there was no one else here besides them, and where could she go since they were on an island in the middle of a sea she didn't know?

She pushed the door open to step tentatively out into the hallway, where she half expected Blaise or Kerrigan to show up and force her back into her room.

She wasn't sure where Kerrigan might be. The most likely place would be the hall since he'd said that he didn't sleep. She wasn't even sure where that was in this large, cold place. Still, it seemed only natural that the great hall would be on a lower floor in the center of the castle.

Relying on instinct, she made her way through the darkened corridors and down the spiral stairs until she reached the first floor.

Sure enough, it opened onto a giant hall that was lined with trestle tables. Ornate banners that were mostly threadbare hung from the rafters over her head. But she wasn't paying attention to them. Her gaze focused on the man before the roaring fire who wore armor blacker than sin.

Kerrigan sat quietly in a large carved chair with his legs propped on a small wooden stool. At first she thought he was still awake until she drew closer.

His head was propped against his fist, but his eyes were closed, and they didn't snap open at her silent approach.

So much for his prideful boasting. The man slept after all, and that knowledge made him seem much more human.

Shaking her head, she took a moment to study the angles of his perfectly sculpted features that were relaxed for the first time since she'd met him. Dark whiskers lightly covered his chin, cheeks, and upper lip while his long black hair fell over his forehead. He was without a doubt the most handsome man she'd ever beheld.

The firelight danced in the darkest waves of his hair and caressed the planes of his face. He no longer looked like a harsh demon out to destroy everyone in his way. He looked like a man, pure and simple. One with a most kissable mouth. Indeed, he was quite inviting like this. Quite approachable.

And before she could think better of it, she reached out to touch the lock of hair on his forehead. Her hand had barely brushed his brow before he jerked awake with a speed so fast that she was unaware of his movement until she felt something hot and sharp in her stomach.

Her eyes wide from pain, she looked down to find Kerrigan's dagger buried deep there.

Kerrigan blinked twice as he felt the warm, sticky blood run over his hand. It took a full heartbeat before he woke up completely to see Seren standing before him. Her lips trembled as she dropped the red cloth in her hand.

She stared at him with tears in her green eyes that were wide in disbelief.

'Seren?' he breathed.

She staggered back.

Kerrigan pulled his dagger out from her stomach, then caught her against his chest as she fell. 'What were you doing, little mouse?'

'Gift . . .' The word came out as a pale whisper. 'For you.'

He looked to the cloth. Unable to comprehend her intention, he lowered her to the floor. Her long blond hair fanned out around her while her blood soaked her dress.

She choked on her own blood as she stared up at him accusingly.

Kerrigan wiped at the blood on her chin as a foreign emotion gripped his heart. It was sharp and painful, a bitter ache the likes of which he'd never known.

What had he done?

'Shh, little mouse,' he whispered, picking her up to cradle her against his chest as strange emotions tore through him. Fear, sadness, confusion. But the strangest of all was the grief inside him that didn't want her hurt. The part of him that actually ached with the knowledge he'd harmed her.

She was trembling from the pain as her face paled even more. She was dying and he knew it.

'Blaise!' he shouted, summoning the mandrake. He didn't have the powers to help her. His magic could only be used to harm others, never to help.

The air around him stirred an instant before the mandrake appeared.

Blaise gasped as he saw the two of them entwined on the floor. 'Morgen?'

'Nay. She surprised me while I dozed.'

Blaise sucked his breath in sharply as he crossed to the space between them so that he could kneel on the floor by Seren's side.

Kerrigan grabbed the collar of Blaise's tunic in a tight fist as he glared at the mandrake. 'Save her.' He growled the order in a low, deadly tone.

He saw the surprise that registered an instant before the dragon hid it.

Kerrigan rocked her gently in his arms as Blaise placed his hand to her wound. Summoning his powers, the mandrake whispered the ancient words, '*Arra terac sisimea dominay narah.*' He repeated them over and over again.

Seren went completely limp in his arms. A tremor of fear swept through him that she was gone.

But she wasn't dead.

Kerrigan let out a slow, deep breath as he felt her heart still beating. Her skin was still warm.

Aye, she would live. Thanks to Blaise.

He wasn't sure why that knowledge brought an instant relief to him, but it did.

Holding her close, Kerrigan closed his eyes and flashed them from the great hall, back to her room where he could lay her down on the large bed so that she could sleep in peace. Even with Blaise's spell, she would need rest to regain her strength.

'You are a senseless little mouse,' he breathed, covering her with a blanket.

He hesitated as his gaze fell to the large bloodstain on her gown, and his stomach actually clenched. He'd damned near killed her, and the sight of what he'd done sickened him.

Waving his hand over it, he changed her gown to a soft cream silk that was as unblemished as her innocence.

He placed the heavy blanket over her and then paused to lay his cold fingers against the blush of her cheek. Her skin was so warm and soft. The delicateness of her cheeks was only emphasized by the brutish strength of his callused fingers.

He could tear her apart . . .

Instead he only wanted to kiss her.

How very strange. In truth, he didn't like these odd feelings inside him. He had never been a kind man or a kind child. He'd always believed in striking the first blow before it was delivered to him. Better to stun his opponents so that when they struck their blow it would be less forceful. Less painful.

He knew of kindness only from watching other people receive it. And that had made him even more bitter. More cruel. Why should other people have something he'd always been denied? What had been so wrong with him as a child that no one could ever look at him with fondness in their eyes? Or gently touch him?

In time, he'd convinced himself that he didn't need kindness or fondness.

Now, he no longer even wanted it.

'Gift . . . for you.'

Her pain-filled words echoed in his head. What gift had been worth almost dying for?

Curiosity got the better of him. Sealing her door to make sure she didn't leave the room again and find danger, he returned to the hall, where he saw the dark red cloth on the floor.

There was no sign of Blaise, who had most likely retired to his rooms.

Wiping the blood from his hand on his armor before he reached for it, Kerrigan retrieved the cloth from the floor. He held it up to see a tunic that was obviously designed for a man. One that was made of tiny, delicate stitches.

Thoughtful, handmade stitches.

Something inside him shattered. And that made him angry. How dare she make him feel like this! No doubt that was her intention. She would ply him with kindness until she had him tamed and mastered. Until he fed from that delicate hand of hers as she led him about by his nose.

Fuck that. He was no woman's pawn. He bowed before no one. Ever.

Balling the tunic into his fist, he moved toward the fire. But as he started to toss it in, he paused.

The cloth was so soft against his skin. It was her precious cloth that she had wept over. Cloth that had meant everything to her. Why would she give it over to him? He would never give up something he held in such regard to another for any reason.

Burn it!

To keep it would make him weak. It would give her sovereignty over him. It would leave his heart open.

And still he couldn't make himself throw it into the flames. *Do it!* The words echoed forcefully through his mind over and over again.

Closing his eyes, he brought the cloth to his face. Seren's scent clung to the fabric. That woodsy rose smell filled him with a desire so raw, so potent that it was all he could do not to return to her.

Instead he did something he hadn't done in countless centuries. He melted his black steel cuirass from him and pulled off the black tunic he wore beneath it. He replaced the black wool with the scarlet tunic and hissed at the softness of the fabric against his skin. It was as gentle as the brush of a fey's wings.

And it smelled of Seren.

He ran his hand over the perfect material. It fit him as if she'd had his measurements. His little mouse was certainly talented. Her work was without fault.

'Thank you, Seren,' he whispered in the silence of the hall, knowing that he would never be able to say those words aloud to her. Only a weak-kneed milksop would ever thank someone.

He felt the heat inside him build as he summoned his armor back onto his body. He would keep her gift, but no one would ever know it.

Not even Seren.

Seren came awake with a start. She was stabbed! Her heart hammering, she waited to feel the painful throb that had burned like fire in her stomach.

But there was no pain to be felt.

Was she dead?

Terrified, she opened her eyes to find herself alone in her bed. She was beneath the heavy covers, and bright sunlight was spilling in from the open windows.

Had she dreamed it? She looked to the floor where the remnants of her sewing was still exactly where she'd left it. The thread, the shears, the scraps of cloth . . .

Nay, Kerrigan had stabbed her. She was sure of it.

Frowning, she pushed the covers back, then hesitated at the sight of her new cream gown.

Kerrigan had been here. After he'd stabbed her, he must have returned her to her bed. But then why didn't she ache from the wound?

Kerrigan stood silently invisible in the shadows, watching Seren as she awoke. He'd been here all day while she slept, wanting to make sure that she really was fine after his attack.

By the changing expressions on her face, he could read every thought in her mind. At least he could until she lifted up the hem of her gown.

His blood fired as she unknowingly bared the whole of her lower body to him while she looked for a scar from her wound. There wasn't one. Blaise's healing had left her completely unblemished.

The cream fabric pooled at her waist as she ran her hands over her flat stomach. Her thighs were slightly parted, and all he could focus on was the light triangle of hair that teased and beckoned him with thoughts of the part of her it concealed. She lifted one leg up, exposing herself even more to his hungry gaze. It was more than he could stand.

Without thought, he stepped forward.

Seren frowned as she ran her hand over her stomach. There had to be a wound. Didn't there?

She wasn't insane. Kerrigan had most definitely stabbed her.

She pushed herself up on the pillows so that she could better see her skin and raised one leg for balance. All of a sudden, something warm and firm brushed up against the center of her body.

She gasped as a hot, searing pleasure swept through her. 'Kerrigan?' she breathed the name.

All that answered her was another stroke of pleasure that was followed by another and another. Her entire body trembled from the force of it. Never had she felt the like. She shivered and groaned.

Surely it was indecent to enjoy something so wickedly pleasant. But even so, she didn't want it to stop. Biting her lip, she parted her thighs even more. The strokes moved even faster against her, teasing her with ecstasy as she arched her back.

Kerrigan knew he should leave her, but he couldn't. The sight of her enjoying his touch was too much to stop. He let her wetness coat his fingers as he closed his eyes and imagined himself deep inside her.

Aye, that was what he wanted, but he wouldn't take that from her. So instead, he claimed her lips with his.

Seren moaned at the taste of a man she couldn't see. But she knew who it was. There was no mistaking the taste of Kerrigan. The feel of his mouth on hers.

It was so strange to be able to feel him and not see him. It was like some vivid, erotic dream.

She shivered as he left her lips and kissed a blazing trail down her throat. He pulled her gown up higher, until she was completely bared for his pleasure.

Seren cried out as she felt him take her breast into his mouth and gently tease her nipple with his tongue. No man had ever touched her like this. She'd never even imagined it. No wonder women turned wanton. It was hard to even think while her body pulsed and danced in response to his masterful touch.

The entire room seemed to spin as she felt the most incredible pleasure imaginable. It was wonderful.

And just when she was sure she could stand no more of it, her body seemed to splinter into a thousand shards of ecstasy. She actually screamed as wave after wave of delight shuddered through her. She had no idea what this was, but it was incredible. Sublime.

She only wished she could see Kerrigan. That she could return this sensation to him and please him in turn.

Her breathing labored, she lay there not sure if a person could still be alive after such a thing. Unbidden, a single tear of joy slid from the corner of her eye.

Kerrigan took form immediately by her side. She saw the deep concern in his eyes as he looked down at her.

'You are still intact, Seren,' he breathed, taking her hand into his. He led it down to the extremely sensitive flesh between her legs. Using his own finger, he pressed her index finger deep inside her until she could feel her maidenhead. 'I didn't take your virginity from you. I swear.'

A foreign tenderness flooded her at his words . . . at the concern he was showing for her. She knew how rare such a thing was for him.

And in that moment, she wanted the very thing she'd never known before. She wanted him . . . mayhap it was wrong, but she already knew that she had no way back to her world, to her place. Morgen. Kerrigan. The Lords of Avalon. They wouldn't allow her to return to her loom in Master Rufus's shop. Ever. All of that was behind her now. Even if she escaped, so long as they believed she was destined to fulfill some kind of prophecy about Merlin, they would bring her back. She'd seen enough of their magic to know that she couldn't fight them or elude them.

All she had to protect her from the others was Kerrigan. A man who claimed he held no heart, and yet he'd been nothing but kind to her.

And she wanted to show him how much she appreciated his protection. How much she appreciated him . . .

Her heart quickening, she stared up at those dark, soulless eyes and offered him a tender smile. 'Can you show me what it would feel like to have you inside me?'

His eyes blazed red a moment before she felt something thick and hard inside her. Seren shivered at the unexpected pleasant sensation. She hissed as it pounded through her in the most wickedly sensuous rhythm, but Kerrigan was still fully dressed and lying by her side. It wasn't he she felt inside her, but rather a facsimile of him.

His eyes continued to flame as he watched her with a feral tic in his jaw. She saw the strain he felt as he gave her pleasure without taking any for himself. It was inconceivable to her that this man who lived only by his own rules would be so giving. It wasn't in his nature to be like this, and that only added to the delectation she felt.

Again the intense pleasure built as her body shivered uncontrollably. It was unlike anything she'd ever imagined. And she wondered how much better it might be to have him there instead.

Seren couldn't speak as she bit her lip and squirmed in ecstasy. She reached out and seized the vambrace armor on his forearm as her body again shattered.

Kerrigan couldn't breathe as he watched her climaxing again. He wanted inside her so badly that he could taste it. The need was all consuming, and yet he found the strength to keep himself from yielding to his lust.

He wouldn't take that last bit from her. Her body was the one thing that was hers alone to give. No matter what it cost him, he would leave her virgin.

112

Just when he was about to move away, she opened her green eyes and pinned him with a heated stare.

That look held him captive.

'That wasn't what I meant, my lord.'

Kerrigan cocked his head in confusion as she released his vambrace, then moved her hand to touch his. She led his hand over the curve of her stomach, down to the short crisp hairs at the juncture of her thighs.

'I wanted to feel *you* inside me, Kerrigan. Not your magic.'

He lightly skimmed his fingers over her mons as disbelief filled him. 'Why?'

'Because I want to give myself to you.'

Anger coiled through him. He pulled back, only to find her rising with him.

'I have no need of your gift,' he snarled.

'And that is the beauty of a gift, my lord. If someone needs it, then it is charity. It is only when you give someone something that they want and have no need of that it becomes a real gift.'

Still he glared at her, and still she showed him no fear. 'This will change nothing between us, little mouse. One physical act will not endear you to me in any way.'

'I know.'

She shivered as he dissolved her gown from her. Kerrigan held his hand out to conjure the far wall into a mirror. He pulled her from the bed to face it.

Seren swallowed at the sight of her nudity as Kerrigan placed her before the mirrored wall. Still fully dressed in his armor, Kerrigan stood behind her, his eyes piercing her with an unfounded anger.

She looked so small compared to him. So insignificant.

'Is this what you would offer me?' he asked softly in her ear.

She nodded.

He brushed her blond hair back from her neck before he leaned down to inhale deeply against her skin. His breath was hot even though his touch was cold.

He looked up to lock gazes with her in the looking glass wall. His eyes were flames that flickered with an unholy light an instant before his armor vanished. All except his sword, which now lay on the ground at their feet.

Seren trembled at the fierce sight of his naked body. Maybe she should be afraid, and yet she wasn't. She couldn't explain it, but somehow this seemed right. She didn't want to be the bride of some unknown knight. Nor did she wish to be a pawn.

Her life no longer seemed to be her own, and yet this moment was completely in her control. It didn't make sense that she was here with Kerrigan like this. She knew he held no real love for her.

But some part of her craved him with an unreasoning madness. She couldn't imagine being with anyone but him. That need, that hunger, they came from him and she wanted to do this.

Kerrigan reached around her to cup her breasts in his hands as he pressed himself up against her back. Leaning against his chest, she closed her eyes as pleasure swept through her.

'Open your eyes, Seren,' he said thickly. 'I want you to see me take your gift so that you can never accuse me of having stolen it from you.'

From the way he said those words, she could tell that someone must have accused him of such a thing in the past. 'I am well aware of what I'm doing, Kerrigan.'

His face hardened. 'No Lord of Avalon will ever have you once they know you have been defiled by me. You will change your destiny.'

She took his hand into hers and led it to her lips so that she could kiss the hard calluses there. She turned in his arms until she could look up at him. 'I was born the daughter of a weaver, and being a weaver is the only destiny I have ever sought. This will change nothing where I'm concerned.'

Kerrigan couldn't understand her madness. She was throwing away a chance to live as royalty. A chance to live in the gilded halls of Avalon with color and laughter.

If it wasn't for the fact that he could sense no magic, he would think it was a spell making her submit to him. But there was nothing here but the two of them.

Why was she doing this?

Never look a gift horse in the mouth.

But how could he not? 'You accept a demon as your lover?'

'Only if the demon is you.'

Then who was he to argue with her? She was a woman full-grown, far past the age to have known a man carnally. She consented of her own free will to be with him . . .

Kerrigan dipped his head down to taste her lips one more time. He growled at the taste of her as he held her naked body close to his. Never before had he taken a virgin, but he knew that for them the first time would bring pain.

And the last thing he wanted was to hurt her.

Again.

His heart hammering, he closed his eyes and summoned his magic.

Seren gasped as all the walls and the ceiling above

115

became mirrored so that she could see them from all angles. His eyes blazing, Kerrigan swept her up in his arms and carried her to the bed that no longer had a canopy. He laid her down gently before he joined her.

She should be afraid of this, yet she wasn't. Kerrigan had been right, she was changing her destiny by being with him. Master Rufus would never again want her. He would throw her out of his house. Not that this would have any bearing on his decision. He would have tossed her out anyway for having been gone this long without permission or a chaperone.

Like Gilda, she'd be tossed to the nearest stew.

There was no way to return to the life she'd known. The life she'd intended to live. It had ended the moment she'd taken Kerrigan's hand and allowed him to pull her across his horse.

And she knew nothing of the Lords of Avalon. Not really. They were vague, dreamlike entities. Story characters who might or might not be what she'd heard from others. Gawain and Agravain had certainly not been what she'd expected.

But Kerrigan was real and she knew him – at least better than she knew any of the others. And for some reason she couldn't name, she wanted to be with him. To stay by his side.

There was something more to him; she could feel it. He was like a feral beast in the wild that lashed out at anyone who came near it, and yet such a beast could be tamed. A patient hand could bring even the wildest of creatures to friendship.

As a girl, she had been picking berries with her mother when they had found a wolf in a trap. The wolf had tried to attack them, but her mother had very carefully fed and watered the animal while talking gently to it. By the time the wolf had finished its meal, her mother had been able to approach it and free it from the trap.

Afterward, her mother had taken her aside and set her on a stump with her basket of berries in her lap. Her mother's blue eyes had been bright as she held her hands and spoke softly to her. *'One day, my Seren, you'll find another beast such as this one. He, too, will be hurt by the thoughtless cruelty of others – by their fear of him. Remember that no matter how feral he seems, no matter how much he snaps, he is only trying to protect himself. It will take time to show him that you only want to help. Time to teach him that not everyone means him harm. Then he will be yours alone and he will fight to the death to protect you.'*

Odd how she hadn't thought about that in years. Her mother had often been possessed of visions. It was why they'd moved so often. As soon as others learned of her mother's wisdom, they would grow nervous and start whispering of witchcraft.

Now Seren wondered if on that day her mother had been speaking of the man in her bed . . .

Kerrigan most certainly fit her mother's description. He was like the wolf in the wild that snapped every time they neared it.

He'd been hurt; she sensed it. It was why he was so wary of everyone. Wary of her when all she wanted was to touch him.

Reaching up, she cupped his face in her hands. He was so beautiful in the sunlight as he moved to place himself between her legs. It somehow seemed wholly natural that he should be her first, and something inside told her that he would most likely be her last. She couldn't imagine ever wanting another man like this.

Her heart softening, she brushed the hair back from

his face an instant before she kissed him. His whiskers scraped her palms and lips. She moaned at the feral taste of him. At the rawness of his touch.

He pulled back to give her a look so tender that it brought an ache to her chest. He might claim not to have changed toward her, but that look denied all his protestations.

Gently, he moved to kiss a path down her stomach. Seren hissed as her body erupted in chills. Her head spinning, she watched as he spread her thighs wide an instant before he leaned down to take her into his mouth.

She groaned deep in her throat as she balled her hand in his dark hair. It was the most incredible sensation she'd ever known. Biting her lip, she looked up to watch him in the mirror above as he pleasured her.

At least until she felt a strange, pleasurable burn at the center of her body.

'Kerrigan?'

He pulled back to look at her. 'You are a maiden no more, Seren.'

'But you haven't . . .'

He led her hand back to the center of her body to show her that her maidenhead was already gone. Then he pressed her hand against his swollen shaft.

She saw the pleasure on his face as she gently wrapped her hand around him. He was so strangely soft and hard against her palm and fingers. He shuddered in her arms as she explored the length of his shaft. 'Did I hurt you?'

'Nay,' he breathed as if he were indeed being tortured.

Seren had never given thought to what a man would feel like in her hand. But she liked the feel of him there. The look of pleasure on his face. Carefully, she circled the moist tip as his breathing turned ragged. He moved slowly against her hand, letting her feel the way his soft flesh moved in contrast to his hardness.

It really was like petting a ferocious animal. She knew tenderness was not in his nature and the fact that he was being gentle with her now made her feel special. Wanted.

His eyes flared brighter an instant before he kissed her deeply, then moved her hand away from him so that he could bury himself deep inside her.

Kerrigan couldn't breathe at the tightness of her body welcoming his. Using his magic, he made sure that she wouldn't feel anything except the pleasure of his touch.

That would be his gift to her.

In truth he'd never known anything better than the feel of her skin sliding against his. Of her hands skimming over his back as she lightly scraped his skin with her nails. He'd never known real tenderness in his life. His past lovers had always been passing itches with no emotional attachment for him.

But with Seren, it was different. He didn't want to rush to get this over so that he could leave. He wanted to hold on to her. To watch her enjoy his body as much as he enjoyed hers.

More than that, he wanted to be as deep inside her as he could get. Rolling over, he pulled out of her.

She gave him a shocked look. 'Is it done?'

He smiled at her innocent questions. 'Not yet.' Kerrigan pulled her up to kneel on the bed as he moved behind her. He paused as he saw her looking at him in the mirror. Their gazes locked, he spread her thighs wide before he sank himself into her again, going even deeper than he had before.

Moaning, she reached up over her head to sink her

hand into his hair while he cupped her breasts in his hands. His heart pounding in tenderness, he thrust against her.

Seren couldn't breathe as she felt the hard thickness of Kerrigan inside her again. She could watch each of his strokes in the looking glass. She'd never imagined how good a man could possibly feel inside her. There was something wild about this. Something that made her feel even closer to him. Like he was a part of her now somehow.

She knew he most likely would never feel that way, but it was true where she was concerned. She felt a connection to him. A warmth that might even be the stirring of deeper affection.

She honestly didn't think that she could have chosen a better man, and for this one moment in time, she was glad that the guild had denied her cloth. Glad that she'd run away from the others and found Kerrigan.

Maybe this had been her destiny after all . . .

Kerrigan could barely breathe as he claimed her. He'd taken more women over the centuries than he could count, and yet none had ever made him feel like this. He wasn't just another lover to Seren. Another prick to pleasure her until someone else came along. She wasn't Morgen to have an additional man in bed with them, waiting for him to grow tired.

He was the only man Seren had ever welcomed into her body. The only one. In that moment he felt a wave of fierce protectiveness toward her. She was his in a way no woman had ever been his before. And that knowledge did something strange to him. It made him want to claim her. To possess her.

To keep her.

And in that instant, he did something he'd never done before. He lost complete control of himself.

Growling deep in his throat, he felt his orgasm tear through him. It surged with a wave of overwhelming power.

He clutched Seren to him as he buried himself deep inside her and his body exploded in ecstasy. Still he wanted more. He hated that it was over so soon when all he wanted was to stay inside her for a while longer.

Their bodies still joined, he pulled her back to lie against his chest as he settled himself on the bed with her lying atop him.

Seren drew a ragged, contented breath as she laid her head back against Kerrigan's shoulder. She could see her naked body reflected in the ceiling above while Kerrigan's tan hands toyed with her breasts.

She shivered as he withdrew from her body.

His dark eyes burned into hers. 'You are virgin no more, Seren.'

'I know.'

Using his legs, he spread hers wide so that she could see the evidence of their play. His seed was mingled there with her blood.

'And what if you find yourself with my child?' There was an odd note to his voice. One that she couldn't name.

'I will do what I've always done whenever things didn't go as I planned. I will cope.'

Kerrigan didn't understand this woman and her calm acceptance of misfortune. 'Will you not be angry at me?'

'Nay, Kerrigan. I offered myself to you. Why should I fault you for my actions?'

His face hardened as he stared up at her in the mirror. 'I won't ever care for you, Seren. There's no place for a wife and child in my world.'

Seren sighed heavily at his inability to simply enjoy

what they'd done. 'I ask you for nothing, Kerrigan. Can you not understand the term "gift"?'

His voice was dark and ragged. 'No one gives something unless they want something in return.'

Her green eyes stared at him accusingly. 'Fine then. I did want something.'

'I knew it. You were using this to soften me.'

She rolled over to look down at him, face to face. His hard body felt strange beneath hers, and yet she felt no shame. 'Nay. After what had happened with Morgen and her spell while you fought, I wanted to know what it would be like to bed with you. You were right. I am a woman full-grown, and for many years I have wondered at what it would feel like to have knowledge of a man's body. Now I know, and that is what you gave me in return.'

His eyes flared to red flames. 'You are ever witless, little mouse. And I have given you much more than that.'

As she opened her mouth to ask him what he meant by that, Blaise's voice echoed in the room around them.

'Lord Kerrigan, come quickly. We're under attack.'

Chapter Eight

Kerrigan flashed his black armor back onto his body. His natural inclination would be to leave Seren to her own devices, but for once he hesitated. Without him, she was completely defenseless.

He swept her naked body with his gaze and paused at the sight of her bloodied thighs. At the sight of her reddened flesh, disheveled hair, and swollen lips that betrayed their play. His body burned at the memory of her touch.

She'd given herself to him without reservation.

Something foreign pierced his heart. Some emotion he didn't even understand. All he knew was that he couldn't leave her here alone.

Clenching his fist, he covered her with the clothes of a squire – in case she needed to run, she wouldn't have a heavy dress slowing her down, or trailing after her. Without a word, he held his hand out to her. She didn't hesitate at all before she tucked her tiny, finely boned hand into his. The moment she did, he flashed them into the chapel beside Lancelot's tomb.

'Stay here, little mouse, and don't come out. No matter what you hear.'

To his amazement, she leaned forward to kiss him

123

gently on the cheek. 'Be careful.' Even more stunning than her actions and words was the sincerity he saw in those enchanting green eyes.

And you as well ...

The words hung in his throat. All he could do was incline his head toward her before he took his shadow form and went to seek out Blaise.

He found the mandrake in a bower room in the southern tower. Blaise stood before the open window that showed a sky darkened by gargoyles and dragons. It was Morgen's army, and the sight made him curl his lip in fury. Damn the bitch for her timing.

'How did they find us?'

'Don't look at me,' Blaise snapped. 'I was dozing in my bed until I felt the pull of my kind approaching.' He glanced askance at him. 'What were *you* doing?'

'Nothing that should have caused this.'

Blaise snorted in disbelief.

Ignoring him, Kerrigan threw up his arms and raised a shell of magic to protect them from the approaching army. So long as it stood, there was no way for Morgen or her people to reach them. The only problem was that the shield depended on him to remain strong. If he napped or grew weak from hunger, the shield would fail.

And his primary source of food was on the outside of the castle ...

Aye, things were definitely looking up for them.

Seren listened carefully, but all she could hear was the sound of her own heart beating. Whatever could be happening upstairs?

It was terribly quiet for a castle that was under attack.

Suddenly, she felt a presence behind her. She turned

her head and jumped back in terror as she saw a beautiful apparition.

With long dark hair, he appeared to be a man in his early thirties. His features were finely chiseled and perfectly handsome. But what frightened her was the fact that he was completely transparent.

His dark eyes penetrated her. 'Seren? Are you all right?'

She shivered at his questions. 'H-how do you know my name?'

'I know the name of everyone who comes to my home.'

'*Your* home?'

'Joyous Gard.'

A feeling of dread went through her as she glanced to the form of Lancelot on his sarcophagus and then back at the ghost. Aye, they were very similar in features. Too similar in point of fact. 'You are Lancelot?'

He struck his shoulder with his fist before he fell down on one knee before her. 'Aye, my lady, and I am here to protect you.'

Three days before this, the idea of the ghost of a famed knight – who up until a short while ago she had assumed was fictitious – would most likely have made her fear a mental distress of some sort had besieged her. But after she had been sucked into the darkness of Camelot and assaulted by demons, gargoyles, and dragons, this was beginning to seem quite normal.

And that honestly scared her.

But not as much as the thought of what might be happening above with Kerrigan and Blaise.

'I am glad to hear it, my lord. No doubt Lord Kerrigan could use another sword, even if it does belong to a ghost.'

'Kerrigan?' Lancelot sneered the name at her. 'He

is the beast that I am here to protect you from.'

She shook her head. 'He is no beast . . . He is above even now trying to keep me safe.'

'Nay, my lady,' Lancelot said earnestly as he stepped closer to her. 'I don't think you quite understand the position you are in.'

'Aye, but I do. Morgen is after me to return me to Camelot so that she can use me to get the Round Table and destroy the world.'

He shook his head. 'Poor Lady Seren. Do you not understand what you have done this day?'

Apparently not. 'And what have I done?'

'You took the devil into your bed and you now carry his child.'

Seren felt her jaw go slack at his news. How did he know . . . But then he was a ghost. Perhaps they knew all that happened in the world of the living.

Even so, she refused to believe him. 'Nay. 'Tis not possible.'

Those dark eyes singed her. 'Aye, but it is. I know you have lain with him. I can feel the life force of the baby that is beginning to form even now. And once Kerrigan learns that you carry his child, he will destroy you both.'

Unable to comprehend what he was saying, Seren looked at her stomach and placed her hand to it. Was it true? Could she be with child already?

Was it even possible for a ghost to know this?

The thought of her pregnant should scare her and yet it didn't . . . And that was the most frightening part of all.

'Kerrigan has no compassion, my lady,' Lancelot said. 'Did you not notice that in Camelot, there are no children there? None.'

Seren frowned as she thought about that. 'I assumed

they were elsewhere. The parts of the castle I saw weren't exactly conducive to innocent minds.'

He shook his head slowly. 'Nay, my lady. Long ago, Lord Kerrigan was cursed by Morgen. He doesn't eat as we do. He lives off the blood of children. That alone sustains him.'

Seren scoffed at his words. 'You're being absurd. I'm not some little girl to be frightened by tales of demons eating children.'

Lancelot moved to stand just beside her so that he could whisper into her ear. 'Then ask him what he eats and note that he will not answer you no matter how much you plead to know. Because he knows the answer will drive you away from him before he can use you to get what he wants. And once he has what he wants, Seren, then he will kill you and the babe himself. Without remorse or care. Trust me in this.'

The problem was, she didn't trust him at all, and why should she? He was a ghost. He could be devil-sent as quickly as he could be good.

She turned to face him. 'I don't believe you. Kerrigan isn't like that.'

He sighed wearily. 'Poor child. Ask him what he feeds on, and when you believe that I am the one telling you the truth, return here and I will help you to escape him.'

He vanished instantly.

Seren glanced about. 'I truly hate it that you people do that,' she said in a low tone.

'Hate that we do what?'

She let out a startled shriek at the deep sound of Kerrigan's voice coming from behind her. 'That!' she snapped. 'Have you people not heard of doors? Of knocking before you enter? Is there no privacy to be had?'

127

Kerrigan gave her a peeved stare as he crossed his arms over his chest. 'Nay, little mouse. True privacy won't exist for several more centuries.'

'Pardon?'

An amused light glinted in his dark eyes. 'Nothing.' He inclined his head toward the door. 'Come, Seren. You may leave here for a few hours.'

She hesitated at his words and dire tone. 'What do you mean?'

'We are under siege by Morgen's troops. No doubt you will be relegated to this dark place all too soon as we battle them. For now we are in a stalemate. So come above and enjoy the daylight while you're able.'

Seren reached out to touch him, only to have him move away. He glared murderously at her. 'I told you, mouse, your gift sways nothing inside me.'

Yet he had brought her here to protect her and now he was offering her comfort for as long as he could.

So what should she believe? His words or his actions?

Her mother had always told her that words were made to deceive, but that actions never lied.

' 'Tis a pity then, my lord. What we did together most definitely swayed my affections for you.'

His eyes blazed fire at her. 'Do not deceive yourself, Seren. I stabbed you once. I can easily do it again, and next time I won't bring you back from the threshold of death.'

Perhaps, but then, too, she had seen the look on his face when he'd realized what he'd done to her. There had been grief and pain in those dark eyes. Even remorse, and when he'd called for Blaise, the anguish in his tone was too heartfelt to be feigned.

No matter what he said, he did care for her. At least a little.

'As you say, my lord.'

He stiffened at her words. 'You don't believe me?'

She should probably lie, and yet it wasn't in her nature to do so. 'Nay, I don't believe you.'

He whirled on her then so fast that she could do scarce more than gasp as he pinned her back against the wall. He pulled the dagger from his waist and held it balanced against her throat. 'I am not a man for you to take lightly, mouse.'

She should be afraid of him and yet she wasn't. She saw through his actions. If he'd really wanted her dead, she would have died the night before.

'I don't take you lightly, Kerrigan. I know exactly what you're capable of.' She boldly covered his hand with hers and pressed it closer to her throat. 'But I am not the kind of woman to live in fear, either. If you are going to kill me, then get it over with, or never threaten to do so again.'

Kerrigan was stunned by her courage. The darker part of him wanted to kill her just because she'd questioned him. Kill her because of the weakness she had exposed inside him.

But the other . . .

He stared at the shining silver blade that was pressed against the pale, tender skin he'd nuzzled only a few minutes before. And as he remembered the way she had felt in his arms, his anger withered.

'Do it,' she said, bravely. 'I know you've cut the throats of countless others.'

It was true. He'd done so a thousand times. Always without remorse. Without feeling anything.

But he felt something now. Anger, desire, and other things he couldn't even identify.

Kill her and be done with it.

Still he hesitated.

Seren braced herself for the worst. She could see the heat in his red eyes. Heat that said he hated her, and yet there was something else there.

Suddenly the blade pressed closer. So close that she wasn't sure how it didn't break the skin of her throat. She wanted to swallow, but knew that if she so much as breathed, the dagger would wound her.

Mayhap he would kill her after all.

So be it. At least it would be over and she would have no more fears.

Kerrigan growled deep in his throat – the sound of a wild animal as it lunged for the kill.

His hand tightened on her shoulder an instant before he flung the dagger away and pulled her fiercely into his arms. His lips were scalding as they claimed hers. Closing her eyes, Seren inhaled the musky scent of him while he explored every inch of her mouth with his tongue.

She melted from the heat of that kiss. From the sensation of his arms encircling her.

Kerrigan pulled back to look down at her with an accusing stare.

Relieved that she was still alive, Seren reached up to smooth the frown from his brow. 'Then there will be no more threats against me. You have decided.'

His gaze hardened. 'You don't control me.'

'Nay. But you made your choice, my lord, and I shall hold you accountable to it.'

He released her so quickly that she barely caught her balance. 'Bah. You are—'

'A fool,' she finished for him. 'And I am a mouse. But I am not some insignificant matter for you to tread upon without regard. I'm a human being, Lord Kerrigan, and you will treat me as such.'

He curled his lip at her. 'You are a peasant and I am

a king. That gives me full control over your life.'

'And you chose to be kingly with your compassion. You spared my life this day and you saved it last night.'

Still his denial burned bright in that obsidian gaze. 'I hold no compassion nor any regard for life, human or otherwise, and that goes for you as well.'

She ignored his argument. 'I don't believe you.'

His eyes flared to red. 'Believe it, wench. When I was ten years old, I killed my own mother, and I felt nothing but relief the moment her blood coated my hands. So if you expect me to ever mourn your passing, think again.'

But he had felt something when he'd stabbed her. She'd seen it with her own eyes. Heard it with her own ears.

And he hadn't let her coldly die.

'Why did you kill your mother?'

His face turned to stone. 'I no longer recall the reason. It didn't matter to me at the time.'

Seren cocked her head as she realized something about him. 'Did you know that you glance down and to the left when you lie?'

His gaze snapped back to hers. 'I don't lie.'

'And yet by your own admissions you are ever a liar.'

His rage was so great that the very air around him snapped with power. Yet he made no move against her. He merely stood there, glaring at her. 'Out of my sight, mouse.'

Suddenly, Seren found herself in the great hall upstairs, only a few feet from Blaise. He turned toward her with an arched brow. One that arched even higher when Kerrigan didn't immediately join them.

'Angered him, did you?' Blaise asked.

'It would appear so. I seem to have a great knack for it.'

He laughed. 'And yet you live. Amazing. You're the only one I know who has ever done so.'

That was far from comforting. 'Why is he so angry at everything?'

Blaise shrugged. 'It's a comfortable emotion. He understands anger. The other feelings are more confusing. You can be angry and have no feeling other than the anger. But to feel something more tender ... it leaves you vulnerable.'

Blaise was a lot wiser than he appeared. His words reminded her of something her mother might have said.

'Was he always this way?' she asked.

'Aye, for the most part. When Morgen found him and first brought him to Camelot, he was terrified. I could sense it. But he never showed it to them. He was as he is now. An animal that had been turned vicious by those who sought to hurt it. So he attacked until none dared to challenge him anymore.'

A chill went down her spine as he described Kerrigan in a manner that reminded her of her mother's words to her that day when they had found the wolf. Was it possible that Blaise might have known of her memory?

With their unholy powers, she supposed that it was possible, or perhaps it was merely his own perception of Kerrigan.

'And yet you are friends with him.'

Blaise's violet eyes turned dull at her statement. 'Nay. Kerrigan is friends with no one. I am merely his servant.'

'But you hold enough power that you could leave him if you wanted to. Why stay?'

One corner of his mouth quirked up in bitter amusement. 'Perhaps I'm a bit of a masochist.'

She frowned. 'I don't understand that word.'

'Someone who likes to feel pain,' he explained. 'Either self-inflicted or inflicted by others.'

Still, she didn't believe him. 'You don't strike me as such a person. You are loyal to him. I've seen it. There is a difference between serving someone because you have to and liking them. You serve Kerrigan by choice.'

For once he didn't deny it. 'And you are far wiser than you should be, Lady Seren. Such things are bound to lead you into trouble.'

Perhaps, but he was avoiding her question. 'So why do you stay and serve him?'

Pain flashed across his brow before he hid it. When he spoke, his tone was low and sincere. 'Because I know what it's like to be abandoned by everyone around me. I know what it's like to be denied the very things that all children should have. Safety. Love. Regard. Your mother loved you, Seren. You don't know what it's like to grow up watching other children with their parents while knowing that if you reached out to yours all you would get is a vicious slap. A bloodied nose. At least I was lucky enough to have been found by a man who cared for me when I was young. Kerrigan had no one until Morgen took him in.'

And she had seen enough of Morgen to know that she hadn't been overly kind to him, either.

'Do you know why he killed his mother?' she asked him.

Blaise shook his head. 'Nay. He has never mentioned her to me.'

As Seren opened her mouth to ask him more, a sudden jolt shook the castle. The force of it was so severe that she staggered. Even the stones around them seemed to sing out in discomfort.

'What is that?'

Blaise opened the shutters to the windows to show her the group that was waiting there to kill them.

Seren's jaw dropped as she saw the dragons and gargoyles hovering a small distance away. Dragon after dragon was diving toward the castle, only to slam and recoil against nothing before they reached it.

Blaise cursed. 'They're attacking the shield.'

No sooner had he said that than a large boulder came hurtling toward them. Seren instinctively ducked as it came perilously close.

It rebounded harmlessly away.

'What shield?' she asked.

'Kerrigan's. He placed it around the castle before he went to get you.'

She let out a long breath in relief. 'Then we are safe.'

Blaise didn't look so convinced. 'So long as Kerrigan remains strong, aye. But once he grows weak ...' She could hear the doom in his tone.

'Why can't he just take us from here? Flash us out as he's done before?'

'Because he knows what I know.'

'And that is?'

'That you carry his child, and so long as you hold such power within you, Morgen can find us. It's what allowed her to track us here and why her army now sits camped around the castle.'

Seren went cold at his words. 'How do you know I'm pregnant?'

'Can you not feel it yourself?'

She shook her head. 'I feel the same as I always have.'

Blaise's violet eyes bored into her. 'You may feel the same, but you're not. Your destiny has begun, Lady

Seren. If Morgen takes you now, she will have possession of one of the most powerful beings on this earth. Your child will hold the power to resurrect Mordred and to bring the balance of power over to Morgen's side. May God have mercy on all of us then. There will be no one who can stop her.'

Nay, he was wrong. He had to be. 'Kerrigan told me that my destiny was to marry a Lord of Avalon and to have *his* child.'

'Nay,' he said, his voice laden with dread. 'Your destiny was to birth the next Penmerlin and so you will. We only assumed that the father of your child would be one of the Lords of Avalon. That made sense . . . had they found you first. But instead of being born of their goodness, your child was sired by a demon lord. That babe you carry is a powerful instrument who will have a natural tendency toward malice.'

Her heart clenched at his words. 'What are you saying?'

'Blaise is saying that you have truly given me the greatest gift imaginable, Seren. With the child you carry, I will not only be able to rule the worlds of man and mage, but bring them both to their knees.'

Chapter Nine

Seren gave a nervous laugh at Kerrigan's dire prediction. 'Careful, my lord, there for a moment, you seemed so sincere that I almost believed you.'

'He's not jesting, Seren,' Blaise said in a bland voice. 'He means it.'

She felt her mouth open slightly as the full ramification of Kerrigan's words hit her. 'You would use your own child to further your own ends?'

Kerrigan moved to stand so close that she had to tilt her head up to meet his fiery gaze. 'I will do whatever I have to to remain where I am. I won't go back to what I was. Ever. Not for you and certainly not for the brat you carry. I warned you of such and I meant every word of it.'

Apparently so. And yet she couldn't imagine being so callous toward an innocent babe who had no say in his existence. 'What did they do to you to make you care nothing for anyone, not even your own child?'

His laugh was bitter and lacking all humor. 'You never want an answer to that question, mouse. Your feeble mind is incapable of comprehending it.'

She nodded before she stepped away from him. There was an odd calmness to her that she didn't understand. She should be terrified of him, and yet all she felt was pity. Sadness. Anger.

But through those emotions, she also had an epiphany.

There was no way either he or Morgen would kill her now. Not so long as she carried this child.

But unlike them, she refused to use an innocent life for her own gain. Blaise was wrong. The baby knew nothing of evil, and she was going to make sure that it never learned of it.

'I am truly sorry for whatever miserly mother spawned you, Kerrigan. No child should be born to a mother who doesn't love it.' She narrowed her eyes on him to let him know exactly how much she meant her next words. 'But I am not she, and this child is mine, and feebleminded or not, I will fight to my death for it. Do you understand that?'

He looked less than convinced. 'Fight with what? I could break you in twain.'

Seren moved to stand by his side. She lifted herself up on her toes to lessen the difference in their height. And she met that cold, eerie gaze without flinching. 'Prepare for battle.'

Kerrigan would have laughed had she not said those words with such growling sincerity that he actually believed her. 'Why would you fight for a child you don't even want?'

'As you told Morgen, you gave it to me, and I protect what is mine. You should have chosen a more pliant vessel to carry your seed, my lord. This one will never stand to see her child harmed in any manner, and I will do whatever I must to see him or her safe. I assure you, you have battled much, but you have never faced a mother bent on protection of her babe. There is no power on this earth or beyond it more powerful, I assure you.'

He was completely baffled by her conviction. 'I *will* kill you, Seren.'

'You *will* have to.' She stepped away from him and turned to Blaise. 'I would ask one favor of you, please.'

The mandrake exchanged a puzzled look with him. 'And that is?'

'That if I do indeed die before my child is grown that you make sure my baby knows that I gave my life for him. That I would have spared him all pain had God willed it, and that I regretted the fact that I wasn't a warrior to fight, but that I did fight with all I was worth . . . for him.'

Blaise gave a solemn nod. 'I will tell him.'

'Promise?'

'Aye.'

And with those words spoken, she left them alone.

Kerrigan didn't move for several heartbeats as his anger mounted. 'That stupid little fool.'

Blaise still stared after her even though she was no longer in sight. 'She's not so stupid, I think.'

'And what do you know of it?'

Blaise's violet eyes showed some inner pain. 'Truly nothing. My mother was like yours. Selfish and cold. She cared nothing for me. But what I wouldn't have given to have had a mother like Seren.'

A wave of disgust curled Kerrigan's lip. 'Bah! You'd be a weak-kneed sop. Our mothers gave us an even greater gift. They made us strong.'

Blaise met his gaze with an unexpected fire shining brightly in them. 'Cruelty isn't strength, my king.'

'Then what is?'

'A woman who is willing to fight to the death two people she knows she can't defeat to protect a child that is defenseless.'

'That's not strength. That's stupidity.'

138

One corner of Blaise's mouth quirked up as if something amused him. 'And so is holding a castle against your enemies when you know you can't hold it for long. Tell me why you haven't handed Seren over to Morgen?'

Rage shot through him as he fought the urge to reach out and strike Blaise. 'You overstep your bounds, servant.'

Blaise lowered his head with a subjugation Kerrigan knew he didn't feel. 'I do indeed. But I notice you haven't answered my question.'

What was there to answer to such a ridiculous inference? 'What do you think? I love her? I don't. I have nothing but disdain for one such as she.'

And still Blaise's expression mocked him. 'Funny. I have nothing but respect for her. I think she's a remarkable creature and I think, deep down, so do you.'

Growling, Kerrigan took a step toward the mandrake, who quickly and wisely vanished.

His temper was snapping all around to the point that even the air around him was charged with it. It crackled with power and rage. But the truth was, he didn't know what made him angrier. The fact that Blaise had dared to say it or the fact that it was true.

He did respect her. Deeply. No one had ever fought for him. Not by choice anyway. Blaise and the others served him because they were afraid of him.

But Seren . . .

She would die to protect a child she didn't even know. *His* child. And in an odd way, it was almost like protecting him.

'You are a simpleton,' he sneered at himself.

Seren could care less for him, and her bravery had nothing to do with the fact that he was the father of this baby. Like as not, she'd gut him if he ever offered her the chance. Just as Blaise and any of the others would.

139

But against his will, his thoughts drifted to what Blaise had said. The mandrake was right. He would have given anything to have had kindness as a child. Just once in his life to have had someone to even look on him with compassion or care.

'*Get out of my sight, worm. You sicken me. I should have drowned you at birth. I don't even know why I bother to feed you now. Begone from me, you sickening dog. I don't even want to look at you.*'

He flinched at the sound of his mother's voice tormenting him from the past. And it was followed by the look of shock on her face the day he'd finally found the anger and courage to stab her and end her insults once and for all.

He'd felt nothing at that time. Nothing but a relief so profound that it corroborated the priest's words. He was hell-spawned, and to the devil he would eventually return.

So be it. At least he would finally be welcomed someplace.

Seren stood in the open window where she could see the army of dragons and gargoyles who were waiting to drag her back to Camelot.

'You won't win, Morgen,' she said in a low tone. 'Not if I can help it.'

'Would you sell your soul to keep that baby safe?'

She turned her head to find the ghost of Lancelot behind her. 'Such a thing isn't possible.'

He arched a brow at her. 'You don't believe in the devil?'

'Of course I do. But he wouldn't barter my soul for so trivial a matter.'

'What if the devil would? Would *you*?'

It was a perilous question. How far would she go to

keep her child safe? The mere thought of hell terrified her. It, like her future, loomed in front of her with all manner of unknown torments and challenges.

She glanced out the window again to see the army of damned warriors. They might not live in hell itself, but all of them lived in a place of torment, the likes of which she'd never known before. They had no light. No freedom. They knew only Morgen and her cruelty.

It was a place she wanted to avoid and one she definitely didn't want her child to see.

'Nay,' she said in a low tone. 'I wouldn't trust the devil not to trick me. Safe the child would be in Morgen's hands, but I don't want that for him. I would only barter the devil if I could possess the strength and skills to keep him safe myself.'

She saw respect in Lancelot's transparent eyes. 'I know one way that would keep you both safe.'

'And that is?'

'The sword Caliburn. The one that Kerrigan wields. Whoever holds that sword is immortal. With it and its scabbard, you can never be wounded or bleed. You don't need a warrior's training. All you need is to have it in your possession.'

What was it with the sword that all she met wanted to take it from Kerrigan? No wonder the man was so distrustful. But she had no way of knowing if she could wield such a sword or the power it contained. Not without a man's strength. 'Are you serious?'

He nodded grimly.

'How can I trust you?'

'Can you not?'

But what if he lied? Dare she even believe one bit of what he said? 'If I take his sword, he'll kill me.'

'Take his sword and he won't be able to.' Lancelot lowered his voice to a tempting and seductive tone.

'Imagine, Seren, absolute power. Immortality. No one would ever harm you or the babe. Ever.'

Still she wasn't so sure about it, but before she could say anything more, he faded from her.

Irritated, Seren started to call him back until she saw Blaise approaching her from the other end of the hallway.

'What are you doing here, my lady?'

'Thinking.'

Blaise laughed deep in his throat. 'I usually try to avoid that as much as possible as it most often leads me to mischief or mayhem.'

She smiled in spite of herself. The mandrake had a way with words. She actually liked him a great deal.

'So what were you thinking of?' he asked as he neared her.

'Something Morgen said about Kerrigan while we were fleeing Camelot. She told the gargoyles to take his sword. She said that if they took his sword and scabbard that he was naught but a mortal man. Is that true?'

She saw the indecision on his handsome face as he debated on what to answer. 'Do you think it is?'

'Aye.'

'Then you would be wrong. Kerrigan isn't like other men anymore. Morgen saw to that. But without his sword and scabbard he can be killed.'

Seren cocked her head as she considered his confession. 'Why would you tell me this?'

Blaise flipped his long braid over his shoulder before he answered. 'Because I trust you to do what is right. Kerrigan is a formidable enemy, but he makes a far better ally.' Blaise bent low to whisper in her ear. 'He is a lost soul, my lady. Everyone gave up on him long ago and cast him aside as worthless. Don't be like all the others.'

'And if he kills me?'

'I don't think he will.'

How she wished she had his faith. 'That's easy enough for you to say since it's not your life hanging in the balance.'

He smiled at her. 'True. But I have lain in your hands the way to destroy him. What you do with that information is up to you.' He started away from her, then paused. Even though he couldn't really see her, his pale eyes were searing with their intensity. 'Don't disappoint me, Seren. Kerrigan is the father of your child, and he's risked much to keep you from Morgen.'

'And he threatens to kill me with virtually every breath.'

'But you're not dead yet.'

The 'yet' was the key part. But then she had dared Kerrigan to do it and he had tossed away the dagger. It gave her hope that she was reaching him. She could raise her child alone, but it would be much easier if the babe had a father.

'No matter what he blusters, he won't kill you, Seren. Trust me.'

Seren sighed as Blaise withdrew from her. Well, at least now she knew Lancelot had been honest with her about the sword. Take it from Kerrigan and he wouldn't be able to harm her.

Neither would Morgen.

But the last time she'd gone near Kerrigan while he slept, he'd stabbed her and had almost killed her.

There had been only one time when he'd removed his sword . . .

When he bedded her.

It would be a bold move on her part. And if she failed this, his anger would be boundless. She couldn't even blame him. Taking his sword would leave him vulnerable to anyone who came near him.

But it would protect the baby . . .

Her.

Do it, Seren.

It could very well be her only hope.

Hours went by as Kerrigan contemplated the strength of Morgen's army. He could summon the gargoyles in to the castle one by one and slay them. But to deplete the gargoyles would weaken him greatly and leave the dragons unchecked. Since gargoyles were made primarily of stone, only they could successfully battle one of those beasts. Dragons' breath would incinerate any living creature, but in the case of gargoyles, it only charred them a bit and left no lasting damage once the flames cooled.

It made them perfect dragon fodder, which made them valuable allies.

Perhaps he should try and woo some of them to his side. Definitely something easier said than done since, as a rule, the gargoyles hated him. He hadn't been exactly nice to them in the past. Like the mods and graylings, they were servants to do his bidding.

As for the dragons . . .

The mandrakes held no more love for Morgen than the gargoyles did, but the problem was that they cared even less for him.

Perhaps Seren was right. Kindness did have its benefits.

Kerrigan scoffed at that. What was he thinking? Fear was a much more potent motivator, and it was definitely the one he preferred.

But it all came back to one question. 'How did I get myself into this?'

He and Morgen had always existed under a truce.

Now he'd breached it for a bit of fluff that had no use for either of them. Seren's child would be able to command the Round Table and all who had sworn allegiance to it.

More than that, the child would be able to wield his sword, Caliburn. He swallowed at the sobering thought. With the birth of his child, he would become obsolete. It was why he'd always taken care to never impregnate any of Morgen's court, or her. Unlike those not of his bloodline, his child could wield the full power of his sword. With that sword, his child could rise up and slay him. And with Morgen guiding the child, it would only be a matter of time before the fey bitch turned his babe against him.

It was a frightening thought. Like so many before him, he'd laid the foundation of his own destruction. In one moment of thoughtless passion, he'd lost control of himself and sired his heir.

His successor.

He heard the sound of small footsteps approaching. He turned from his window to find Seren entering the room with a large platter of food. She was still dressed as a squire in a brown tunic and hose, with her pale hair plaited down her back.

Frowning, he watched as she placed the platter on a small table not far from him. 'What is that?'

She looked down at her fare. 'Dandelion salad with cowslip and berries. It was all I could find out in the kitchen gardens. I made a light sauce with the berries and water for the salad. It should be quite tasty.' She met his gaze. 'I thought you might be hungry.'

He was famished, but there was nothing there that could nourish him. 'Nay, Seren.'

'You haven't eaten anything all day.'

'I am quite fine without.'

She placed her arms on her hips as she continued to argue with him. 'You can't go without food. Blaise said you must keep your strength up or else the shield will fall and the others will attack.' She held up a bowl of berries. 'Humor me, my lord, and eat a few.'

He stared at the small blackberries. They looked so harmless and yet if he ingested them, his stomach would cramp and undignify him before her. 'I can't eat those.'

'Then what would you like? Perhaps I could make that instead.'

He cocked his head as he caught a strange tremor in her voice. It was slight . . . subtle. Yet it was enough to make him wonder. 'What is this really about?'

And then he saw it in her eyes. That darkness that had marked many before her. Aye, she wasn't used to being dishonest, and it showed now in her entire demeanor. She was lying to him. 'I know not what you mean.'

'You do,' he said, drawing near to her. 'Tell me.'

He expected even more lies from her.

She didn't bother. Stiffening her spine, she met his gaze with the sincere honesty that had marked her from the moment they first met. 'I heard that you feed from the blood of children. That you would feed on our child once he was born.'

Kerrigan snorted at the absurdity of that. 'Nay, little mouse. I find nothing nourishing about the blood of children.'

He saw the relief plainly in her green eyes. 'Then what would you like to eat?'

Unlike her, it was in his nature to lie. Always. The truth was as foreign to him as was trust. There was no need to be honest with her, and yet the sadistic part of himself wanted her to know the truth of him. Let her understand exactly who and what he was, and then she would give up all her inane dreams that he might protect her or the child.

He smiled coldly at her. 'What I like to eat, little mouse, is life.'

A deep frown creased her brow. 'I don't understand.'

'I know.' He moved to step around her so that her back was against his front. Pulling his glove off, he laid his hand over her chest, between her breasts. 'Haven't you wondered why I'm so cold to the touch?'

'Aye.'

Kerrigan leaned forward and inhaled the special scent of her hair. It fired his blood even more than being able to feel the heat of her body. All he had to do was move his hand a tiny degree and he would be caressing her breast . . .

He pushed that thought aside as her heart hammered its strength against his palm. He could feel the strength of her life force. Feel the electricity he needed to regenerate his powers.

All he had to do was close his eyes and he could draw it off her. Pull it inside himself until he consumed her.

'In order to live,' he whispered in her ear, 'I drain the life off others.' He watched as her nipples hardened under the fabric of her tunic, teasing his desire.

'I still don't understand.'

Kerrigan couldn't stop himself from flicking his thumb over one taut peak. She trembled in response, but didn't pull away. He cupped her breast as he pulled her back against him. The hunger of his body was second only to his hunger for her life.

The demon inside him was awake and it wanted her. The only thing that held it back was the man who didn't want her dead. At least not yet.

He forced himself to return his hand to the valley between her breasts, just over her heart. 'I'm nourished by the essence of others.'

Seren gasped as she felt a sharp pain pierce her heart. She tried to move away from Kerrigan, but he held her in place.

He laid his whiskered cheek to hers, and for the first time his body was warm. 'You should feel the rush of it, little mouse. The feel of someone's life force moving through you, invigorating you.' He nuzzled her neck, before he moved his hand away from her. 'I live off the strength of that human essence. The electricity that runs through a heart. I literally suck it into my body to feed myself.'

'And what happens to the person you draw this electricity from?'

'If they're human, they die. If they're Adoni, they can survive it. At least on occasion.'

She gaped at his harsh words. 'You kill people and steal their souls?'

'Nay, little mouse, the soul holds nothing for me. Give it to your God or your devil. I care not which. As for death . . . better them than me.'

Stunned by his confession, she turned in his arms. But before she could speak, she heard the large rustling of wings. A dark shadow appeared in the window an instant before three gargoyles flew into the room.

Rage and fear mingled inside her. How had they breached his shield?

Kerrigan moved around her to engage them. Seren looked about for some way to help, but there was nothing she could do. As she had said earlier, she wasn't some warrior to fight. But how she wished that wasn't so.

Kerrigan caught one of the gargoyles by the tail and used it to slam it into the wall. The gargoyle shrieked before it jerked its tail free, then dove at him while a second one came at his back. They caught him between them, and pummeled his body with their fists.

The third gargoyle flew at her. Seren gasped before she ducked it and hid herself beneath the nearest table. As the gargoyle came after her, Kerrigan sent some kind of sorcerer's blast from his hand at the gargoyle that splintered it into pieces. Dust from the stone scattered everywhere, making her cough as the stone dust invaded her lungs.

Then Kerrigan spoke in a language she couldn't understand. His words rang out clearly in the hall in a deep cadence that was almost like a song. A heartbeat later, the other two beasts dissolved.

Seren sat beneath the table, covered in dust, as she realized exactly how much power Kerrigan commanded. For the first time, she was scared of him. Scared of this man who claimed to have no compassion.

A man who killed others just so that he could live. It was monstrous.

'You're safe, Seren,' he said quietly. 'They're gone now.'

Her entire body shaking, she crawled out from under the table to see nothing but the powdered remains of the gargoyles.

Kerrigan leaned against the table with his arms supporting his weight. His black hair framing his handsome face, he looked a bit pale and worn. And as she neared him, he pushed himself back and leveled a menacing glare at her.

'How did they get inside the shield?' she asked.

His breathing labored, he raked a hand through his tousled black hair. 'When I took the spark from you, it opened a slit in the shield. I can't feed and hold the shield at the same time. Not unless I wish to kill you.'

Seren wrapped her arms around herself as a foreign coldness consumed her. 'So this is the life you have. You kill in order to live, and you live in fear of those who want to kill you in return.'

She couldn't imagine the horror that was his existence. The loneliness. Surely he did live in hell and had done so for countless centuries. 'Tell me something, my lord, is this the life that you would give to your child?' She looked up at him and narrowed her gaze. 'Truthfully.'

She took his hand and led it to her stomach so that she could hold it over her womb. 'Is this really the existence you want him to know?'

Kerrigan closed his eyes as the warmth of her washed over him. She feared him now. He could smell it, and yet there was no joy in his having caused it. In fact, it pained him.

He spread his hand out so that he could feel the tiny spark of power that called out to him and to Morgen. In time, that spark would manifest itself into a fetus and then a living, breathing person.

Whoever controlled the child controlled that child's powers.

An unbidden image went through his mind. He saw himself as a callow youth. Bitter and angry, his face still stinging from his mother's latest slap, he'd been lugging water from the well to his mother's hovel.

Three men had been riding by on horseback when his mother, being ever eager for coin, had called out to them to ask if they'd like to spend some time in her bed.

A knight dressed in a brown and gold woolen surcoat had sneered at her and her peasant's homespun rags. At least until his gaze had fallen to Kerrigan.

'How much for an hour with the boy?'

Stunned, Kerrigan had frozen in place. He didn't know what shocked him most: the man's question or the calculating gleam in his mother's light eyes.

Her gaze had gone from him back to the knight. 'He's a virgin, my lord. Surely that's worth at least a silver mark.'

Horrified to a depth he'd never known, he'd watched as the knight dismounted to pay his mother the silver coin.

Time had seemed suspended as the knight approached him. The summer breeze had swept its blistering heat over his body while the other two men had laughed and made comments on how they should have thought to offer for him first.

'I'll take a turn with him when he's finished. Two bits for the bastard since he'll be virgin no more.'

His mother had laughed along with them. 'Done.'

Terrified, he'd been unable to move.

Until the knight had reached for him.

Kerrigan had swung his bucketful of water over the man, then beat him with it. The other two men came to help, and somewhere in the fighting, Kerrigan had grabbed the knight's dagger. Shaking in indignant outrage, he'd begun stabbing without thought as to the repercussions. He'd been blinded by his fear. Blinded by his anger.

And when everything had settled down again, he'd found himself covered in blood, standing over the bodies of the men. His face had throbbed from their beating. His entire body had ached.

Then in true scavenger form, his mother had come forward to search their purses for more coin.

Kerrigan had gaped at her.

Their deaths hadn't even fazed her as she pocketed any item of value they had. 'We'll need to bury these bodies somewhere.' She'd glanced to the horses that carried their armor. 'Think you we could sell that for more?'

'You were going to sell me to them.'

She'd looked at him crossly as she rose to her feet. 'What are you squawking over, chicken? I've sold myself for you enough times that it's only right that you pay for me for once.' She'd grabbed him by the hair and gave a yank as one corner of her mouth had turned up into a mocking smile. 'And now that I know what you're worth, we'll be—'

Her words had ended in a choking gasp.

Kerrigan had felt nothing as he watched her eyes turn glassy. He'd felt her blood running over his hand before she'd staggered back and fallen.

And still all that he'd felt was emptiness. And relief.

Until the fear had set in that someone would learn of what he'd done and kill him for it.

He'd dropped the dagger and run with all his strength. And in that one moment, he'd set his future into motion the same way Seren had the instant she'd reached up and taken his hand.

And now he looked into those large green eyes that held no hatred of him. No scorn.

But they were fearful, and that saddened him.

'You haven't answered my question, Kerrigan,' she said softly. 'Would you barter your child to this life so that you can have the world? Is it really worth it?'

She lifted his hand and held it between hers. 'All people are born with goodness inside them. All. And I know that somewhere deep inside you is still that goodness you were born with. You may never find it for me, but I pray you, my lord, find it for your child. Don't let him learn brutality from your hands. You

152

were tender with me when you created him. I know you can find that same tenderness for him. I know it.'

His chest tightened at her words. He'd never loved anything in his life. Nothing. He didn't even think he was capable of such a tender emotion. There was no goodness in him. There never had been. 'And if you're wrong?'

'I'm not wrong.'

In that moment, he realized the full strength of this woman.

He fought for himself. For *his* wants and *his* desires. But Seren . . . she fought for others.

He laid his hand against the smoothness of her cheek and stared into those eyes that seemed to glow from a fire that ran soul-deep.

'How can you have faith in me after all you have seen? All you know about me?'

Her features softened. 'It doesn't make sense, does it? But then the fact that the two of us are locked inside a castle while an entire army waits to kill you and capture me doesn't make sense, either. Why are we here?'

He gave a short laugh. 'I know not.'

Her eyes turned light and teasing. It was a look that no one had ever had with him before. 'And to think I'd really hoped that you had a plan of some sort.'

He enjoyed this light bantering. The absence of malice and mistrust. 'So did I. It seemed like a good idea when we came here.'

The light faded from her eyes as her face turned serious again. 'What's to become of us, my lord?'

Kerrigan stroked her brow with his hand as he marveled at the strength of her. At the way she was willing to take them all on for a tiny child that she didn't even know. 'That is the question I keep asking myself. I could fight my way through Morgen's army, but I can't protect you while I fight. They'd take you the minute the shield went down. Not to mention that her army is actually mine and I don't really want to diminish my own forces. I might need them later.'

'Then we will have no choice except to go back to her.'

Kerrigan released a long, tired breath. 'It's not quite that simple. Morgen now has a serious reason to want me dead. Sooner or later, she will find the means to do so, and then you'll be on your own.'

He saw the spark of fire in her eyes before she spoke. 'She won't win this.'

'And how do you know?'

'Good always triumphs over evil. 'Tis how every story ends, and this one is no different.'

Kerrigan forced himself not to laugh at her naivete. 'Need I remind you that evil has already triumphed. Arthur is dead and Camelot is in our hands. This isn't a story, Seren. It's reality, and in reality, there are no guarantees.'

Seren refused to believe that. She looked up into those dark eyes that smoldered with power and remembered the feral look of the wolf that had eventually licked her mother's face in gratitude.

Kindness is key, my Seren. That and your courage will save you.

She opened her mouth to argue when all of a sudden, a tremendous jolt went through the castle. One so fierce that even the stone walls groaned.

Kerrigan stumbled into her.

'What is that?'

Kerrigan couldn't answer as another such invisible wave went through the castle. He hissed as he fell to his knees.

Seren took a step toward him. He growled like a

snarling beast, then slapped his hand against the floor. His eyes turned back to their red flames as he came to his feet.

She followed after him to see what appeared to be a giant tree in the hands of the gargoyles. They flew with it toward the shield, slamming the tree into the invisible wall like a battering ram against the door.

As they made contact, another ripple went through, forcing Kerrigan to stagger back.

'What is that?' she asked him.

His face pale, he gave a dark, sinister laugh before he answered. 'In short, our doom.'

Chapter Ten

Seren narrowed her gaze on him. 'I don't like the sound of the word "doom." It's rather ominous.'

'Not half as ominous as that army will be when it breaches the shield, kills me, and takes you.'

She gave a fake shudder. 'I can feel the warmth of your sunshine, my lord. It overwhelms me so.'

Kerrigan actually smiled at her sarcastic words. 'Are you always so pert in the face of danger?'

'Well, until I met you, the greatest danger I faced was making Master Rufus angry. His anger certainly pales in comparison to yours and Morgen's.'

She said the words lightly, and yet they set an indignant fire deep inside him. One that didn't like the thought of someone harming her. 'Did he ever hurt you in his anger?'

Seren looked away.

His anger doubled. 'Seren, answer me.'

She shrugged as she moved away from the window. 'I'm his apprentice, my lord. He was in full right to punish me whenever I overstepped my bounds.'

He took her arm, pulling her up short. 'Punish you how?'

Her green eyes cut through him as she looked up at

him. 'How does anyone punish an insignificant servant?'

Kerrigan didn't know why, but the thought of another man laying a hand on her went through him like acid. 'He struck you?'

'Does it matter?'

'To me it does.'

She glanced down at his hand. Kerrigan let go as he realized his grip must be biting.

'Why?' she asked simply. 'You have told me repeatedly that you hold no regard for my life. What then does it matter how I'm treated by my master?'

It shouldn't matter. He shouldn't care at all. And yet . . .

'Why do you wish to return to such a life?'

'Because it was *my* life, Kerrigan. Mine. And it was a good one. I had friends who loved me.' Her gaze turned dreamy. 'Wendlyn is a beautiful girl who works beside me in the shop. She has a crush on the butcher's son who comes by to deliver meat to Mistress Maude. Then there is Mildred, who weaves off to the side. She doesn't say much, but she hums often to herself. And there's Robert, Master Rufus's son who will turn eight this year. He's a bit mischievous, but a good lad nonetheless who oft fetches us supplies when we need them.'

He could hear the love in her voice as she spoke of the people who'd made up her world. 'But if they treat you badly—'

'I never said they treated me badly. All of us have an off day or two. We are human and should be forgiven our faults.'

He shook his head at her. 'You astound me, Seren. I've never met anyone with your capacity for caring.'

She lifted herself up on her toes until their gazes

157

were almost level. 'Then you've been spending time with the wrong sorts of people, my lord. Perhaps you should get out more.'

He laughed out loud, amazed at the sound of something he hadn't heard in a lifetime. 'Perhaps I should.'

As Kerrigan turned back toward the window and the army that was still pounding his shield, he sobered. With every pounding beat of the battering ram, he could feel that strike against his powers.

They were weakening him. Each blow shattered through his body, pounding painfully.

'Aw, screw this,' he snarled an instant before he threw his hands out and sent a shatter bolt of lightning through the gargoyles and dragons.

Seren was stunned as the very air around them shimmered from his powers. Even her hair stood on end as what appeared to be lightning shot from Kerrigan's fingertips to the gargoyles who were battering his invisible shield.

The tree splintered into tiny pieces that rained through the air. The gargoyles went hurtling toward the ground. Kerrigan started to laugh, until he stumbled again. The lightning shot back into his body as he braced his hand against the stone sill.

His face was even paler than before. His hands were shaking as he grimaced and turned to press his spine against the stone wall. He leaned his head back and laughed shakily. 'That was a most idiotic expenditure of my powers, but it was worth it.' His dark eyes were gleaming as he gave her a crooked smile. 'Did you see them fall?'

She shook her head at him. There was something about him that reminded her of a little boy who'd been punished for doing something he knew not to, and yet was proud of what he'd done. 'It was quite lovely the way they hurtled through the air. And did it gain you anything?'

'Nothing but satisfaction, and there is much to be said for that.'

She rolled her eyes. 'Are you all right?'

He drew a deep breath before he pushed himself away from the wall. 'I'm not fallen or defeated yet.'

'Good. I hope you can continue to say that.'

He squeezed her hand and then stiffened as if he'd realized what he'd done and it somehow embarrassed him. He let go immediately.

He glanced back out the window. 'Pity I don't want to expend more energy. I'm sure I could take down a mandrake or two while I'm at it.'

She patted him on the shoulder as she would Robert in the shop whenever he was particularly proud of some accomplishment. 'And I'm equally sure that they are grateful you don't.'

He rubbed his hand over his chest. 'Remind me not to do that again, by the way.'

'Does it hurt?'

'Only when I move . . . or breathe.'

'Then I would say not to breathe, but that could have consequences most dire.'

'No doubt. Now if you'll excuse me, I should like to go lie down for a bit.'

Seren was rather surprised by his words. 'You would admit that to me?'

Again he gave her that almost charming lopsided grin. ' 'Tis less damaging to my ego than passing out and less dangerous as well.'

'Then come,' she said, reaching her hand out to him. 'I shall lead you back to your room. Unless you wish to pop us there.'

He took her hand and tucked it into the crook of his

arm. 'Nay. We'll have to use our feet. I can't afford another blast to my powers right now.'

Seren didn't say a word as she led him through the castle, back to her chambers. She kept her hand in his arm while they made their way very slowly upstairs.

'Where do you think Blaise has gotten off to?' she asked. 'I haven't seen him at all.'

'Hiding most like. He won't come unless I summon him.'

'Why didn't you summon him to fight the gargoyles?'

'There wasn't much he could do to fight them. Had he engaged them, he would have been harmed.'

Seren released him to open the door to his room as those words went through her. He'd thought of someone other than himself. She considered pointing it out to him, but then thought better of it. Kerrigan seemed to like thinking of himself as evil. But as she learned more of him, she saw less of the demon and more of the man. He wasn't the callous devil he presented to the world.

There was a heart that still beat within him, and it gave her hope that he would be the father her child would need to protect it from Morgen and her plans.

Without another word to her, Kerrigan went to lie upon the bed. That alone told her just how weak he must be. He wasn't the kind of person to show his weakness to anyone.

She stood back as he reclined with one leg drawn up.

'Is there anything I can get you, my lord?'

'A Tylenol would be great.'

She frowned at his peculiar word. 'A what?'

'Nothing, little mouse. There is nothing else I need.'

'Then I shall leave you to the quiet.'

He didn't respond as he closed his eyes and settled back. But she had to admit that even while he rested, he made a fearsome sight with his black armor covering a body that was rife with strength.

And she noted the way he kept both of his hands on his sword as if ready to attack anyone foolish enough to draw near it. Poor man that he couldn't even rest peacefully. No wonder he'd stabbed her when she'd neared him.

How many times had Morgen or one of her men tried to take the sword from him so that they could replace him as king? She couldn't imagine having no friend or haven.

Feeling for him, Seren left the room. She wasn't sure where Blaise had gone to, but she wanted another word with the specter of Lancelot.

It didn't take her long to return to his crypt. The torches had burned down to a light so low that she could scarce see. It was so cold now that her breath formed a small cloud around her head. She heard the scurrying of mice in the darkness, but nothing else. Only the pounding of her own heart.

'Lancelot?' she called. 'Are you here?'

'Behind you.'

She turned to face him.

He shimmered faintly between this world and his own. His rugged face held an ethereal beauty that was almost feminine. Yet he exuded masculine power and intensity. 'Are you ready to leave here?'

'Nay,' she said honestly. 'I have spoken to Lord Kerrigan and he has told me that you are the one who spoke falsely.'

Shock registered on his face. 'Me? How so?'

'You said that he fed on the blood of children. He doesn't.'

He tsked at her. 'How do you know he isn't the liar then?'

'I believe him and what he had to say about it,' she said with conviction. 'But I want to know why it is that you lied.'

'And I still say that I am not the liar, my lady. Have you seen Kerrigan feed yet?'

Seren hesitated. 'Nay, not exactly, but he placed his hand to my chest to show me how he draws his strength from the living.'

'And did he draw that strength from you?'

'I felt the tingle of it.'

'But he didn't feed, did he?'

Seren folded her arms over her chest as she moved away from him and considered his words.

Lancelot moved to block her retreat. 'I am on your side in this matter, Seren. Kerrigan is a powerful demon who can command the elements as he did to attack the gargoyles. Is it not possible he used such a trick with you?'

Aye, it was possible, and she knew it. Still, she believed Kerrigan. 'Why are you making me doubt him?'

'Because he is evil to the marrow of his bones, and evil will never do what is right. Your only hope to survive this is to trust *me*. Steal his sword and scabbard, and I will take you from here to a place where no one will ever be able to harm you or your babe again.'

Seren stared at him as his words chased themselves around in her mind. How good he made it sound. How tempting.

'You know something, Lancelot?'

He arched an expectant brow.

'I don't trust *you*. You've done nothing yet to help

me. You tell me to grab his sword and then you'll help. If you're really good and he isn't, then you'll help me without condition. Until you do, I think I shall trust myself and myself alone. Because in this, I am the only one who truly has my best interest at heart, and that is the only thing I don't doubt. God save you.'

And with those words spoken, she turned about and started for the door.

'Seren, wait.'

She hesitated at his call. 'Aye?'

His shimmering eyes pierced her with anger. 'Go, throw your lot in with your devil, and when he devours you and your child, remember that you were offered a chance to save both your lives.'

His words set off her anger. How dare he say such. 'Have no fear. I will bear full responsibility for everything.' She headed out of the chapel.

Seren didn't know if what she did was right, but she hoped it was. As she'd said, she had no one else to trust. Her instincts had always been keen. She could always tell an honest client from a dishonest one. It was one of the things Master Rufus valued most about her.

Kerrigan wasn't as evil as he appeared. She truly felt that he was as Blaise had said. When given kindness, Kerrigan did respond to it. He would protect her and he would love this baby. She knew it.

As she started up the stairs, Lancelot appeared before her, blocking her way. She drew up short while he continued to glare as if he couldn't bear the sight of her.

'You're a feebleminded woman.'

'I beg your pardon!' But before she could say anything more, a strange haze engulfed her. Seren tried to move, only to find that she couldn't.

163

'Had you obeyed me, we might have let you live in blissful ignorance of what befell your lover. Oh, well. Now you will deliver that sword to me and we will kill Kerrigan together. Now go.'

Something inside Seren rebelled at his words, but even so she found herself on the stairs again.

'Kill Kerrigan.' The command repeated itself over and over in her mind until she could hear nothing else.

It spread through her, consuming her. Drowning out all arguments and all feelings. There was nothing inside her except a demanding blackness that held her in the tightest of grips . . .

Aye, she must kill Kerrigan.

Kerrigan lay on his side with his eyes closed as he tried to stay focused on the shield that was again being battered by Morgen's troops. A cold sweat covered him. What he really wanted to do was sleep, but he didn't dare.

He'd pulled off all his armor and wore nothing but the tunic Seren had given him and a pair of breeches. Caliburn lay beside him, barely a hand's breadth away.

As he heard someone enter the room, he reached for the sword to take it by the hilt. He rolled to his back to see Seren entering.

He let go of Caliburn and relaxed. She was truly a vision as she drew near him. Even dressed as a lad, she was all woman, and she was the best thing he'd ever seen in his life. 'I thought you were leaving me to rest.'

A tender smile softened her face and stole his breath. 'I was thinking that I might be able to help you with that.'

He was about to ask her how when she placed her hand to his hip. All rational thought fled his mind.

Her eyes were dark and hungry as she dipped her head toward his and captured his lips with her own. Kerrigan growled at how good she tasted. He'd never known anyone sweeter. He cupped her head in his hand as he pulled her back so that she could lie atop him.

She nipped and tugged at his mouth with a boldness that surprised him. 'My little mouse is hungry.'

She smiled at him before she whipped his tunic over his head and tossed it to the floor. And as she climbed onto the bed to straddle him, a tremor of suspicion went through him.

She hadn't mentioned the tunic . . .

No sooner had the thought gone through his head than she grabbed Caliburn from his side. Kerrigan rose as she launched herself from the bed. The leather scabbard slid across his bare stomach before it clattered to the floor. She retrieved it quickly and pulled the sword free of the scabbard.

'What is this?' he demanded angrily.

He saw the sword's power fill her eyes until they flickered like fire in the dim light of the room. Power surged through the room while the sword acclimated itself to her.

Her eyes rolled back into her head as she shook all over. Lightning flashed, raising the hair on his body as it crackled.

Kerrigan froze. He'd been evil when he found the sword. Seren was good. He had no idea what the power of Caliburn would do to her. Unlike Arthur's Excalibur, this sword had been created by the fey to channel the darker powers. It wasn't meant to be held by a decent human. It was meant to be controlled by a dark Merlin.

'Seren,' he said firmly, yet he took care to not

frighten her in any manner. With that sword, she could kill him easily. 'Look at me.'

More lightning flashed as her pale hair whipped around her shoulders as if caught in the midst of an invisible wind. Her face went from human to ghastly, then back again.

'Seren, put the sword down. Slowly.'

'Nay,' she said breathlessly. 'It is part of me.' She moved to swing it at him.

Kerrigan held himself completely still. 'If you swing that sword, Seren, you will kill me. Instantly. That's the power of it. I wear no enchanted armor to deflect the blade. It will cut through me like a scythe through wheat.'

Seren could see Kerrigan only through a blazing haze. His voice was distorted in her ears and sounded demonesque. She'd never felt anything like this. She was drunk on her own power, on the knowledge that no one could hurt her or her baby so long as she held this sword in her hands.

She was all powerful. Not even Morgen could touch her now.

Throwing her head back, she laughed at the victory. The entire world could be hers . . . Hers!

No one could stop her.

Ever!

'Put. The. Sword. Down.'

'Nay,' she snarled at him. She smiled evilly as she relished the battle to come. 'Take it from me if you're able.'

He held his hands out in surrender. 'I'm not able to take it from you, Seren, and I know it. You're going to have to look me in the eye and kill me. *Me*. The father of your child.'

Hissing, she angled the sword up shoulder high,

grasped it in both hands, and started toward him.

Kerrigan held his breath as he waited for the hot sensation of the blade plunging through him.

It would be what he deserved.

And then just as the blade should have skewered him, Seren slammed her body into his, forcing him to take a step back. She threw one arm about his neck and buried her face into his shoulder. 'Help me,' she whispered in a small, agonized voice that sounded more like the woman he knew. 'Take it from me, Kerrigan. I don't want it.'

'I can't,' he said between clenched teeth as he held her against him. 'No one can take the sword from the one hand that wields it. So long as it is free of the scabbard, I can't do anything. You have to let it go.'

She screamed out as she tore herself away from him. He could see how much pain she was in. The sword wasn't designed for her. She lacked the bloodline or magic to carry it. And if he didn't get it back, the sword would burn her alive.

Summoning his own powers, he approached her slowly until he could pull her back against him. He held her to his chest and covered her soft, warm hands with his cold ones. She trembled against him. The scent of roses enveloped him as he leaned his head down to help steady her.

His heart thundered as he sought to help her any way he could. 'Reach down inside, Seren, and force your will onto the sword.'

She let out a cry of despair. 'It wants me to kill you. I don't want to . . .'

He gentled his voice as he spoke softly to her. 'The sword serves you, not the other way around. Focus on what *you* want.'

'I want the pain to stop.'

167

'Then hand the sword to me.'

Kerrigan jerked his head up as he heard the last voice he expected. It was a voice he hadn't heard since the day he'd found Caliburn in the forest. And just as then, it was the same tall, dark-haired man who had tried to convince him to forsake Morgen and travel the road of the straight and narrow.

It was a path he'd gladly refused.

'Brea? Why are you here?' This was a member of the Tuatha Dé Danann, a group of powerful and ancient Celtic gods who were supposed to fight only on the side of good.

The old god glared at him with hatred and malice. 'I'm here to set things right. Caliburn should never have been used by you or your kind. It is a sword meant for the gods and Brighid is tired of seeing it misused.'

Brighid was the sister to the Lady of the Lake, the nymph who had forged King Arthur's sword, Excalibur. The two swords had been created together in order to bring balance so that no one Merlin would be the more powerful. Caliburn was the steel and Excalibur was the stone.

One sword to rule and the other to destroy. One a sword of light and the other a sword of darkness. It'd been a cruel twist of fate that Kerrigan had been the inheritor of Caliburn's power.

Kerrigan glared at the god. 'Caliburn is mine by right of birth and of conquest.'

Brea looked at Seren. He held his hand out to her. 'You know what must be done, Seren. Return the sword to the side of good where it belongs.'

Seren cried out as she fought against the god's powers. 'Good doesn't lie.'

Kerrigan didn't know who was more stunned by her words. He or Brea.

The god frowned at her. 'What?'

She trembled visibly in his arms, but made no move to leave them. 'You lied to me. You told me . . .' She leaned her head back against Kerrigan's shoulder. 'Take your sword, my lord. I don't want it.'

The moment her words were spoken, her hands fell away, allowing Kerrigan to take it back.

Brea cursed. 'Imbecilic chit. Have you any idea what you've done?'

Seren was whispering to herself. An instant later, she shot a lightning bolt of her own at the ancient god. 'I will not kill for you or anyone else. Ever.'

Brea's face hardened. 'Then you have damned the world of man to darkness. I hope you can live with that.' He vanished.

Kerrigan held the sword with the point against the floor as Seren turned to face him. Her eyes were once again the beautiful green shade that rendered him captivated. He saw the relief in her pale features and the fear.

She ran her hands over her arms as if to warm herself. 'How do you handle the sword's power?'

'I get a lot of aches in my head from it.'

She gave a short laugh before she sobered. 'It burns like fire. It felt like it was trying to devour me.'

He nodded. 'Power consumes. Always.'

She looked down at her open hands, then clenched them shut as if she'd seen something in her palms that had frightened her. 'I don't want that kind of power in my hands. Ever again. Only God should have the power of life and death over another.'

Kerrigan was completely battled by this woman. Men killed to possess one tiny iota of what she'd had in her hands a moment ago. No one had ever taken this sword who hadn't fought to the death to keep it. No one.

Until her.

She'd handed it over without the least bit of reservation. It didn't make any sense to him. How could she have given away that kind of power?

She placed her hands over his. 'I understand you now. The sword speaks to the worst part of you. To the animal that wants only to consume and kill others.' She looked up at him from beneath her long lashes. That open, honest look burned him. 'Let go of it, Kerrigan. For once, stand here with me without the sword whispering to you.'

The sword cursed him in his head and demanded he hold tight to the hilt.

Kerrigan had always listened to it.

For once, he didn't. He let go of the sword so that it fell against the stone floor, then cupped her face in his hands.

Seren trembled as Kerrigan claimed her lips. His scent invaded every part of her while he explored her mouth with his. Their breaths mingled as she ran her hands over his back.

Giddy with her victory, she pulled back so that she could hug him close.

Until her eyes fell to the floor where the sword lay.

His foot was on it.

'Kerrigan!' she castigated as she pulled away. She put her hands on her hips before she looked back up at him. 'You cheated.'

He offered her a wicked grin. 'A man can only do so much,' he said unabashedly.

She shook her head at him. 'You really can't let it go, can you?'

'I spent the whole of my youth hungry and beaten, wanting and aching for things that were beyond my grimy grasp. So long as I carry Caliburn, I know that no one will ever be able to mock or belittle me again. No one.'

She heard the anguish in his tone. The pain that not even the centuries could erase. 'But that sword is cold comfort on a lonely night.'

'There you're wrong. It comforts me on a level unimaginable.'

'And I would offer you even more comfort. If you would take it. Put your weapon away, Kerrigan. For one afternoon.'

She knew the sword was still whispering to him. Somehow she could hear it now.

Stepping into his arms, she embraced him again.

Kerrigan couldn't think as Seren reclaimed his lips. The taste of her mouth nourished him in a way that defied description. She pressed her body closer to his as her tongue swept against his.

He could feel her nudging the sword away from him with her foot. It should anger him, but it didn't. It only amused him. Pulling away from her, he kicked the sword up from the floor and placed it in the brackets that were embedded in the stone above the bed. It would be within arm's reach, but not in their way.

He turned back to find Seren pulling her tunic over her head to bare her body to him. His breath caught in his throat as he saw the puckered tips of her small breasts.

Using more magic than he should, he conjured a large gilded tub of hot water and placed it before the hearth.

She gasped as it appeared.

'I thought you might wish a bath,' he said as he closed the distance between them to help her remove her breeches.

'Aye, thank you.'

171

As she stepped out of them, Kerrigan paused. He was kneeling before her with his gaze level on her belly. Deep inside her, his child was already growing. *His* child. A tiny part of him and her . . .

He looked up to find her staring down at him with a tender smile on her face as she played idly in his hair. In all his life, he'd never known anything like this one quiet moment.

'Is something wrong?' she asked, fingering the frown on his brow.

'Nay.' He rose up from the floor so that he could pick her up and place her into the tub.

Seren sighed as the hot water lapped against her cool skin. Kerrigan kissed her lightly on the lips as he gently stroked her breasts with his cool hand. She wrapped her arms around his neck, drawing him closer to her.

His breeches melted from him an instant before he joined her in the tub.

'Careful, my lord, you're expending your strength.'

'I know, but I didn't want to wait for you.'

She tsked at him. 'Some things are best when savored.'

'And others are best when devoured.'

Seren bit her lip at the wave of desire those words conjured.

He sat back in the tub, then pulled her forward to straddle his waist while he soaped a small cloth.

Seren leaned forward to nibble his chin. His whiskers scraped her lips, making them tender, and yet she loved the prickly sensation against her tongue. Nothing had ever tasted better than her demon knight. As he soaped her breasts and teased them, Seren closed her eyes and imagined what she wanted for her future.

How she wished she could keep Kerrigan with her,

like this. Just the two of them.

But she knew that she couldn't, and she didn't want to think about the future right now. In the past, she'd always known her plans. To become a journeywoman who owned her own shop and to find a decent man to marry.

Now ... now she didn't know what the morrow would bring. She couldn't even begin to conceive it. She would be a mother to a powerful child that she would have to protect. Seren had no idea how she would even begin to manage such a new life.

Scared, she held Kerrigan close. He was an anchor for her. He was solid and real, and at least for this moment, he was keeping her safe.

Kerrigan held Seren close as she hugged him with a fierceness that astounded him. It wasn't a sexual hold, it was one of comfort. Her cheek was pressed against his as she held him in a death grip.

'Are you all right?'

'I'm frightened, Kerrigan. I don't want anything else to change.'

'Everything changes in time, Lady Mouse. It is the way of things.'

She sat up with her expression imploring him. 'Can't you take your powers and make it stop? Can't you find some way to lose us here in this one moment for eternity?'

How he wished. But that wasn't possible. He cupped her cheek in his hand. 'Nay. Those are far beyond my abilities. I don't know of anyone who can do such a thing.'

'How I wish I could,' she breathed. Then she fingered his lips, her face tender as she studied his features. It was as if she were trying to commit them to memory. 'You are so beautiful. Were you always like this?'

'Nay. I used to be warm.' And then he realized as he spoke that for the first time in centuries, he was warm again. Warm in a way that didn't make any sense.

His heart pounding at the thought, he kissed her deeply. Her hands skimmed his body as she returned his caresses. Unable to bear the separation, he lifted her up and placed her on top of him.

Seren moaned as Kerrigan filled her with his thickness. He leaned back against the lip of the tub to stare up at her. 'Take your pleasure from me, Seren.'

She wasn't sure what he meant until he lifted her up ever so slightly, then slid her back down on him. She hissed at the sensation of his long, deep stroke. Taking his cue, she rode him slowly, deeply.

Seren knew how limited their time together was and it sweetened the moment all the more. For all she knew, this could well be the last time she was with him. Morgen could take them at any moment. War and necessity could force them apart.

They could even die . . .

She shivered in fear as she considered all the things that could happen.

Kerrigan ran his hands over her breasts as they kissed and she continued to stroke his body with hers. He didn't know why, but in her arms, nothing else seemed to matter. He didn't care that there was an army outside waiting to separate them.

Didn't care that Morgen wanted him dead or that an angry god wanted her sword back.

None of that mattered. For the first time in his life, he could see beyond himself. This wasn't just about him and his needs. It was about Seren's.

The baby's.

He didn't just want to take his pleasure from her and

leave; he wanted to give it back to her in return. Closing his eyes, he savored the sensation of her breasts on his chest, the feeling of her warm, soft skin sliding against his. She nipped his lips playfully before she pulled back to smile down at him.

His heart hammered at the seductive sight of her. Wanting more, he lifted his hips, driving himself even deeper into her body.

Seren groaned in pleasure as Kerrigan pierced her. She lifted his hand from the water to hold it in hers. His hand was so much larger. So strong. Her hand looked almost childlike in comparison. How she wished she had beautiful hands . . . like a lady. But her hands showed the scars and cuts of a peasant who worked hard for a living.

Yet Kerrigan didn't seem to care about any of that. His eyes blazing, he lifted her up and pressed her back against the opposite lip of the tub. Still inside her, he knelt between her legs as he took over thrusting for her.

She let go of his hand to hold herself up in the water. With her hands braced on the side of the tub, she leaned her head back as he moved even quicker.

Kerrigan growled at the sight of Seren open and inviting. The water pooled around her breasts, the peaks of which jutted up. Unable to stand it, he leaned down to capture one in his mouth. He teased the soft nipple with his tongue as he moved in and out of her body.

Seren buried her hand in his hair an instant before her cries of ecstasy filled his ears. He smiled in satisfaction as she came for him. He watched the pleasure play across her face as he continued to ride her.

She was truly beautiful.

And then he allowed himself to find his own piece

of paradise. Burying himself deep, he shivered as his body burst into a thousand spasms.

Kerrigan didn't move for several heartbeats as complete satisfaction engulfed him. This was the most perfect moment of his life, and he wondered what it would be like to have more afternoons like this. To be able to stay with a woman and not have to worry about her deceiving him or trying to take his power from him.

Seren only gave. She asked for nothing in return.

Amazed by her, he got up and carried her from the tub to the bed.

Seren smiled as Kerrigan picked up the covers and joined her in the bed. Completely content, she lay on her back while he lifted himself up on his arms to tease her lips with a playful kiss.

He pulled back to stare down at her. 'I'm growing weaker, Seren.' His tone was angst-ridden as he confided that to her. 'I won't be able to hold the shield past tomorrow.'

Her stomach clenched at the thought of what would happen to them once the shield was gone. 'What will Morgen do to you?'

'You should be more worried about yourself. Morgen won't need you once that child is born and, knowing her, she won't wait until it's born. She'll most likely cut it from you the instant it's able to live on its own.'

Seren sucked in her breath at what he described. Surely not even Morgen was that cruel. Was she?

She felt tears sting her eyes at the thought of never seeing her child alive. Of never holding him in her arms. 'I won't be here to protect him?'

He shook his head.

Anger scorched her. How could this be, and yet she

knew of their magic. Knew of Morgen's cruelty.

In the end, this wasn't just about her. 'Then promise me two things. Please.'

Kerrigan had never made a promise in his life to anyone. At least none that he had any intention of keeping. Most likely, he wouldn't keep these, either, but he was curious as to what she'd ask of him.

'Aye?'

'Promise me you will protect the baby for me. That you will make sure no one ever hurts him.'

Her request baffled him. 'Why is that so important to you?'

'Because it's what a mother does.'

Kerrigan still didn't understand the request. But there was no need to deny it, either. 'And what is your other request?'

'Marry me in secrecy before I show my pregnancy.'

Kerrigan stared at her in complete stupefaction. That had been the last thing he'd expected her to ask. 'Marry you?'

She nodded grimly. 'I won't be here long enough for you to worry over and I don't expect you to honor the vows. But I want my child born in wedlock. I don't want him to be stigmatized by something he had no part in. If Morgen takes him early, no one need know that he wasn't legitimately conceived.' She reached up and closed his mouth, which he hadn't realized was gaping open. 'Please, Kerrigan.'

He didn't know what to say to her. The last thing he wanted to tell her just then was that he wouldn't be around much longer himself. Once the child was born and lived, Morgen would kill him, too, and hand his sword over to the child to wield.

'Seren—'

She placed a finger over his lips to silence his

words. 'Please, Kerrigan,' she repeated. 'For the child who won't be able to fight for himself.'

He nibbled the tip of her finger, before he pulled it away from his lips. 'I won't do this for the child, Seren. But I will do it for you.'

Those words brought tears to her eyes. Kerrigan stiffened as the tears fell down her face.

So his strong little mouse did indeed cry. Not for her lost freedom. Not for her sacrificed virginity . . .

She cried over mere words.

Before he could move, she seized him and pulled him down for a kiss that left him dizzy.

He'd never tasted anything like it, and it caused his body to stir again. Aye, if these were to be his last moments of freedom with Seren, then he wanted to spend them inside her for as long as he could.

Just as he slid his knee between her legs, a knock sounded on his door. 'What?' he roared.

'I need a word with you.'

Kerrigan growled in frustration at the sound of Blaise's voice. Now the mandrake made an appearance?

Now?!

The last thing he wanted was to leave this bed, but Blaise seldom made such requests. It must be important for Blaise to disturb him. 'Give us a moment.'

Seren kissed his cheek before she scooted out from underneath him so she could dress. Normally Kerrigan would flash himself back into his clothes. But the last thing he needed was to drain any more of his powers. He'd used enough removing their clothes.

He pulled on his breeches and then noticed that Seren held the red tunic in her hands. A slight smile hovered at the edge of her lips.

'You were wearing it?'

He nodded.

Her smile widened. 'Then I hope it brings you good luck. The same luck that brought you to me.'

He snorted. 'I wouldn't count that as luck, mouse. More like ill fortune and madness.'

'Nay,' she said with a shake of her head. 'It was a great day.' She moved to place the tunic on the bed next to him. 'I'll wait in the great hall.'

Kerrigan nodded. He was trying to fasten his greave on his right leg when she opened the door to the hallway. Every time he came close to lacing it, it slipped. Holding it with his hand, he was trying to tighten the laces, which were at an awkward angle. This was a lot harder to do by himself without magic.

'Having problems?'

Kerrigan pulled the sword from the wall into his grip. 'No. Why?'

'You look like you're having problems. You know, all you have to do is insert tab A into slot B and buckle or lace.'

'Shut up.' Kerrigan balanced the sword on his leg while he struggled with the armor.

While he worked the first one, Blaise pulled the red tunic from the bed where Seren had placed it. 'Ooo, look,' he said in a playful tone. 'It's really soft. Red, what a different look for you, oh dark one who always wears black.'

Kerrigan paused to frown at him. The mandrake was acting most peculiar. 'What has gotten into you?'

There was an amused gleam in Blaise's violet eyes. 'If you're so low on power that you're not even using it to dress, then I know you won't take a shot at me or choke me. I may never get another chance to taunt you again without risking bodily injury. Therefore, this has become a moral imperative.'

He narrowed his gaze on the mandrake. 'I really hate you.'

'I know.' Blaise put his arms into the tunic. 'Now watch me closely. Here's how you dress. You put your arms in like this, pull it over your head, and settle it onto your body.'

Kerrigan glared at the fool. He didn't know why, but the thought of Blaise wearing the tunic Seren had made for him moved him toward violence. 'Take that off. Now.'

'I don't know. I kind of like it.' He batted his eyelashes at Kerrigan. 'Does the color look good on me?'

'It looks like shit. Now take it off.'

Blaise tsked at him.

Kerrigan picked the sword up from his knee. 'You know why armies wear that color red, don't you?'

'Never knew they did.'

'They do, and there's a reason for it.'

'And that is?'

'It hides bloodstains.' Kerrigan let fly his dagger as he spoke.

The dagger flew straight to its target ... Blaise's shoulder. But instead of penetrating the fabric and wounding him as Kerrigan had intended, it stayed in place, vibrating back and forth.

Both men gaped as Blaise reached out to touch the wobbling dagger.

Kerrigan couldn't breathe. It couldn't be.

'What the hell ... ?' With his sword in hand, he crossed the room to pull the dagger from Blaise's shoulder. He stared at the dagger, half expecting a trick, but the dagger didn't appear damaged.

How odd ...

'I knew it,' Blaise said under his breath.

'Knew what?'

'Your little mouse is a Merlin.'

He shook his head in denial. It wasn't possible. Originally bred from the Adoni, Merlins were always ethereally beautiful. They were powerful. Seren's beauty was inside, no doubt, but she didn't have the physical perfection of their breed. Never mind their magic.

Blaise nodded slowly. 'Aye, Kerrigan. Think about it. What is able to weave a cloth so strong that no mere mortal weapon can penetrate it?'

'The Loom of Caswallan.' It was one of the thirteen sacred objects that had been given to Arthur when he'd been king of Britain. Each one enchanted, those objects had given the ancient king the power he needed to rule his people and bring peace to his kingdom.

After Arthur's fall, the Penmerlin had returned the objects to the Waremerlins, who watched over them and sent them out into the world to hide them from Morgen. Since that fateful day, Morgen and their court had been trying to find the missing objects and return them to Camelot.

His sword had been one of those objects. It was why Morgen had tolerated him to live. She needed his bloodline to have full control of it.

Now another Merlin had been found, along with the object that her bloodline commanded. No wonder the prophecy had said Seren's child would be the next Penmerlin. Seren herself held those powers.

'Do you think Morgen knows?' he asked Blaise.

'I don't know. But the bigger question is, if Morgen does know, does she know where the loom is? That combined with your sword, her table, and one more object and Merlin would give her enough juice to raise Mordred back from his nearly dead state.'

Letting out a deep breath, Kerrigan was beginning to understand some of Seren's fears about one person ruling the entire earth. If that person wasn't you, and if they were particularly angry at you, it was bad indeed.

Morgen would kill them all before this was over.

Unwilling to think about that, he growled before he stabbed the dagger into Blaise's stomach with all his strength.

'Pardon?' Blaise said when the dagger did nothing more than become lodged in the weave of the scarlet cloth. 'What was that about?'

'I was just making sure the cloth was impervious.'

'Well, the next time you wish to test it, I suggest we put it on you first and then *I* wield the dagger.'

Kerrigan gave him a dry stare. 'Give it over now.'

Grumbling, Blaise complied as he whisked the tunic off.

'So what brought you here?' Kerrigan asked as he took his tunic back.

'We have a gargoyle at the gate.'

Kerrigan rolled his eyes at the absurd comment. '*A* gargoyle? You disturbed me for this? God's blood, have you been by the window lately? I think you need to go count again.'

He jerked at the next buckle in his armor as he mumbled under his breath. 'Interrupt me for something so incredibly absurd. A gargoyle at the gate. There's an entire army of them flying over our heads, and he's just now noticed. Where have you been anyway that you've missed all the action up until now?'

'I was trying to rest, if you must know. But that has nothing to do with the little summoning you missed.' Blaise made an irritated noise in the back of his throat.

'I said *a* gargoyle is at the gate, not eight hundred.'

Kerrigan paused. 'What do you mean?'

'Garafyn is outside, wanting a parley.'

He straightened as those words went over him like a cold shower. 'Garafyn? Morgen sent Garafyn to talk to me? Does he even have a tongue?'

'Apparently so. But I'm with you. Who knew? I thought he was mute. Turns out he's a really crusty bastard who wants you to come out and chat with him for a bit.'

'Why?'

Blaise shrugged. 'I'm just the servant. He wouldn't talk to me, which is why I've come to fetch you. But since it is the gargoyle king wanting an audience, I thought it might be important.'

Kerrigan was still baffled. Garafyn had been one of the original knights of the Round Table. Cursed into his gargoyle state by Morgen, he wasn't exactly friendly to anyone except his fellow cursed beings.

He couldn't imagine what Garafyn wanted with him. The gargoyle never interacted with anyone he didn't have to.

Wasting power he knew he shouldn't, Kerrigan flashed himself back into his armor, including the red tunic.

'Hey!' Blaise snapped. 'Give us the shirt, mate. I might need it since I don't have a magical sword to protect me.'

Kerrigan gave him a droll stare. 'The tunic wouldn't help you anyway in dragon form. You'd tear it the instant you shifted and then I would be obligated to kill you for it.'

Blaise considered that for a minute before he nodded. 'Good point. You keep it.'

Shaking his head at the incorrigible beast, Kerrigan

walked past Blaise, through the castle, then out to the bailey.

He saw Garafyn standing off to the side of the shield with his hands on his hips, looking greatly peeved. Then again, most gargoyles looked that way even when they were happy. Not that they were happy often. The bad part about being cursed was that very few things happened that were good or fun.

Garafyn stood at an even six feet. His face was contorted, with large, overgrown fangs that had to make talking painful. More than any of the others, he was hideously formed. It was as if Morgen had taken special care to mutilate the man's appearance. Even Garafyn's wings were strangely shaped. They were sharp like a bat's, with spikes protruding from each bend.

His eyes were a deep bloodred that seemed to glow, and he watched Kerrigan carefully as he approached.

Once he stood before the gargoyle, Kerrigan arched a taunting brow. 'Well?'

Garafyn spoke in a low, bored tone that was filled with mockery. 'I am here at the behest of the queen of Camelot. I—'

Kerrigan frowned. 'What?'

Garafyn let out an exasperated breath. 'You know, the bitch on the throne? The one who thinks she's the greater evil, which ironically is true since no one else is a bigger bitch, but that's beside the point. She wanted me to talk to you so here I am roasting in the sun and praying that one of those damned dragons doesn't lob a glob of shit on my shoulder. God knows I get enough of that from the pigeons.'

Blaise had been right, Garafyn was a crusty bastard, and he bore an accent that was reminiscent of some New York cabdriver. But Kerrigan wasn't in the mood for it. 'There's nothing either of you could possibly say that I would ever care to hear.'

Garafyn cleared his throat before he made an odd clicking noise with his mouth. 'Fine. But tomorrow when they strip that sword from you and drag your carcass off in chains, club the woman in the head and slice her open in a few months' time, remember that the gargoyle schmuck tried to talk to you, but you had better things to do like go plan a funeral. G'head. Have a nice death.' He turned to leave.

Kerrigan curled his lip. 'Garafyn?'

The gargoyle paused to look back.

'What say you?'

Garafyn glanced to the army that was waiting at the bottom of the hill before he met Kerrigan's gaze with a glint in his red eyes. 'You ready to parley?'

'Depends on what you have to say.'

Garafyn moved back to the shield. He wiped his hand over his chin before he grimaced at the sight of his own stony skin. It was obvious he hated being a gargoyle.

'Look, we both know that I hate you and I hate the bitch below. But I've been thinking. You've no way out of this whole debacle. You can't feed with the shield up and you're too weak to safely transport the three of you out of here with your magic. And even if you do, there's not many places you can go that old bitch hound can't find you while the little peasant carries that baby.'

Garafyn scratched his cheek as he continued his rant. 'So where does that leave you? I'll tell you where that leaves you. Screwed. Completely, utterly, and with relish. But you know, screwing men has never been to my taste. So I'm thinking of something a little more to both our tastes.'

'And that is?'

Garafyn let out another sound of disgust. 'You know, she's not *that* stupid. Stop looking so damned agreeable. Throw your arms up over your head and act indignant.'

Kerrigan frowned. 'What?'

'Look pissed so the bitch thinks I'm here giving you her terms of surrender.'

He grimaced at the gargoyle. 'You've got to be kidding me.'

'Do I look like I'm kidding?'

Nay, he looked quite serious. Kerrigan let out a disgusted breath of his own before he did as the gargoyle suggested.

Garafyn rolled his eyes. 'Acting isn't your forte. Put your arms down.'

Kerrigan snarled at him. 'I don't like to play games.'

'Trust me, this isn't a game. We screw this up and the bitch of the damned is going to turn me into a countertop.'

'We don't have countertops yet.'

'Yeah, look around, we're not supposed to have gargoyles and dragons, either, but they seem to be here, huh? Trust me, countertop is in my future, and with my luck, the bitch will use me to prepare some nasty-smelling shit on top of me. But I guess it's better than being stuck in the twentieth century as a damned lawn ornament for a dog to piss on.'

'Would you stay on the topic? And what is your point anyway?'

'Fine,' Garafyn growled. 'The point is this. All of us down there around Morgen's camp know that you're about to fall. Come tomorrow, I can lead my Stone Legion up here and run the risk of your chiseling off a vital piece of my anatomy, or I and a couple of my friends can hold the angry horde back long enough for you to recharge your magic and get all of us out of here.'

Kerrigan realized that Garafyn was staring at his star medallion. It was one of the symbols of a Merlin's power. A conductor, the medallion allowed a Merlin to use natural powers to boost his own. In the hands of a mundane being, it could be used to give him magic. Their amulets could allow creatures such as Garafyn to escape Camelot and live in peace.

Garafyn, like the rest of his Stone Legion, was a slave to Morgen . . . and to him. If Garafyn or any of his crew left Camelot, Morgen could pull them back without effort.

But with the amulet, that would change.

'Is that all you want?' Kerrigan asked him.

'No,' he snapped in that thick, oddly New York accent. 'I'd like to a be human again. And throw in some world peace, just because. But since that's never going to happen, I just want to be out of this hellhole and out from under the scrutiny of a woman whose head I'd like to crush.' There was no missing the sincere hatred on Garafyn's face as he mentioned Morgen.

The gargoyle paused as if some painful memory tugged at him. 'My consolation is that you weren't here in the glory days of Camelot. I have no real beef with you except for the fact that you've been known to blow a few of us into dust for no particular reason. That, I have to say, has pissed me off in the past, but then again, you did mostly blast the natural-born gargoyles more than my cursed legion.'

He paused as he thought about that. 'Then again, I've been known to do the same myself when they piss me off. So, believe it or not, I can live with your temper tantrums. What I can't live with is another day of watching the queen bitch dance around in her red dress to crap-ass music. I've had it with her and those mewling lips of hers. That face and her friggin' requests for me to go to the twenty-first century to bring her back some Starbucks. Have you any idea how hard it is to fetch a cup of Starbucks when you look like *this*?' He scowled in distaste. 'There's only so many people who will buy the lie that I'm making a Spielberg film, you know?'

And again the gargoyle had sidetracked himself onto another topic.

'How can I trust you?' Kerrigan asked, bringing him back to the current subject.

Garafyn shrugged. 'Basically you can't. But I'm the best shot you got.'

That wasn't true. He was the only shot Kerrigan had, and they both knew it. 'All right. How do I know who to take with me? I assume you want only your men saved and not the other gargoyles.'

'Yeah, I don't give two shits about the other gargoyles. As for my men ... oh, we'll be obvious. We'll be the ones with our backs to you, fighting the others off.'

That made sense. But Kerrigan knew that where they would have to go to escape Morgen wasn't exactly conducive to Garafyn's form. 'Don't you care where I'm going to take you?'

'As long as it's out of Morgen's reach, no. If you can make it so I never see another of these pricks, hell, no.'

Kerrigan looked down the hill at the others. He couldn't see Morgen, but he knew she was down there. He could feel it. 'What are you going to tell *her* about our conversation?'

'That you're a dickhead who wouldn't listen to reason.' He looked over his shoulder at a large tree. 'I'll make sure they're all down there by the oak at ten tomorrow. None of them will be near you so that you'll have time to feed. You stay in the castle, bring down the shield, and feed on the girl. The mandrakes will have to take human form to enter the castle, and since they prefer to not fight that way, Morgen will send us in first. I'll come running in with my guard.'

How strange that Garafyn would do that. He was taking one hell of a chance. 'You trust me to not leave you behind?'

Garafyn sobered as he narrowed those eerie red eyes on him. 'Three days ago, I wouldn't have trusted you with shit. But I've seen you with that woman. She trusts you, so I'm thinking maybe she knows something I don't.'

Kerrigan snorted. 'You're either brave or a complete idiot.'

'I try to avoid being either of those since both will get you killed ... and usually painfully. Now look pissed for the bitch.'

Kerrigan made a face.

'Oh forget it. You need some acting lessons.' He stepped back from the shield. 'I'll go tell Morgen that you refused her offer.'

'What was her offer anyway?'

'You know the spiel. Hand over the woman and your sword and she'd let you live. Blah, blah, blah.'

Aye, that was the spiel all right. All these centuries later, and Morgen wasn't a bit more original. No wonder he was bored with her. 'Tell her I refuse.'

'Don't worry. Even if you hadn't, I'd say it just so that I could get the whole Linda Blair head-spinning routine going. It's the only time I find Morgen funny.'

Garafyn inclined his head to him. 'See you tomorrow.'

Kerrigan watched as the gargoyle made his way down the hill toward the others. It was incredible that such a beast would ally himself to him. But then the old saying went through his mind: *My enemy's enemy is my friend*.

He didn't know if he could really trust Garafyn and his guard or not. This could all be an elaborate plan to get him to lower his defenses.

Then again, if they were deceiving him, there was one flaw to their plan. One he doubted Morgen had thought about. There was only one person in the castle he could feed from.

Seren.

And she carried his child. If he bungled this, he would kill Seren and the baby, and Morgen would lose her best shot at raising Mordred from the dead. Neither proposition boded well for him.

But at least the latter wouldn't kill him. No matter what he might argue verbally, he was beginning to suspect the truth. Seren was starting to mean a lot more to him than just a nameless pawn to be used.

Now he just needed to teach his little mouse to roar.

Chapter Eleven

Kerrigan let out his breath slowly as he entered the great hall to find Seren and Blaise sitting off to the side of the hearth in carved chairs, talking.

Talking.

That thought drew him up short as he watched them. They sat like two old friends who were laughing together while making small talk over nothing.

It seemed somehow incongruous that a small peasant maid and a powerful mandrake would chat in such a manner. Graylings, sharocs, Adoni, all that he could accept. But this . . .

This screwed with his head.

'Well?' Blaise asked as soon as he sensed Kerrigan's presence.

Kerrigan moved to stand beside Seren's chair, where he draped his arm over the back of it. She watched him expectantly as if she thought he had some great plan to get them out of this. How he wished it were so. The truth was, he'd be lucky not to get them all killed on the morrow.

'I'm going to drop the shield tomorrow before I'm completely out of power.'

Suspicion darkened Blaise's eyes. 'And do what?'

'Regain my strength and get us out of here.'

Even though he knew Blaise couldn't really see Seren, the mandrake looked at her before he returned to Kerrigan's gaze. 'And how are you going to recharge your powers?'

Kerrigan glanced down to Seren, whose face went instantly pale.

She placed her hand over her stomach. 'You'll kill me.'

'Nay,' Kerrigan said slowly. 'Like Morgen, you're a Merlin. You should be strong enough for me to—'

'What new madness is this?' Seren asked as she shot to her feet. 'Me? A Merlin? Are you insane?'

'It's true,' Blaise said quietly as he continued to sit. 'You are the same as Kerrigan and Morgen ... well, I take that back. Unlike them, you're not evil.'

She shook her head in denial. 'The both of you are mad.'

Kerrigan placed a comforting hand on her shoulder. He could well understand her fear at finding this out, especially like this. But it changed nothing. 'Tell me something, Seren. The loom you used to make my tunic ... where did you get it?'

'It was my mother's.'

Blaise asked the next question from his chair. 'And where did she get it?'

'It belonged to her mother before her.'

'Aye,' Kerrigan said, 'because they were both Merlins sent out into the world to protect your loom. Just as the nameless man who fathered me must have carried the blood of Caliburn's Merlin. I doubt my father, whoever he was, ever knew of his heritage. But given the actions of your mother, I think she may have known exactly who and what you were. What she was.'

Seren couldn't breathe as he spoke. In a way, it all

made sense. Her mother's gift of foresight. Her ability to heal and to care. She'd had what the local priests called unholy powers. But there had been nothing evil about her mother. She'd been a good and decent woman who only wanted to help others.

And now that Seren thought about it, her mother had always been skittish, as if looking for someone who might be after them. As a girl, she'd thought nothing of it. But now that she considered it, she remembered how many times her mother would stay up into the wee hours of the night as if afraid to sleep. How she would always make their beds someplace where they could quickly flee if they needed to.

Her mother must have known about Morgen and her servants.

But most of all, she remembered the day her mother had gifted her with the loom for her birthday. Seren had wrinkled her nose in distaste of the old, scuffed-up piece. It'd been small, no more than three of her mother's hand spans in width.

Still, her mother's face had beamed with pride as she set it on the table before Seren. 'This has been in our family for generations, little Seren. It belonged to my mother and to hers before her. Now I'm gifting it to you.'

'But I don't want it,' she'd whined. 'Can I not have a new one?'

Her mother had shaken her head as she lovingly brushed the hair back from her child's face. 'This is a very special loom, my Seren. One that will come to mean the world to you one day. And with it, you will make a destiny all your own.'

Even so, Seren had poked her finger at it in distaste. She'd wanted a new doll, not some silly old loom. Even if it had been in her family, what did that matter?

All her mother ever thought of was work.

Laughing gently at her, her mother had wrapped it back up in a piece of brown cloth. 'Keep this put away, child. Always. Let no one know that you have it.'

'Why?'

'Because it, like you, is very special and dear, and I don't want anyone to take either one of you away from me. One day you will know exactly what to do with your loom. Until then, keep it with you and hidden.'

No sooner had her mother packed away the loom than Seren had forgotten those words. Her mother had arranged her apprenticeship only a few weeks later, and then her mother had died.

After that, Seren had hated the loom that reminded her of the mother she'd lost. She'd kept it hidden away, along with all the painful memories of her mother's death. It was only after Mistress Maude had caught her last year using the store loom for her personal project, and punished her for it, that Seren had remembered her mother's loom.

There in the faint moonlight of the room she shared with the other apprentices, after everyone else had gone to sleep, she'd carefully unwrap it and bring it out at night to weave. And as she worked, the loom had ceased to be such an eyesore. It'd become beautiful to her, and in time, it'd become a friend.

There were times when she could have even sworn that it talked to her. Madness surely, which was why she'd never mentioned it to others. But she knew in her heart that the loom had somehow helped her make her cloth. That it directed her stitches.

Could it really be magical?

Nay, her mother would have told her if it were. Her mother would never have kept such a secret from her. 'I don't believe you.'

Blaise gave a short, evil laugh. 'Well, I'll offer to stab Kerrigan to show you proof of it if he promises not to kill me for the affront.'

Kerrigan narrowed his eyes on the mandrake as he pulled his dagger from his belt, then handed it to Seren. He removed the black steel vambrace from his forearm and exposed a portion of the red tunic sleeve. 'Try and stab the fabric you created.'

Seren honestly thought the man was insane. Both of them. The last thing she wanted was to harm him, but still he insisted that she stab him with the weapon.

Taking the dagger, she stared at him. 'This is ridiculous. I'll only make you angry when I cut you.'

'Nay, I promise. Try and stab the cloth.'

Hesitant, she did as he asked. Sort of. She touched the dagger's tip lightly to the cloth and tried to push it in just enough that she would do nothing more than prick his skin.

The cloth held it.

Frowning, Seren pressed it harder, and still the tip of the dagger refused to breach the scarlet cloth.

Nay . . . surely she was dreaming.

She tried even harder to stab it. And again nothing happened.

'This can't be,' she whispered as she fingered the undamaged cloth. There wasn't a single thread pricked by the dagger's tip. 'I cut it with shears and I stitched it together. Why won't it part now?'

'Neither of those is a weapon of war,' Blaise said in a low tone. 'You can't be stabbed with a sword or dagger, but a pair of shears . . . deadly stuff.'

Kerrigan nodded. 'The loophole.'

Seren scowled at the two men as they continued to talk about things that confused her. 'What has the cloth to do with an archer's window?'

Kerrigan looked confused an instant before he appeared to understand her. '"Loophole" is another word for a way out of something, Seren. A small out. Such as, your cloth is impervious to weapons of war, but not to common everyday instruments such as shears or needles.'

'Beware a fence post or farmer's hoe,' Blaise added dryly. 'The tip of one would go right through it.'

Kerrigan nodded. 'It would seem that that is why you were able to sew and shape the cloth, but when I tried to stab Blaise earlier with my dagger, the cloth protected him.'

Blaise gave her an impish grin. 'Every one of the sacred objects has a secret that will render it useless. Usually the Merlin who was given the weapon knows the source of its weakness as well as its strengths. Your mother probably died before she could share the loom's secrets with you.'

Seren still didn't want to believe it, but how could she not? There was no denying that the dagger was no more effective against the cloth than it was against the armor.

'I'm a Merlin,' she breathed. 'But why don't I have powers?'

'You do.'

She looked up at Kerrigan as he took his dagger away from her and sheathed it. 'How so?'

'When Brea was here—'

'Brea was *here*?' Blaise snapped, interrupting him. 'When?'

Kerrigan held his hand up to silence him. 'You shot the lightning blast at him. I thought at first it was a holdover from your having taken Caliburn from me.'

'She took Caliburn, too? When the hell did all of this happen?'

Kerrigan gave him a peeved glare. 'While you were sleeping. We were also attacked by three gargoyles.'

Blaise gaped. 'And I slept through all that?'

'Apparently. I always said you were worthless. Now we have proof.'

Blaise made a face at him.

'Children,' Seren snapped, trying to keep them on topic, 'could we please stop fighting?'

The men turned hostile glares toward her.

'Well, you were behaving as such, and if you persist, I shall make you go to separate corners.'

Blaise's expression turned wicked. 'I'd rather you give me a spanking.'

Kerrigan's eyes flamed. 'Try it and you'll have a disembowelment instead.'

'Children!' But even though she said it harshly, she was totally enchanted by their playful air. It was such a welcome change from Kerrigan's normal frightening demeanor. Who knew that he could tease in such a manner?

'Back to the point,' Kerrigan said. 'Seren has manifested powers. To what other extent she has them, I don't know.' His gaze turned dark as he faced her again. 'We need to find that loom of yours before Morgen does. Whoever has it can use it.'

That was simple enough. 'I left it in my room, tucked in my small chest where I keep all my personal items.'

Blaise gave a low whistle. 'You go for that loom and Morgen will know it in a heartbeat.'

'Aye,' Kerrigan conceded as he turned toward Blaise. 'You'll have to do it.'

'Oh no,' Blaise said, his eyes wide. 'I'm not suicidal. Skewered and basted dragon is not something I want to see on a menu.'

'It will be if you don't go. Neither of us can afford for Morgen to find that loom. Imagine an army of Adoni swathed in cloth that no sword can pierce.'

Blaise looked sick to his stomach. 'And imagine trying to convince an army to attack them with shears. It's almost comical.' He sighed. 'Very well. Get us out of here and I shall go for the loom.'

'They won't let you.'

The men stared at her. 'How so?' Kerrigan asked.

'It's in our room where no man is allowed to venture. Not even Master Rufus is allowed there. Mistress Maude makes certain that we are safe from any male company.'

'Then what do we do?' Blaise asked.

'Teach me to use my powers.'

She could see the instant hesitancy in Kerrigan. 'I don't think that's a good idea.'

'Why not?' she and Blaise asked together.

He looked at the mandrake. 'You know the reason. Once she begins to learn, the battle begins.'

Blaise rubbed his chin thoughtfully. 'She was born of goodness. She should do fine.'

'What battle?'

The men ignored her once more. 'Why hasn't she felt her powers before now, Blaise? I'm thinking her mother must have bound them.'

'To hide her most likely.'

'Or to protect her.'

Seren whistled. The men looked at her with widened eyes.

'Good sirs,' she said between her clenched teeth, stressing each syllable carefully, 'please notice that I am here in this room with you and would like to be included in this discussion since it is about me and my future.'

'Sorry,' Blaise said sheepishly.

Kerrigan made no such apology. 'Inside of every being there is a constant war being raged. The part that tells us to do what is right and what is decent and the part of us that is self-serving. The part that wants what it wants regardless of who is hurt getting it. Think back to when you held my sword. You heard its voice. Felt its lure. Now imagine that call amplified to such a state that it becomes deafening to all else.'

She remembered that sound well. It had been frightening. Truly. 'It was deafening, and I did return the sword to you.'

Blaise made a sound of disbelief. 'You returned Caliburn? Are you mad?'

'Nay,' she said, looking at him. 'Its power wasn't meant for me.'

'And it scared you,' Kerrigan said.

'Aye, it scared me.'

His dark eyes caressed her with warning. 'Now imagine that power belonging to you. Solely. That is the power of a Merlin. You can destroy or you can create, but you can never do both. The final decision of how you use your power is entirely up to you. But once chosen, it can't be undone.'

Seren let her gaze drop to the floor as those words echoed in the quiet room. Now she understood Kerrigan and what had turned him into who and what he was. 'You chose to destroy.'

He nodded.

'Why?'

'I had no knowledge of good or decency. When the Lords of Avalon showed up, wanting me to join them, I laughed in their faces. Why should I use my power to help those who had spat on me? To the devil with them all.'

Seren cocked her head as she stared at his handsome face. 'And yet you are helping me.'

He looked away.

'There is no shame in doing something that is right, Kerrigan,' she said softly. 'People lash out at what they don't understand. And I am sorry that they lashed out against you. But it doesn't mean that you can't change.'

'She won't turn,' Blaise said quietly. 'It's not in her nature.'

Kerrigan hesitated. He wasn't so sure. He knew just how seductive that darker part of power was. Seren had only come up against it briefly. It permeated everything until it consumed like a fire. She was a small woman who knew nothing of malice. Nothing of power.

'I don't want to ruin what you are, Seren. The power *will* change you. It always does.'

Still she met his gaze unflinchingly. 'And I want to be able to protect myself. You can't give me the strength of a warrior, but you can give me the magic of a sorceress.'

He couldn't fault her for wanting that, and if he failed tomorrow, she would be alone in the world. Alone with his child.

God's blood, how he didn't want to teach her something that could eventually hurt her. But he didn't really have a choice in this. If something happened to him, she would be defenseless, and he better than anyone knew what happened to the defenseless in this world.

He couldn't leave her like that. Leave her prey to something like him. Not when he had the ability to stop it.

'You realize there isn't enough time to train you?

Whatever you learn, you won't be able to use it.' At least not if he went by conventional means.

Disappointment filled her eyes.

The sight of her defeat slammed into him.

Don't. Besides, what do you care? She's nothing but a pawn to carry your child. But he knew better than that. This little mouse had come to mean a great deal to him, and that scared him more than facing all of Morgen's army with no sword and no armor.

He bit back a curse at the truth. And he knew what he had to do. He only hoped that by helping her, he wasn't about to destroy her.

Chapter Twelve

'Blaise,' Kerrigan said quietly to the mandrake who was still in his chair. 'Give us the room.'

Blaise's eyes flared as if he understood what Kerrigan was about to do. For a second, he expected Blaise to argue.

He didn't.

Instead the dragon got up and headed for the door with that silent walk that had always reminded Kerrigan of a ghost gliding.

He waited until they were alone before he returned to Seren's side. He still couldn't believe he was about to do this. Never in all these centuries had he ever helped anyone.

No one.

But Seren was right. He couldn't stand by and see his child abused as he'd been. He couldn't leave it alone in the world. Morgen would kill them both if she had a chance and raise the child in who only knew what manner. His best course of action would be to arm Seren so that she could fight the bitch as an equal. If he unlocked her full powers, then she could be quickly trained and shown how to use them to fight Morgen and her army.

Hoping he was making the right decision, he unbuckled the sword from his hips and forced himself to prop it against the chair. But it was hard. He never liked to let the sword go for more than a few seconds at a time – something that had often pissed off Morgen since he'd always made love to her with it in his grasp.

But all that was behind him now.

Seren wasn't sure what to expect as Kerrigan pulled her back to his front. He leaned his cheek against her head as he murmured something in a language she didn't understand. Wrapping his arms around her, he rocked her gently in his embrace as a strange redlike haze encircled them.

Breathe easy. The words were spoken inside her head as Kerrigan continued to chant softly in her ear. But it was hard to obey. The haze seemed to choke her. It was too thick to breathe. She felt as if she were drowning. Gasping. It was unbearable, and her lungs burned from the effort.

Just as she was sure she would die from it, she felt a sharp pain at her neck. A scream lodged in her throat as she dug her nails into Kerrigan's thighs.

Kerrigan growled at the taste of Seren's innocent blood. His stomach cramped in pain, but he ignored it. This was a ritual that was older than time. One practiced by the very first of their kind.

Originally, the blood ceremony was used to marry the powers of the Pendragon who ruled the people to the Penmerlin who commanded the elements. The Penmerlin would be killed afterward, leaving the powers solely with the newly crowned Pendragon so that he could better rule his people.

But he had no intention of killing Seren. Pulling back, he licked his lips as he turned her around in his arms. Her eyes were no longer her own, they were now black from the dark magic that had corrupted him. The magic that fed and nourished him.

She was drunk from it. She was no longer pure. No longer innocent.

His heart breaking at what he'd done to her, Kerrigan opened the neck of his armor and bent his head for her. She wasted no time in taking what he offered.

Kerrigan cursed as she sank her teeth into his neck and pulled his powers into her own body. They were joined now. Two souls sharing all the knowledge of a Merlin's abilities. His blood carried in it all he'd learned. All he'd experienced.

Unlike him, Seren wouldn't have to learn her powers. They would course through her now, along with the ability to wield them.

The room began to swim as he was weakened even more.

She clutched him to her as she greedily drank his essence. Afraid she would consume too much, he pulled back.

She advanced on him.

Kerrigan caught her in his arms. 'Enough, Seren! If you take too much, you'll kill me.'

Her eyes were no longer human, they were completely red with the black pupils showing him a reflection of himself. He looked pale. But he was still in control here. Not her.

'I want more.' Her voice was deep, demonic.

Kerrigan ground his teeth at the sound he despised. He'd given her the very worst of himself. And he hated it. 'Nay.'

Seren shrieked as that word echoed in her head. It was strangely painful, and the new creature inside her rebelled at its utterance. It clawed at her, demanding that she take Kerrigan now and make him pay for the pain he caused by denying her.

How dare he tell her nay!

She leaned her head back as an invisible wind whipped through the room, sending her hair flying about her. It was warm and wicked, licking her flesh, making her wanton. She licked her lips hungrily as her entire body demanded appeasement.

She'd never felt anything like this before. It was power. Raw and uncomplicated. Hissing, she let it pour through her until she was able to channel it into the palm of her hand. With a laugh, she unleashed it against the table that was closest to her.

The table splintered into ashes.

Oh, this felt good. Too good. Nothing could stop her now. Giddy with that knowledge, she started for the door, only to find Kerrigan in her way.

'Where are you going, little mouse?'

'There's no mouse here,' she said in a voice that seemed to echo in her head. 'I'm going to face the bitch and kill her.'

'Nay, Seren. You're not that strong yet.'

'Watch me.' She started past him only to have him grab her. She sent a blast at him that he deflected.

Enraged, she moved to attack him.

He wrapped himself around her, pinning her limbs so that she couldn't move.

Seren screamed out.

'Shh,' he whispered against her ear. 'Let the power flow through you. Don't let it consume you. Give it a few minutes and it won't hurt anymore.' His deep voice began a soft, gentle lullaby that her mother used to sing to her long ago when she was just a child. It reached down deep inside her and touched something alien. Something soft and quiet.

Her anger retreated as she remembered being a small child in her mother's lap.

'Be good for me, Seren. Always.' It was her mother's tender voice she heard crooning to her, not Kerrigan's.

And then the evil returned. It sneered and fought against those tender thoughts. It wanted vengeance and gore.

What do you need with goodness? Banish it. Laugh at it. You have your own power now. You need no one else. Take it and use it to hurt all those who dared to hurt you ...

That voice was overwhelming and cold and it brought with it a flurry of images that burned her.

Indeed, something inside her crackled and popped, and unleashed a torrent of memories that weren't her own ...

She saw a younger Kerrigan. Dressed in meager rags, he was only ten-and-eight summers in age. He shook in terror as he held his sword above his head. It burned in his grip, yet still he held it tightly within his desperate grasp. He could hear the echoing laughter that rang in the trees of the dark forest that surrounded him, but he saw nothing of the woman who made such a sound.

'Show yourself,' he snarled, his grip tightening on the hilt even more. 'I have no fear of you.'

'Perhaps you should.'

He jumped forward as the heavenly voice whispered in his ear. Turning about, he gaped at the sight of the woman before him. Dressed in a gown so red that it was inhuman, she was the most beautiful woman he'd ever seen. Her pale hair and skin were a stark contrast to the vibrancy of her dress.

'Who are you?'

She licked her lips as she gave him a seductive pout.

206

'I am Morgen, queen of the fey.'

He angled his sword at her, ready to kill her if she tried to take it from him. 'I don't believe in the fey.'

She gave him a mocking smile. 'Then explain the sword you hold at my throat. Explain how it killed the men who were after you without touching them.'

He had no explanation of how the men had been struck down. It was magical and not born of this earth. Even now he could feel the life force of the weapon he held. Feel the power of it. It was changing him somehow. The sword seemed to be alive, whispering its will into his mind.

The woman held her hand out to him. 'Come with me, boy, and I will make you a king.'

He scoffed at her outrageous offer. 'King of what? Peasants? Beggars?'

'Nay,' she said in her voice that was rife with promise and seduction. 'I can give you riches and power beyond your wildest imaginings.'

He found that even harder to believe. 'I have quite an active imagination and I am no fool. No peasant becomes a king unless it is king of the lowest, and of that I have no need. I've been a ruler of *them* since the hour of my birth.'

Morgen cocked her head as she studied him curiously. 'So mistrustful, my evil heart. But have no fear. A peasant can become king when he isn't really a peasant.'

Her words gave him pause. 'What say you?'

She reached out and boldly brushed the blade of his sword aside with her hand. With no regard of the danger, she approached him slowly, swinging her hips suggestively. 'You were hidden, boy, by those who were afraid of your birthright. They knew that you were destined to find this sword and to become the

207

greatest king the world has ever known.'

Kerrigan closed his eyes at her words. Dare he even begin to believe or to hope? A chill went over him. One that was intensified as she raked a cold finger down his right cheek.

'Come with me and I will show you a world of wonders where you will never again know hunger or want.'

He couldn't breathe as he thought of that. How he wished it were so. All his life he'd had nothing. Never enough food. Never enough clothing.

Never dignity.

His entire existence was one of burning, painful wants. Of a yearning so strong that it had left blistered scars on his soul.

'Morgen!'

Kerrigan opened his eyes as he heard the sharp cry of a woman's voice. This newcomer stood tall and proud, like an Amazon warrior. Her long red hair was plaited and drawn off her sharp, angular face. She was pleasing enough in looks, but there was a harshness to her features that made her seem jaded and cold.

Not to mention she wore the golden armor of a man. It gleamed in the dim light, obscuring any trace of womanly curve to her body.

A knight stood by her side. Only two inches taller, he had a face that would rival any woman's for beauty. His features were fragile and perfect and set off by the mass of wavy golden hair that fell haphazardly around his face.

Kerrigan had never seen anything like them or the strange golden armor they wore.

Morgen moved to stand beside him so that she could drape one long, shapely arm over his shoulders. 'Well, what have we here? The Monk and the Frigid. What an interesting combination Merlin has sent this time.'

The woman drew her sword and stepped forward. 'He belongs to us. Move away from him, Morgen, or perish.'

Morgen laughed out loud. 'You can't kill me, and we both know it. Now sheath the sword, Elaine, before I use it to mess up that pretty face of yours.' She took a minute to breathe in his ear. His body hardened instantly.

Laughing again, Morgen toyed with his ear as she continued to talk to Elaine. 'You know the rules, Queen Frigid. We both have an equal shot at our little man here. He is the one who has to choose which path to follow. Your way or mine . . .'

Elaine cursed.

Morgen ignored her. 'What *will* he do?' She sucked her breath in sharply as she stepped away from him to taunt the other two. 'The suspense is killing me . . . Oh, the agony and horror of waiting.'

'Then I say we drag it out,' Elaine said dryly. 'With any luck you'll perish and end this war once and for all.'

Morgen curled her lip until she looked back at Kerrigan. Her face softened into the tenderest of expressions. 'Come with me and I will give you whatever you desire. Wealth. Power. Women. No one will ever mock you again.'

Kerrigan's heart raced with desire. It was too much to hope for, and well he knew it. All things had a price. No one ever gave up anything without wanting payment for it. 'And what is the cost of that?'

'There is no cost. You will join my fey army as their leader and king. You will have your every wish fulfilled.' Morgen returned to nuzzle his neck and purr into his ear. 'Even *I* will be yours.'

He drew his breath in sharply as an image of her

naked and in his bed flashed through his mind.

'Stop that, Morgen,' Elaine snapped. 'You can't plant images into his head. 'Tis against the rules.'

Morgen shrugged before she stepped away. The images vanished from his thoughts. 'Fine then. Make him your offer and let him see your virtue.'

Elaine tried to soften her face in the same manner as Morgen, but it didn't have the same effect. It only looked as if she were in pain. 'Come with us and you will join the side of all that is good and decent in the world.'

'We are champions of right,' the man said. 'My name is Galahad, and we serve a higher order. Chastity, sacrifice, and humility are our oaths. Join us and know that your life will be spent making other lives better.'

Elaine grimaced at Galahad as if she could kill him for his offer. As it was, she did strike his shoulder so hard that he grimaced in pain.

Kerrigan stared at the two of them in disbelief. Were they serious? What did he need with chastity? Indeed, he'd spent the whole of his nights trying to find women to ease that burden from him.

As for sacrifice and humility, he'd been bred to them both, and quite frankly had had more than enough of it in his short lifetime. To hell with that.

Galahad held his hand out to him. 'Give us your sword, lad. Join our order, and you will have the family you have never known.'

And there was another thing that had never served him well. Even if he knew who his father was, he was certain the man had been a bastard of some sort. Not to mention, his own *sweet* mother had once tried to sell him.

Family . . . they could shove that as well.

Morgen licked her lips hungrily. 'Swear your sword to me, boy, and you will have the power to make anyone who tries to teach you humility turn into toads. Let the monks have their chastity and family, and let us live our lives to their fullest. Take what you desire and make it yours.'

There was no decision to be made here. At least not for a boy such as him. He'd entered this world damned from birth as a nameless bastard. If he had to leave it, then it would be on his own terms.

He turned to Morgen. 'I will go with you, my lady. And I will be your champion.'

'Chastity,' Elaine sneered at Galahad. 'You had to pick that one, huh?'

Morgen laughed in triumph as she turned toward Elaine and Galahad. 'Welcome to my world, boy. I promise you, you will be glad you chose my cause ...'

Seren closed her eyes as those memories faded, to be followed by others of Kerrigan and his service to Morgen.

Like all the others before her, the queen had lied to him.

There was no peace in her service. He had power, and wealth, but nothing else. There was no comfort. No friendship. No warmth. Only lies and enemies had awaited him.

The sword was as much a curse as it was a blessing.

Overwhelmed by his emotions and her own, Seren felt herself slipping. Falling.

She didn't want to live like that. Alone. Suspicious. Cold. Ever watchful and angry. Ever cruel.

Closing her eyes, she saw herself again at the loom in their small shop. Wendlyn was there, laughing while they worked. Marie was handing them more thread. The sun was bright as people walked before their window, peeping in at them.

'When I am married,' Wendlyn said cheerfully, 'I shall bring peppermint tarts here for all of you and tell you tales of how great it is to own your own shop.'

Marie laughed. Her blue eyes twinkled with good-natured humor. 'Well, when I am married, I shan't have enough time away from my husband to be visiting the likes of you.'

Sara, who was far too skinny and pale, had scoffed at her. 'What of you, Seren?'

Seren had paused in her work to stare dreamily out the window at a passing couple with a small child between them as they crossed the street. 'When I am married, I will come back with my husband and liberate whoever is still working here. I shall offer you all jobs and we will eat peppermint tarts until our bellies ache.'

Wendlyn had leaned over then and given her a hug. 'Our Seren, ever thinking of us first.' She'd squeezed her hard before she returned to her work. 'You will have your husband. I know it. And he will be a fine man indeed.'

'Aye,' Marie had agreed. 'Only the best for our Seren.'

Only the best . . .

Seren opened her eyes to find herself sitting on the floor in Kerrigan's lap. He had his arms wrapped around her as he continued to rock her gently.

The voices of the past were silent now. All gone. They left a peculiar emptiness inside her. She felt the same and yet she didn't. She had more knowledge now. It was as if she were somehow connected to the universe around her. She could feel the force of it. The beauty. The power.

Her body trembling, she reached up to place her

hand to Kerrigan's cheek. For once, his skin wasn't cold. It was almost a normal temperature. His whiskers scraped her palm as he opened his eyes to stare down at her.

Time seemed suspended as their gazes locked and held. There was nothing more hidden between them. She had glimpsed this man's heart and found it every bit as cold and merciless as he had claimed.

In his life, he'd known nothing but suffering as those around him used him for their own purposes. The insults of his past echoed in her head. They stung and they mocked.

And she learned that there were some scars that never healed. Some pain that time didn't dull.

Her poor Kerrigan . . .

Wanting to comfort him, she pulled his head down so that she could capture his lips with her own.

Kerrigan cupped her head in his palm as he opened his mouth to welcome her inside him. He'd had no idea of what sharing his powers with her would do to them.

Now he knew.

For the first time in his life, he'd seen another existence from the inside of it. He'd heard the gentle sound of her mother's voice. Had heard the laughter of the women she worked with. The acceptance. The love. It boggled him.

But more than that, it tore him asunder. Now he knew what he'd never known. He was privy to normality. To kindness and caring. No wonder his little mouse was so calm and gentle.

Pain seized him as he realized that such a life was forbidden to something like him. There would never be such decency in his world. No laughter or comfort. He'd made his decision long ago to be a demon lord and to live among others who were cruel like him.

His child, however, was another matter. He wouldn't allow it to be born in Camelot. Not with Morgen and her court there to corrupt and ruin him.

No matter what it took, he would see Seren and this child safe.

Somehow he would find a place for them so that she could live and give love to a part of him that he would never know. A part of him that he wouldn't see or hold. His child . . .

It was for the best.

Pulling back from their kiss, he offered her a smile. 'You've been through much this day, my lady. You should rest.'

Seren drew a deep breath as her fingers lingered on his mouth to toy with his lips. 'I am tired, and at the same time, I'm not.' She glanced up from his lips to those dark eyes that smoldered with his fire. She remembered now what they had looked like as she'd seen him before Morgen had entered his world. 'Your eyes used to be blue.'

'That was a long time ago.'

Seren leaned back against his chest so that she could see him better. 'Tomorrow we will stand together and we will fight Morgen.'

He shook his head. 'We can't. It will still take some time for you to get used to those powers inside you. There are times even now when mine get the better of me.'

'Perhaps, but I feel so peaceful right now. At ease. It's as if I've always had my powers.' She kissed his scarred knuckles and inhaled the warm scent of his skin.

Kerrigan wished he could make her understand the truth of what she was feeling. But to be honest, he was enjoying this moment with her. He was warm. Most of all, he was at peace. There were no angry voices that wanted to strike out and hurt whoever was near him. There was no pain.

There was just the two of them lost in this one moment.

But tomorrow would be a different story. Tomorrow Morgen would meet them and he would be weak. Seren would have her powers, but no real experience wielding them. Their only hope rested in the hands of a grouchy gargoyle who might or might not betray them.

Damn. How he wished that he could take them someplace far away from here. Someplace where there was no Morgen, no magic.

Your life is ever one of wanting.

It was true. Wanting more was what had led him to be here with her. It was what had led him to her.

And on the morrow, it would be what most likely led him to his death. Because as he held Seren in his arms, one thing became painfully clear. His exchange with Seren hadn't changed her nearly as much as it had changed him. He wasn't what he'd been . . .

You were changed before you initiated her.

It was true and he knew it.

Caring for her was a weakness. It left him vulnerable, and he held no doubt that Morgen already knew it was his Achilles' heel. If he made one misstep, one tiny miscalculation on the morrow, Morgen would win and he would be dead.

Chapter Thirteen

Kerrigan spent the night lying in bed with Seren. The demon within him wanted to leave her, but the man didn't, and that was the part he'd been listening to. His sword was fastened on the wall above his head while they were entwined naked underneath the covers.

His body ached from the strain of the shield, and even now he could hear the gargoyles and dragons outside, trying to tear through it. Tomorrow, he hoped, they would be free of this.

Oblivious to the sounds outside, Seren was draped over his chest, sleeping peacefully while he toyed with her silken hair. Her breath tickled his chest and made his nipple pucker every time she exhaled.

He knew that he should leave. He had no business allowing this little creature into his withered heart.

No one could ever be trusted. Yet she filled him with unknown emotions that weren't violent or cold. And as he lay with her in his arms, he began to have even more peculiar thoughts.

He imagined her holding his child . . . caring for it.

In his mind, he could see himself as a merchant, working in his shop with her by his side as their children ran about, laughing and playing. He could see the sunlight streaming in through the large windows, high-lighting the pale hair of a young daughter as she laughed and tried to catch the beam in her chubby hand.

Seren's sweet voice filled his ears with praise for their daughter's accomplishment . . .

'Oh, you are an imbecile,' he breathed, banishing those images. What an insipid dream. Merchants and peasants were pawns. They were fools and beggars.

He was a king. Granted, king of the damned, but king nonetheless. And the world was his for the taking.

His coronation had been in blood and in fire. In truth, he liked it. He didn't want to be kind or compassionate. Ruthlessness was the only thing that served a man well. The weak suffered while the mighty took what they wanted.

And he was mighty.

He would never again be that pathetic, thieving peasant who was mocked and belittled by others. Those days were blissfully past, and they would never come again. He would make sure of it.

Kerrigan felt the warmth draining out of him. The fire returned to his eyes. Leaning his head back, he felt the magic flow through him once more like chilled wine that invaded every corner of his soul. Aye, he was formidable, and he fully intended to stay that way. Strength was all that was respected in this world and in Camelot. And his strength more than all the others.

His resolve set, he moved out from under Seren and dressed himself in his armor.

Refusing to look at her, he pulled Caliburn down and strapped it to his hips. The time for weakness was past. This had been a nice interlude with Seren, and he would make sure that his child didn't suffer. But in the end, he had to return to what he was.

The king of the bad asses. There was no place in his world for a consort. There was only room at the top for one person and that was he. He didn't need Seren and her petty emotions tying him to her. All he needed was his sword and his magic. To hell with everything else.

Seren sighed as her dream turned to a sweet, warm day as she'd known in her youth before she'd become an apprentice. Her mother had taken a job with the tailor of a small village in Yorkshire.

While her mother worked, she was playing in a field not far from the cottage of the woman who watched after her. She wore her pale green kirtle that her mother had stitched with yellow dragons along the hem. It was her favorite gown.

With her head thrown back, she was turning circles in the field, watching the beautiful blue sky spin around and around above her.

'Seren?'

She paused in her play at the sound of her mother's cadent voice. She stumbled a bit as the dizziness hit her. 'Aye, Mother?'

As her mother drew near and her dizziness passed, she realized that she wasn't a little girl anymore. She was a woman full-grown.

She was herself.

Pausing in front of her, her mother brushed the hair back from her face and smiled sweetly at her before she kissed her brow. 'You've changed much, my little treasure.'

A stinging wave of grief consumed her as she heard her mother's blessed voice again. Tears welled in her eyes. 'I've missed you, Mama.'

Her mother's lips trembled. Unlike Seren, her mother was one of the most beautiful of women. Her hair was a darker shade of blond, with honey gold highlights. As a child, she'd spent hours brushing her mother's hair at night before her mother plaited it. Her hair had always smelled of spring flowers. It'd been softer than the best woven silk. Those precious memories flooded her now and made her ache to her very soul.

'I have missed you, too, my Seren,' her mother said in a tender voice. 'I hear you whispering to me sometimes in the quiet haven where I stay.' Her features showed her own pain and grief as she cupped Seren's cheek in her palm. 'Many times, I've wanted to answer you, but couldn't. But you were never alone, my precious daughter. Never.'

A tear of joyful sorrow slid from the corner of her eye. 'Why are you here now?'

Her mother reached under the neckline of her golden gown to pull out a small medallion. It reminded her much of the one Kerrigan wore. It held the same star with a dragon. 'It is past time for you to have this.'

Her mother placed it in the palm of her hand and closed her fist over it. She held Seren's fist in both of her hands. 'Your great-great grandfather was the one who betrayed his king and set all of this into motion. He allowed evil to seduce him, and he made a fatal mistake that destroyed the fellowship of Arthur's Table. We are of the bloodline of Emrys Penmerlin, and the daughter you carry now will one day meet the same challenge as our progenitor. I don't know what she'll choose. But if she follows in his footsteps, the world will be forever lost to Morgen and her demons.'

Her mother wiped away the tear from her face. 'Don't cry, Seren. Not for me. I'm at peace, child. I kept you safe until you were able to grow up, and now . . . your life is up to you. It will be what you make it.'

If only it were that simple, but Seren knew better.

There was so much that wasn't in her control. 'What of Kerrigan?'

Her mother's gaze turned distant, as if she were hiding something from her. 'His path is his own as well, and it's not for me to say. But you must be strong, child. Listen with your heart, and don't let others deceive you.'

'But how will I know if they're deceiving me?'

'Seren?'

She turned at the sound of a deep masculine voice. Her mother began to fade.

'Mama, wait! Please don't leave me.'

But her mother vanished anyway.

'Mama!' Seren woke up with tears in her eyes to find Blaise standing beside her bed.

He blinked twice at her. 'Sorry, Seren, I'm not female.' He frowned. 'Actually, I'm not sorry that I'm not a female, but I am sorry that I'm not your mother . . . Then again, I'm not really sorry about that, either. Basically, I'm not sorry at all, I just felt the need to say something.'

Irritated at him, Seren glanced about the room. There was no sign of her mother. No sign of her dream . . . at least not until she realized that there was something in her hand.

Looking down, she found the medallion right where her mother had placed it. Her heart raced at the sight of her medallion, but she kept it from Blaise. She didn't know why. It just wasn't something she wanted to share.

'Where's Kerrigan?'

'He's in the hall, waiting for you.' Blaise moved forward and handed her the scarlet tunic that she'd made for Kerrigan.

Seren frowned.

'He wants you to wear it. Just in case.'

Her frown melted into a smile at his thoughtfulness. 'I'll be down in just a moment.'

Blaise nodded before he left her alone.

Her thoughts churning over her dream, Seren scooted out of bed. There was a chill in the air. Or was it in her body? She couldn't really tell. All she knew was that it was frigid and eerie.

Dismissing the feeling, she quickly fastened the necklace and donned her clothes, then joined the men downstairs.

Unaware of her appearance in the great hall, Kerrigan was again dressed in his black armor while Blaise was dressed in a brown tunic and hose, with his white hair left free to hang down his back.

'Do I look like a woman?' Blaise asked Kerrigan, who was sitting in one of the chairs before the hearth.

'Aye.'

Blaise looked completely offended by his quick response. 'Excuse me?'

'What?' Kerrigan gave him an innocent expression. 'You want me to lie?'

Blaise folded his arms over his chest in an angry gesture. 'I don't look like a woman.'

'Then why did you ask me?'

'Seren thought I was her mother when I went to wake her.' He reached up and wrapped his hand in his hair. 'Maybe I should cut this.'

'Wouldn't help. Then you'd just look like an *ugly* woman.'

Releasing his hair, Blaise glared at him. 'Oh thank you, Lord Darkness. Do me a favor, never hire yourself out to work for a suicide hotline.'

'Suicide hotline?' Seren asked as she moved closer to them. 'What is that?'

Blaise turned to face her. 'It's ...' He paused and looked as if he were searching for a way to define it. 'Never mind. It truly won't make any sense to you.'

She was beginning to wonder if they spoke in esoteric fashion on purpose just to confuse her. 'Well, if it makes you feel any better, you don't look like a woman. Kerrigan does.'

Kerrigan snorted from his chair. 'Hardly.'

Blaise considered that for a moment. 'Only if the woman is tall, hairy, and bearded. Come to think of it, you do remind me of a hag who used to live in Camelot.'

Kerrigan narrowed his red eyes on the mandrake. 'Shut up.'

Seren tsked at Kerrigan and the venom he was releasing. 'He's in a mood, isn't he?' she asked Blaise.

'Aye, and he's been like that all morning. What? Did you not share the blanket with him?'

'I said *enough*.'

Seren scowled at Kerrigan's angry tone. He reminded her of the day she'd first met him. Blustering and threatening. Gone was the tenderness he'd shown her lately. 'Did I do something wrong?'

An unnamed emotion flitted across his face before he shook his head. He rose to his feet. 'We have to meet the gargoyles soon. Before we do, I have to explain what's going to happen. When I drop the shield, I will have to feed from you immediately. You will have to submit to me. If you choose to fight, it could very well kill you. Do you understand?'

Aye, she fully understood that. She didn't like it, but she understood it.

She nodded.

'It's going to hurt, Seren,' Blaise said quietly. 'Probably a lot.'

She swallowed at his grave tone. 'How badly?'

It was Kerrigan who answered. 'Bad enough that you will want to run away, but if you do, I won't be able to control it. If I lose control . . .'

She was dead, most like. Seren drew a ragged breath at the seriousness of their situation. 'Very well. I shall endure whatever pain you cause.'

Blaise gave her a look of respect. 'You're a braver man than I am.'

'Woman, you mean.'

He screwed his face up at her. 'There you go again, calling me a woman.' He met Kerrigan's gaze. 'I swear, she's giving me a complex.'

Seren shook her head at his play, not that she understood that last bit exactly. But she had a good idea of the gist of it.

Looking at Kerrigan, she sobered as she noticed that he lacked their humor.

She approached him, only to have him move away. 'Are you sure that you're all right, my lord?'

'I am fine.' His tone was sharp and clipped.

Sighing, she nodded. 'So when does the shield fall?'

'As soon as we go outside.' Kerrigan looked past her, to Blaise. 'Once I have enough power, I'll transport all of us from here into the future where Morgen won't be able to follow with her army. I figure the twentieth century should do.'

Blaise sighed. 'Seren won't understand anything there.'

'Does it matter? At least there if a dragon or gargoyle pops through, they'll get shot down by the humans before they come near us. They may be fierce, but not even they can survive napalm or an armed missile. Once radar registers them, they'll be dealt with and they know it. It should keep them out of our way at least for a while.'

'What is the twentieth century?' Seren asked.

Blaise let out a deep breath. 'A world unlike anything you can imagine.' He looked back at Kerrigan. 'It'll mess with her sensibilities.'

'Can you think of someplace better?'

'Not really. You're right about their weapons. But do you think that'll keep Morgen at bay?'

'Nay. However, the Adoni will only be able to come through the portal two at a time without alerting the military. We should be able to handle that with little problem.'

Blaise nodded. 'What about the gargoyles who are with us? They don't exactly blend during daylight hours.'

'Let them find a building to sit on. They're not my problem. All I promised them was an escape from Morgen. What they do after that is their business.'

Blaise looked at her. 'Have you ever noticed that he really enjoys being evil?'

'Aye.' But the strangest part of all was that there was something about that that she found alluring, almost endearing. 'What can I do to help in this?'

'Don't die,' they said in unison.

'I can honestly say that I will do my best to stay alive.'

'Good,' Blaise said as he walked over to the window to look outside. 'Garafyn is leading them down the hill as he promised.'

Kerrigan was staring at her with an undefinable expression that tugged at her heart. There was something about it that reminded her of the boy she'd glimpsed the day before when they had shared their blood.

He wasn't as cold toward her as he was pretending, and it was the man in him that set fire to her blood.

There was something about being in his presence that made her ache to want to touch him.

But they didn't have time for that now.

Kerrigan turned his gaze away from Seren toward Blaise. 'Remember that shifting us through time will weaken me even more, and I won't be able to recharge from Seren again. It'll be up to you and the gargoyles to fight whatever might follow us through.'

Blaise inclined his head. 'Have no fear. We can handle it.'

Kerrigan removed his left gauntlet and tucked it into his belt. 'Then let us get this over with.'

Blaise headed out first.

Seren paused by Kerrigan's side. The sunlight played in the dark waves of his hair. His eyes were black now, restless, and she wondered at what was causing his dour mood. 'I trust you, my lord. I know you won't hurt us in this.'

Kerrigan couldn't breathe as he stared down into those clear, trusting green eyes. God's blood, he couldn't remember ever being so naive. Even now he half expected Garafyn to betray them. It would be in the gargoyle's nature.

Just as it was in his nature to destroy.

Only he didn't want to destroy Seren. Frowning at her, he laid his hand to hers. She had more strength and courage than Morgen's entire army.

He bent down to inhale the scent of her hair before he placed a tender kiss to her lips. She tasted of innate goodness, of sweet womanhood, and in truth he wanted more of her. He wanted to take her upstairs and spend the rest of the day making love to her.

But he couldn't. They had a battle before them that wouldn't wait. He only hoped that he wouldn't fail her.

Pulling away, Kerrigan led the way from the castle,

out into the bailey where Blaise was waiting for them.

He paused by the mandrake's side. 'If I fall, take my medallion and get Seren out of here immediately. Hide her wherever you can.'

'I will do my best.'

'Good. Now let me go and do my worst.'

He saw Seren meet Blaise's cautious gaze before they followed him onto the old wooden drawbridge. Reaching out for his dwindling powers, he summoned the earth's mist to help blind their enemies. So-called dragon's breath, it was the same spell that Emrys Penmerlin had once summoned so that Uther could lie with Igraine and father King Arthur on the unsuspecting noblewoman.

The thick fog rolled forward, and through its dampness, he could feel Morgen. She knew the source of the fog and she was livid. He sensed her gathering her army . . .

She called the dragons down before they flew into each other and ordered the gargoyles to climb the hill.

'Adoni! Ready your arrows!'

But she would never order them to fire and he knew it. The chance of blindly striking Seren and killing her was too great.

Now was the time.

Taking a deep breath, he brought down the shield. The pain in his head ceased immediately. Grateful for that reprieve, he turned toward Seren. He spread his left hand out, only to pause as he met her open gaze.

She trusted him.

His heart stopped beating as he saw the tenderness in her gaze.

Do it.

This was their only chance to escape. He narrowed his gaze before he placed his hand in the valley between her breasts. He felt the instant surge of her life force as he drew it out. It was warm. Invigorating.

But he'd barely started when Seren let out an agonized cry. Her eyes filled with tears as she bravely stood her ground. As promised, she made no move to pull away. No move to break his hold. She merely stood there with her lips trembling as her tears overran her eyes and fled down her cheeks.

The pain was excruciating, and still she stood strong like an ancient Amazon.

Kerrigan cursed as he snatched his hand away. He couldn't do this. Not to her. Not like this.

Seren staggered back. He caught her against his chest as his heart thumped in sympathetic pain.

'I'm sorry,' he whispered softly.

'Are you strong now?' Her words came out in ragged breaths.

Nay, he wasn't. But he couldn't bring himself to hurt her again. He looked up and met Blaise's unblinking stare through the fog and realized that the mandrake knew what had happened.

He knew that Kerrigan had backed down. But there was no scorn in that violet gaze. No hatred.

If he didn't know better, he'd almost think that Blaise was proud of him.

'Looks like we fight our way out then.' Blaise instantly took dragon form.

Drawing his sword, Kerrigan turned to find Garafyn and Anir nearing them. With a wave of the fog curling behind them, they flew in and landed before him. Their eerie yellow and red eyes glowed, and that was the only way he could really see them, since their gray bodies blended in almost perfectly with the fog.

'Let's go,' Garafyn said.

Blaise tilted his head so that he could look with one

eye at the gargoyle. 'I thought there would be more of you?'

'The others fell behind. Screw 'em. It's every rock for himself. We don't have time to wait.'

Blaise lowered his dragon's head to speak in a low tone. 'We have a small problem.'

'No,' Garafyn said sternly, '*we* don't. Let's go.'

Kerrigan shook his head. 'We can't.'

'Why not?'

Kerrigan braced himself to fight them. 'I can't feed from her.'

A flap of Garafyn's wings parted the fog enough for him to see the angry look on the gargoyle's face. His eyes glowed eerily red in the mist. 'Can't or won't?'

'Can't.'

'Bullshit!' Garafyn growled. 'You've killed people for what? Six hundred years or something like that? I've seen you do it countless times. Don't go getting . . . stupid on me now. Damn.' He looked over his shoulder as he tried to peer into the fog. They could hear the others, but not see them. 'We're about to become a driveway here, Kerrigan. Do something.'

Kerrigan snorted. 'I thought you were going to be a countertop.'

'No, I just shafted the Queen Bitch who we both know isn't real forgiving. I don't even rate a countertop at this point. Not unless you grow a ball and suck the juice from your pet here.'

Blaise moved toward the gargoyles. 'I think you should just kill them, Kerrigan.'

Anir hissed at Blaise. 'Then suck off the dragon,' he said to Kerrigan. 'He's a worthless piece of scale.'

Kerrigan sneered at them. 'I don't suck energy off any male. Ever.'

Seren took Kerrigan's hand. Morgen's army was

closing in on them and her heart pounded at the ferocious sound of creatures advancing. Their steps and grunts echoed around them. It stirred the mist and rebounded off the stone walls.

They were coming closer and closer.

Any second, they would be surrounded ...

Suddenly, Seren heard a voice whispering inside her head. Instinctively, she knew it was a spell like the ones Kerrigan had used in the past.

It was her magic speaking to her, she realized. It was the powers that he had awakened the day before. Closing her eyes, she listened to it and repeated the words out loud. As she did so, the air around her seemed to sizzle and burn. Something crackled in the fog, sparking colors around them.

'What is she doing?' Garafyn asked.

'Getting us out of this.' Kerrigan pulled her into his arms and began to chant with her.

Seren followed his lead. She heard men screaming while the two of them combined their magic.

One minute they were there on the drawbridge, and in the next, they were standing out in the middle of an open field. There was no sign of Morgen or her army.

Opening her eyes, Seren looked around. They appeared to be in some kind of forest in broad daylight. She frowned as she saw something fly overhead. At first she thought it was a dragon, only its wings didn't move. It was huge and silver ...

'What is that?'

Kerrigan looked up at what she was pointing to. 'A plane.'

She frowned. 'A what?'

'Big. Silver. Bird,' Garafyn said irritably, stressing each syllable as if she were simple-witted. 'People climb into it and they fly from one place to another.'

Seren looked back up to see it again, but it was already gone. 'Are you jesting?'

'Nope.'

Unable to believe it, she wanted to see the plane again. But as she glanced around, she realized that Kerrigan didn't look well. His features were pinched and drawn.

'Are you all right?'

'Never better,' he said sarcastically.

Blaise changed back into a man. 'Anybody have a guess on when and where we are?'

Kerrigan sheathed his sword. 'I'm not sure. It looks vaguely like upstate New York. Stirling Forest, I think.'

Seren frowned at his words. '*New* York? What happened to the old one?'

The men ignored her question.

Blaise turned toward Garafyn and Anir. 'We need to hide the gargoyles. Beasts, go find a building to squat on.'

Garafyn curled his lip. 'Dragon, go find a—'

'Enough,' Kerrigan said, cutting them off. 'Blaise is right. The last thing we can afford is someone seeing all of us together.'

Garafyn growled at him. 'Yeah, well, I'm sick of pretending to be a lawn ornament.'

'What is a lawn ornament?' Seren tried again.

Garafyn let out a disgusted breath. 'A statue that sits on a yard where dogs piss all over it.'

'Yeah,' Anir said, 'in short, it's us. I really hate New York.'

Blaise snorted. 'Hey, at least it has a lot of buildings for you to hide on.'

Garafyn didn't look amused.

Kerrigan gave the gargoyles an evil glare. 'Feel free

230

to return to the Middle Ages or Camelot any time you want.'

'Yeah, right,' Anir said. 'Like those people don't tie us to a stake and torch us. Really messes with their head when they realize stone don't burn easy. As for Camelot, fuck that.'

'Yeah,' Garafyn snarled. 'Especially after we just screwed over Queen Bitch.' He looked at Kerrigan. 'Where are you guys going?'

Before they could answer, something bright flashed beside them.

Kerrigan turned as an Adoni came through to land before them. He made a sound of disgust. 'Don't you people have a home?' Drawing his sword, he lunged at the Adoni, only to have him step back.

The instant he did, Garafyn snapped his neck.

The Adoni fell dead at Kerrigan's feet.

Kerrigan curled his lip. 'Did you have to do that?'

'I thought I was helping.'

'I need to feed, and that would have been a great source of food for me.'

Garafyn held his hands up in surrender.

'Anyone got a suggestion on where to hide before another jolly good friend finds us?' Anir asked.

'I'm thinking Pluto,' Garafyn said under his breath.

Kerrigan didn't acknowledge that strange word at all. 'We need something mobile. They'll have a harder time pinpointing us if we're in motion.'

'Wait,' Anir said with a note of warning in his voice, 'I saw this episode of *X-Files*. The guy's head explodes the minute Mulder reaches the West Coast. I don't want that to be us.'

Seren was completely baffled by their conversation. 'Please, someone, tell me what's going on.'

Garafyn gave her a droll stare. 'We're discussing

how we're going to die. Anir is voting for head explosion. My vote is disembowelment. *Painful* disembowelment.'

'Shut up,' Blaise said before he turned to Seren. 'We need to find something to move us around quickly.'

'I'm sure there are horses—'

'Too slow. We need something that moves much faster than that and doesn't get tired.'

Kerrigan rubbed his head as if he had an ache between his eyes. 'I have enough energy left to conjure us a mobile home. I think. But I'm going to have to feed soon and—'

His voice broke off as another Adoni appeared. His eyes flamed red an instant before he saw Seren. The air crackled as two more came through.

The Adoni rushed them.

Anir grabbed one while the other two went for Seren. Kerrigan swung his sword to drive one back.

Seren used her powers to blast the other, but it had no effect on him. She struck out, and her blows glanced off him.

The Adoni grabbed her hair and laughed. The air around them shimmered as if he were about to take her back through time.

Panicking, she saw Kerrigan toss the one he was fighting toward Blaise, who then engaged him so that Kerrigan could run toward her.

Before he could reach them, Garafyn grabbed the Adoni who held her and flipped him on his back. 'One vegemite Adoni made to order. Eat 'em up, grump.'

Seren cringed as Kerrigan placed his hand over the Adoni's chest. The creature screamed out in pain while Blaise killed one and Anir finished off the Adoni he was fighting.

She watched as the color came back into Kerrigan's

face even as it faded from the Adoni. She wanted to look away, and yet she couldn't. She was mesmerized by the brutality of what Kerrigan had to do to survive. Damn Morgen for doing this to him. It wasn't right that Kerrigan had been turned into this because of one woman's sadistic nature.

But even as that thought went through her, Kerrigan let out a relieved sigh. When he came to his feet, he was again the fearsome knight she'd met in London.

Garafyn appeared to smile. 'Good to the last drop, huh?'

'Don't start with me, Garafyn,' Kerrigan warned. 'I'm now in position to pull your wings off your back and laugh while I do it.'

'Point well taken.'

Kerrigan led them over to what appeared to be a road, only it had an odd black surface to it. She'd never seen anything like it. It was hot, with lines, both broken and straight, painted over it. No sooner did they reach it than a giant . . . something appeared out of nowhere.

It looked like a big, long box with wheels. It was too big to be a wagon.

'Is this a house?' she asked.

'Kind of,' Anir said. 'It's a mobile home.'

She was baffled by his words. 'How can a home be mobile?'

Anir laughed. 'Step inside and see.'

Kerrigan opened the door. 'He's right, Seren. We need to get inside and get out of here before more come through.'

Seren followed Blaise into the peculiar device. Blaise pulled her toward a table that was flanked by two benches while the gargoyles came in and tucked their wings around them. Kerrigan joined them, then shut the door.

'I'll drive,' Blaise said.

'Duh,' Garafyn said. 'Kerrigan needs to rest. Anir and I would get us pulled over since I don't think cops are used to seeing statues driving, and queenie over there would kill us since she's never seen a highway or car beforc.' He paused as if another idea just occurred to him. 'You do know how to drive, don't you?'

Blaise gave an evil smirk. 'Guess we'll *see*, huh?'

Garafyn looked sick to his stomach. 'I really hate mandrakes.'

Kerrigan shook his head at the gargoyle. In a strange way, he was beginning to like Garafyn, and that actually scared him.

'Relax,' he said to Garafyn as Blaise moved to the front to take the wheel. He looked up at the mandrake. 'Make sure you stick to the back roads.'

'What? You don't want a major fight in a U.S. city?'

'I could care less about that. But we need to move fast, and I don't want to hit a traffic jam.'

'Good point.' Blaise took a seat, then started the engine while Kerrigan moved to the small row of seats so that he could close his eyes and rest for a bit.

Blaise pulled them onto the road and started down the empty highway.

Seren scooted out of her bench and followed Kerrigan to the back. All things considered, she was being remarkably calm, but then after Camelot, the marvels of the twenty-first century were probably mild for her.

'What?' he asked as she sat down by his side.

'They're going to find us again, aren't they?'

He sighed at the fear he heard in her voice. Part of him wanted to comfort her, but he didn't know how to do that. So instead, he chose to be honest. She had every right to know what they were up against. 'Aye.'

'Then what are we going to do?'

He opened his eyes to see the concern that burned bright in her green eyes. 'We're going to keep running, Seren. It's all we can do.'

'But for how long?'

'As long as it takes.'

'You know,' Garafyn said from the table. 'It would be easier to hide if you two split up. The power of three Merlins is pretty damned hard to miss. But one ...'

'I won't leave her unprotected,' Kerrigan growled.

Garafyn scowled. 'Since when do you have a conscience?'

'I don't have a conscience.'

'Then why are we protecting her?'

Kerrigan didn't answer. In truth he didn't know what to say. He honestly had no idea why he was doing this. There was nothing to be gained by protecting her. Not really.

They were only delaying the inevitable. Morgen would find them again and again. She would be relentless.

He angled his head so that he could meet Seren's gaze. 'You know, you've been nothing but trouble since I first met you.'

Instead of being offended, she smiled. 'I was minding my own business, my lord, when you came and took me away from everything that I knew.'

Smiling, he reached up to brush a stray piece of hair back from her cheek. Her skin was so soft. Warm. In all his life, he'd never known kindness until she'd taken his hand and followed him into hell itself.

The only problem was that angels couldn't live in hell and demons couldn't live in heaven.

Kerrigan listened to the hum of the engine. Seren

didn't belong here in this time period. She would have to learn a new language. Relearn how to do the simplest of tasks. She knew nothing of surviving in this world.

'Who was the idiot who planned this escape anyway?' Kerrigan asked bitterly.

It was Blaise who answered. 'That would be the two who have rocks for their brains.'

'I resent that,' Garafyn said indignantly. 'It wasn't like either one of you had a better suggestion.'

Kerrigan didn't comment as he continued to stroke the softness of Seren's cheek.

Where could they hide? Really?

They were two gargoyles, an albino dragon, a demon lord, and a simple maid whose only dream was to be a weaver. They were far from inconspicious. Not to mention the fact that Seren would soon grow heavy with her pregnancy. Then she wouldn't be mobile. She wouldn't be able to run or to fight. He didn't know what kinds of demands this pregnancy would have on her powers.

She needed to be with other women. With someone who could help her through this. Someone who could protect her even better than he could.

He knew nothing of children or childbirth. He only knew how to take life.

If he had one wish, it would be to have had one day of peace alone with Seren. One day to have spent with her not as her captor or her protector, but as a man, pure and simple. But there was nothing simple about his life. As for pure . . . he would laugh if he could.

Nay, it was over. They'd given it a good run. But in the end, he knew the truth.

'Garafyn. Anir.'

The gargoyles looked at him. Kerrigan leaned up

and pulled the medallion from his neck. He took a moment to study the piece that he'd found near the stone where his sword had been buried. Morgen had been the one to explain its significance to him. In the hands of a Merlin, it amplified his power. It could also serve to return a Merlin home to Camelot should he be weakened out in the world of man. In the hands of the gargoyles or others who had no magic, it would allow them to channel certain powers.

With it, the gargoyles would no longer be seen by Morgen. They could hide from her. But more than that, they would have the ability to travel through time without a Merlin opening a portal and sending them through.

Though they'd still be cursed into the stone bodies of gargoyles, Garafyn and Anir would be free.

Sighing, he tossed the amulet to Garafyn, who caught it with one taloned hand.

The gargoyle gaped as he realized what it was.

'Payment for services rendered.'

The gargoyles exchanged a stunned look.

'You're not going to keep us enslaved like Morgen has?' Garafyn asked.

Kerrigan shook his head. 'There's been enough slavery. You're free.' From the corner of his eye, he saw the weepy look on Seren's face.

Garafyn's hand actually shook as he placed the medallion around his neck. Two seconds later, the gargoyles vanished.

'That was truly kind,' she said softly. She was so beautiful as her tiny hand held his. How could something so small touch him so deeply?

Still, he scoffed at her sentimentality. 'What do I know of kindness?'

A gentle smile curved her lips as she lifted his hand

to place a sweet kiss to his knuckles, which were scarred by a lifetime of fighting. 'You're learning.'

Nay, he wasn't. He was what he'd always been. Cold. Calculating. Because if he wasn't, he would never be able to do what he was about to do.

Kerrigan caught Blaise's frown in the rearview mirror, but he quickly averted his gaze. Garafyn was right. The only hope they had was to separate.

And it was the last thing he wanted to do.

Taking a deep breath, he closed his eyes. 'Brea! If you want your sword back, come and take it.'

Chapter Fourteen

Kerrigan heard Seren gasp beside him as he summoned the Celtic god to them with his powers. He only hoped that Brea was listening. But then given how much the Tuatha Dé Danann wanted the sword back, it was a good wager that Brea would show.

So much for being a bad ass. He was about to become a first-rate chump. And for what?

A cheap piece of peasant . . .

Kerrigan clamped down on that thought in anger. That wasn't Seren and he knew it. She was so much more. And he hated that he knew the truth of her. Because in the end that was his downfall. The moment he'd looked into her eyes and seen something more than a disposable pawn to be used, looked into her heart and seen the innocent compassion, he'd set his own course for destruction.

Damn, he was a fool. And he was becoming an even bigger one by the minute.

Blaise pulled to the side of the deserted road as Brea flashed into the seat in front of Kerrigan and Seren. Dressed in a pair of jeans and a turtleneck, Brea looked completely at home in this time period. The god's dark eyes were full of suspicion as he stared at them.

'Why have you summoned me?'

Kerrigan paused as he considered his many reasons, none of which made a bit of sense. He really didn't know why he was doing this other than the one basic fact that it was the right thing to do.

You've never done the right thing before ...

It was true. He hadn't, and yet he couldn't seem to keep himself from doing this. *That's what you get from trading blood with the innocent. It's her purity that's corrupting you.*

Then again, her innocence had corrupted him the instant she put her tiny hand into his and allowed him to pull her across his horse.

He'd been wrong when he thought she had destroyed her future by that one foolish act of trust. It was his future that had been destroyed by one act of selfishness.

Nay, it wasn't selfishness that was his undoing. It was something else entirely. Something he'd never felt before.

Compassion. Warmth. And another emotion he didn't dare name because it wasn't meant for something like him. It was a noble emotion for those who were worthy of it.

It was an emotion for someone like Seren.

He met Brea's gaze levelly. 'I want you to take Seren to Avalon.'

Kerrigan wasn't sure whose face appeared most stunned by those words, but he had to admit that Brea's expression was most comical. Too bad he didn't feel like laughing.

Seren's face paled as she wrapped one hand around his biceps. 'I won't go without you,' she said, her voice breaking.

Those words spoke to a part of him that he'd never

met before. A part of him he'd thought was completely defective.

His heart.

And it was breaking now. But this had to be done. There was no choice. Not if he wanted to keep her safe.

He placed his hand over hers and gave a gentle squeeze of reassurance. 'I'll join you there.'

Brea narrowed his eyes on him. The god knew he was lying and by the look on Blaise's face, he did, too.

Seren's eyes were filled with pain as she looked up at him. She trusted him, and he hated that he was breaking that trust. 'Why won't *you* take me?'

He savored the softness of her hand under his. It was such a tiny hand, and yet it had the strength to shake him to his foundations. To make him do things he'd never done before. To make him care for someone when he knew what he really should do was walk away.

Taking a deep breath, he did what he did best. He lied. 'I can't, Seren. You'll need an escort through the veil, and I gave my key to the gargoyles.'

Her green eyes sparked at that. 'I have a key.'

He was stunned when she pulled a matching medallion from beneath the red tunic and handed it to him. He clamped his jaw shut to keep from gaping. 'Where did you get this?'

'My mother gave it to me in a dream.'

Now that was interesting, and if they had more time, he'd question her further about it. But her possession of an amulet changed nothing. If anything, it only strengthened his resolve.

'You'll still need Brea to make the introductions for you at Avalon and to make sure that nothing happens to you.'

'But why aren't you coming?'

'I have to go and get your loom before Morgen finds it . . . if she hasn't already. You go ahead with Brea, and I'll join you in Avalon as soon as I can.'

Kerrigan got up as Blaise moved toward the back where they were seated. 'Watch her,' he said sternly to the mandrake. 'I need to have a word with Brea outside. Alone.'

Blaise nodded at the same time Seren protested. She was getting up to follow after him.

'I'll be right back,' Kerrigan promised as he gently pushed her toward her seat.

She narrowed those green eyes on him threateningly. 'You'd best be, my lord.'

Cupping her supple cheek in his palm, he inclined his head to her before he took Brea outside so that Seren wouldn't be able to overhear them. They were parked beside a small pasture where he could see a few small calves and cows grazing. Luckily there were no other cars about to notice his peculiar clothes or to ask if they'd broken down.

But that wouldn't last. They needed to get out of here before someone stopped and questioned them. Or worse, before Morgen found them again.

'You said something about the sword?' Brea prompted as soon as he left the RV.

Kerrigan nodded as he closed the door to make sure that Seren couldn't overhear them. 'You promise me that you'll personally protect her and I'll give you the sword in trade.'

Brea still looked less than convinced of his sincerity. 'There's a 'but' in there, I sense it.'

The god was astute, which given his status and birth wasn't all that surprising. 'I want your word that when my child is old enough, the sword will be released to him or her.'

'That's it?'

Kerrigan nodded.

Disbelief darkened Brea's brow as if he were still having trouble believing that his hearing wasn't defective. 'You would trust my word?'

Kerrigan found that hard to believe, too. But he had no choice in this. It was the best he could offer for Seren and their child. 'If you swear by the goddess Danu, aye. I know you'll have no choice except to stand by it.'

Brea scowled at him. He moved closer as if he sensed something out of the ordinary. 'What has changed about you?'

Kerrigan stepped away from him, uncomfortable with the intensity of the god's attention. 'What are you talking about?'

The god cocked his head as if he were studying an unknown object. 'You are not what you were when I first tried to take Caliburn from you in Joyous Gard.'

Those words set fire to his temper. He didn't like knowing that his emotions were so obvious to another. He didn't want anyone else to know of his weakness for a small slip of a woman who should mean nothing to him.

And yet she meant everything.

'Don't be a fool. Nothing about me has changed. I am as I was.'

Brea's frown only increased. To his surprise, the god hesitated at his offer. 'If I take Caliburn, you realize you will be mortal again. You will bleed.'

'I know.'

'Morgen will kill you for the battles you two have fought.'

Kerrigan clenched his teeth. There the god was wrong. Morgen was far too vindictive for that. She wouldn't kill him. She would do her damnedest to make him wish and beg for death.

That was one satisfaction he would never give her.

But he didn't say that to Brea. Instead, he faced the god man to man. 'Give us your word that you'll take her to Avalon and make sure that none there harm her or the baby.'

For once, Brea didn't argue. 'You have my word.'

'On the blood of Danu.'

'On the blood of Danu.' Brea held his hand out. 'Now give me the sword.'

Kerrigan shook his head. He couldn't do that. Not yet. 'If I do, Seren will know something is amiss the instant she sees me without the sword on. Take her, and I will give it to you once she's safely hidden within the walls of Avalon.'

Brea scoffed. 'Do you think for one minute that I trust you, demon? Especially after all you have done in the past?'

'I give you my word.'

Brea curled his lip. 'That's as worthless as your life.'

He couldn't fault the god for those words. Brea was right. 'Seren won't go with you if she suspects anything.'

Brea stepped back, then held his palm up toward the sky. A light flashed an instant before another sword appeared in his hand. It was made of brightly polished steel with a leather-wrapped handle and a dragon's-eye stone set in the hilt.

Kerrigan scowled at it. If he didn't know better, he'd swear it was Caliburn.

'It has no powers,' Brea said as he held the sword out toward him. 'But she won't know that unless she touches it.'

It was a good plan, and for once he had nothing more to add to it.

Sighing, Kerrigan inclined his head before he unbuckled Caliburn. He could hear the sword screaming in his head. Hear it begging him not to let it go. *I am yours . . . We belong to each other.*

For centuries the two of them had been together . . .

It was all he'd ever had to call his own. All that had ever really mattered to him. The power. The strength. This sword had made him king. It had turned a boy into a man.

In all his life, this sword was the only thing that had ever taken care of him.

Kerrigan held Caliburn tight in his fist as the power of it consumed him. So long as he held this sword, no one could touch him. No one could harm him.

He was letting go of everything.

Don't be stupid . . .

He looked at the tinted windows, knowing that Seren couldn't see him. But she was in there, and he was the only one who could protect her from Morgen.

The sword or his mouse . . .

Cursing, he handed the sword to Brea even though it burned his hand to do so.

The look of shock on the god's face was truly priceless. He stared at the sword in his hand as if he half expected it to vanish. 'You really let go of it.'

Kerrigan didn't say anything as he snatched the fake sword from Brea's other hand and fastened it around his hips. 'She's not to know of this. Ever.'

Brea didn't respond. He merely continued to stare at Caliburn as if it were an apparition.

If only it were. The absence Kerrigan felt inside him at the loss of Caliburn was a pain more profound than any he'd ever felt before. It was as if a vital part of himself had been lost. And it took all his will not to take it back.

But he couldn't, and he knew it.

Without looking at Brea, Kerrigan brushed past the god and headed back into the RV.

He entered it at the same time one of the Adoni manifested by the driver's seat. Anger tore through him as he unsheathed his fake sword. The male Adoni lunged at him. Kerrigan hissed as the Adoni caught him a blow to the lips that cut them. For the first time in centuries he felt the sting of the blow, tasted the salt of his own blood.

His eyes flaming, he drove his sword through the Adoni's body, then pulled it free.

'We haven't much time,' he said to Seren and Blaise as he approached them. 'If we're not moving, they can find us.'

He noted the way Blaise stared in disbelief at his cut lip, but luckily Seren didn't understand that part of the sword's power.

Wiping the blood away, Kerrigan pulled Seren to her feet. 'You have to go with Brea now.' He met Blaise's frown. 'I need you to go with her as well and protect her.'

'Nay,' Seren said quickly as she stopped in the middle of the RV and refused to go farther. 'I'll go with Brea, but I'd rather Blaise go with you to get the loom in case something happens and you need him.'

Kerrigan started to argue, but knew better. They didn't have time to waste. Besides, Blaise would make this easier. He'd be able to send the necklace and loom back with the mandrake to Avalon.

Nodding, he ushered Seren down the narrow aisle to the door and out to the side of the road where Brea was waiting. Luckily the god had the sword hidden from their sight.

Kerrigan let out a relieved breath as he moved her to stand before Brea.

Seren felt her heart sink as Kerrigan released her hand. There was something not right in this. Something she couldn't name. It was as if an air of hopelessness engulfed him.

What was he planning?

'You will be careful?' she asked, cupping his face in her hands so that she could feel the prickle of his whiskers against her palms. Even so, he avoided looking straight at her.

'Aye. I will be careful.'

'Promise?'

That succeeded in making him look at her. 'I promise.'

She took a moment to study the dark red embers of his eyes, the bit of shadow on his cheeks. Her knight was the most handsome man to ever live.

'I shall be counting the minutes until your return.'

The dark sadness returned to his eyes. 'As will I.'

She pulled him into her arms. He held her in a gentle embrace that warmed her through and through.

Then he tightened his arms and pulled away. 'You must go now, Seren.'

But she didn't want to. She never wanted to let go of this man. Reluctantly, she started to pull away, only to have Kerrigan capture her lips in a stinging kiss. She moaned at the taste of him, at the way he held on to her as if he never wanted to release her.

Groaning, he pulled away again, then wrapped her in his arms and leaned his cheek against her head. His arms tightened an instant before he stepped away. 'I shall see you anon.' Even as he spoke the words, he held her hand tightly in his.

Her heart pounded at the thought of being without him for even a moment. She handed him her necklace so that he would be able to join her in Avalon with the loom. 'Anon. Quickly.'

He nodded, and as he released her hand, a horrible premonition went through her. She opened her mouth to speak of it when two more Adoni appeared.

'Take care of her,' Kerrigan snarled to Brea as he turned to fight them.

'Wait,' Seren said, but it was too late. The god had already touched her arm.

Her last sight of Kerrigan was of him engaging the two Adoni warriors.

The next thing she knew, she was on a peaceful beach with a bright sun above her. Seren squinted against the glare as she looked out over the clearest, bluest ocean she'd ever seen. Gulls cawed over her head while the water lapped gently against snow white sand. Land jutted out to her right, forming a sheer cliff that rose up high toward the sun.

On top of the cliff was a golden castle glinting in the daylight. It was beautiful. Mesmerizing. There was a lush, green forest that separated her stretch of beach from the castle on the cliff.

'This is Avalon?' she asked Brea.

'Aye.'

'It looks like heaven.' Her voice was scant more than a whisper. How she wished Kerrigan were here to see it. It was so much prettier than Camelot.

This looked like the place where King Arthur would have held his court.

Brea smiled at her. 'Not entirely. Nothing is ever perfect. But this is close and you will be very happy here.' He held his hand out to her. 'Come, child.'

She followed him up the beach toward the castle. As they drew near the forest, an incredibly striking blond woman appeared before them. The woman wore a white gown that was trimmed with gold. The weave of the fabric was flawless. It reminded Seren of a perfect field of snow.

There was an air of unmistakable kindness to this newcomer. It bled from every part of her. Just being in her presence filled Seren with warmth.

'Brea,' she said in greeting. 'I see you found our wayward steward.'

'Not exactly. Rather she found me.' He paused. 'Aquila Penmerlin, meet Seren.'

The woman smiled sweetly. 'Call me Merlin, Seren. Most people do.'

Before Seren could respond, the smile faded, to be replaced by a peculiar frown as Merlin looked back at Brea. She rubbed her arms as if something chilled her. 'You have Caliburn?'

Seren's heart stopped at her words. 'Nay. Caliburn is with Kerrigan. Isn't it?'

Brea looked a bit sheepish before he shook his head. The air around him glowed an instant before Kerrigan's sword appeared in his hand.

Seren's jaw went slack as she recognized the weapon.

The god handed it not to Merlin, but to Seren. 'I have a feeling you'll need this one day.'

She refused to take it. 'How did you come by this?'

'Kerrigan gave it to me in exchange for my bringing you here. He wanted me to make sure that the sword went to your child.'

Pain tore through her as her premonition now made sense. 'He's not coming back.'

There was no sympathy in Brea's eyes. 'He would

have had to come here in order to bring the loom to you, but I'm thinking it's why he allowed Blaise to go with him. Instead of Kerrigan bringing you the loom, Blaise will.'

Seren grabbed his arm as her rage mounted at her own foolishness. Damn Kerrigan for this! 'Take me to him. Now!'

Brea pried her hand from his arm. 'I can't. I promised Kerrigan that I would bring you here, and I have to stand by my word.'

She turned toward Merlin. 'Can you send me to him?'

Unlike Brea, Merlin's blue eyes were dark with sympathy. It was obvious the woman felt compassion for her. 'I'm afraid I can't, Seren. I'm sorry. I don't know where he is. Kerrigan is too powerful for me to track.'

Seren closed her eyes as a wave of hopeless despair claimed her. And in that moment, she hated Kerrigan. How could he just abandon her like this? Abandon their child?

He hadn't even tried to join her. He'd merely handed her off to the Celtic god and left her to her own end.

Stung by his actions, she took the sword in both of her hands. She could feel the hum of its power. Feel it cooing to her. But for once she was in control of it.

Because I have Kerrigan's blood . . .

It had to be. There was no other reason that the sword was so calm to her now.

'I can't believe he relinquished it,' Merlin said in a low, reverent tone to Brea.

'I can.' Seren knew a part of Kerrigan that no one else did. It was a part he never showed to the world.

It was the part of him that she loved. Nay, that

wasn't true. She loved all of him. Even that nasty, grousing part that growled.

And somehow, she was going to find him again . . . and then she was going to kill him.

Kerrigan drew a deep breath as they finished off the Adoni and dissolved the RV from the side of the road.

'The traveling had been a good thought,' Blaise said as he folded his arms over his chest.

Kerrigan felt his jaw tic from his anger. 'While it lasted. Damn Morgen and her persistence.' That bitch would never leave him in peace. Not while Seren held so much power within her.

'So how are you going to get Seren back?'

Kerrigan didn't answer.

Blaise narrowed his violet eyes on him. 'You are going to get her back . . . Right?'

He made sure to keep his features blank. 'She's better off in Avalon.'

'Yeah, but what about gaining control of the Table? You can't do that without her.'

'What do I need with a table? I can't even eat.'

Blaise looked even more confused. 'What? Did the Adoni knock something loose in your head when they hit you? You know? World domination. Power. Wealth. Hello? Who are you and what have you done with my master?'

Before Kerrigan could answer, four more Adoni came through the portal.

'Oh, lay off, you bitch,' Kerrigan snarled as he caught the first Adoni with an elbow to his nose. He was getting really tired of this fight.

Another caught him about the stomach and threw him to the ground. Kerrigan grunted in pain as the weight of the beast damned near crushed him. He could feel his ribs starting to break. Bending his leg, he kicked the Adoni off and let out a relieved bellow once the weight was free of him.

Blaise was fighting another.

Kerrigan unsheathed his sword and engaged the Adoni. He caught one through the shoulder, but as he was pulling back, the other sliced his arm.

He turned with a hiss to drive his sword through his attacker, before he spun about to finish off the other.

Seeing the blood that coated him, the last two Adoni vanished instantly.

Blaise cocked his head. 'Why did they ...' His voice trailed off as he saw the bleeding wound on his arm. 'I wasn't imagining that earlier, was I? You *are* bleeding.'

Kerrigan let out a long, tired breath. There was no need to corroborate the obvious. 'We need to get out of here before they return with more. I'm sure they're reporting to Morgen even now that I was wounded.'

Blaise stared at him in disbelief. 'Are you insane? Do you know what would happen to you if Morgen caught you now?'

'Believe me, I know.' It was the stuff of nightmares and children's stories.

Blaise held his arm out to him. 'We need to go get that loom before they find it.'

Nodding, Kerrigan did something he'd never done before. He reached out and took Blaise's outstretched arm so that he could use his magic and return them to Seren's time.

They flashed into an empty alleyway behind her weaver's shop. Kerrigan took a moment to return his armor to a fashion more suited to this time period so as not to raise any suspicions. Likewise Blaise adjusted his clothing to a pair of brown breeches and a dark blue surcoat.

They didn't speak as they made their way around to the front of the store. Kerrigan paused as he saw a young boy rush past him, into the building to squeal at the women who were working, before he bounded up a wooden staircase to disappear.

Robert. He remembered Seren telling him about the boy who belonged to the store's owners. And she had liked the lad a great deal.

Strange emotions curled through him as he opened the door and entered with Blaise one step behind him.

The store was rather small. There were four women off to his left who were working quietly on their looms. Even from this distance, he would see how worn their hands were ... just like Seren's. His gaze lingered beside an attractive brunette where there was an obvious vacant loom before the window.

Seren's place. That was where she'd spent so many years, working for the owners of this shop. That was the window where she would watch people drift by outside as her entire life was spent slaving away for others.

But for Damé Fortune, she'd still be here now, just like her friends. There was even the half-finished cloth she must have been working on before he'd taken her.

'May I help you, my lord?'

He turned at the sound of an older woman's voice to find the shopkeeper's wife. 'Mistress Maude?'

She looked surprised that he knew her name. 'Aye, my lord? Do I know you?'

'Nay, goodwife. I've come here to collect an old loom that belongs to Seren of York.'

The old woman's eyes flared angrily at the name. 'There's nothing here that belonged to that bit of rub—'

Her words were choked off as Kerrigan took her by the throat and squeezed tight. His rage took hold, but he made sure to keep his eyes dark and not let them flicker red. 'Careful who you insult, old woman. Her name is Seren and you will not defame that name. Understand me?'

Gasping for air, she nodded her head.

Kerrigan released her.

'So much for my thinking you'd changed,' Blaise said under his breath in twentieth-century English so that the woman couldn't understand him.

Kerrigan didn't respond to Blaise while he glared at the woman who was rubbing her bruised throat. 'I want Seren's possessions and I want them now.'

Still coughing, the woman stumbled against the apprentice who was closest to her. When she spoke, her voice was thick and deep. 'Get up, you lazy cur, and get His Lordship whatever he wants.'

The girl nodded before she quickly got up to do her mistress's bidding.

Kerrigan followed up the stairs after her. She led him to an attic room that was at the far end of the shop.

He hesitated as he saw the meager furnishings that made up their dormitory. Each girl had been relegated to a small pallet with a thin, paltry mattress that sat on the floor. Each bed had one small, flat pillow and one threadbare blanket. To the right of each pallet was a plain trunk. There was nothing warm here. Nothing welcoming. It was no better than the bleak atmosphere of Camelot.

Yet this was where his little mouse had dreamed of her modest merchant who would one day claim her ...

Anger welled up inside him.

'Who are you, girl?'

She paused before one of the pallets to look up, then she caught herself before she met his gaze. Her eyes fell back to the floor. 'Wendlyn, my lord.'

'Wendlyn,' he said, softening his voice as he recalled her from Seren's memories. 'You two are friends.'

She nodded as she opened the lid to the ark that was nearest the window. 'All of Seren's belongings are in here, my lord.'

Kerrigan had to duck to enter the room. He didn't speak as he approached the trunk that held almost nothing. There was a modest cloak for the colder weather. A pair of patched hose, an old kirtle, and a ragged white chemise. He moved them aside to find a single pair of leather shoes that had a hole in the bottom of each sole.

Pain hit him hard as he realized that this was all his little mouse had in the world. And she'd been so proud of it. After all, she'd had potential . . .

His heart heavy, he gathered up each item until he found her small loom resting in the bottom, wrapped in a piece of brown cloth. It looked as worthless as the rest of her belongings. Yet it was priceless to him. If not for this loom, he would never have known that Seren existed.

As he pulled it out, a small pendant fell free from the brown cloth it was wrapped in. Kerrigan frowned at the sight. He reached into the chest to find the heraldic dragon of Avalon. The symbol of Arthur. He knew instantly that it must have belonged to her mother.

'Why is this in here?'

The girl glanced at the pendant, then looked away. 'We are peasants, my lord. The necklace belonged to Seren's mother. Had Mistress Maude known about it, she would have taken it from her and sold it for her upkeep, so Seren kept it hidden. She would take it out sometimes at night and pray for her mother, then she would hide it away again.'

He could just imagine her doing that. His hand shaking from his raw emotions, he ran his fingers over the trunk's lid and imagined Seren opening it up every day and carefully closing it. He felt connected to her.

But she was his past now . . .

Taking a deep breath, he gathered up everything and rose. As he started away, the girl's voice stopped him.

'My lord?'

'Aye?' He looked back to find her staring at the floor, her brow knitted by worry.

'Might I ask after Seren? Is she . . . is she well?'

Her concern for his mouse warmed him. 'Aye, Wendlyn. She's hale and healthy, and in a much better place than this one.'

He saw the relief on her face. 'Would you please tell her that I asked after her, my lord? And let her know that I wish her well?'

'I will indeed.'

'Thank you.'

He inclined his head before he left the room and found Blaise waiting for him on the stairs.

'Are you all right?'

Kerrigan glared at him. 'Do I not look all right?'

'Nay. You look strange.'

He grimaced as he brushed past the mandrake. It wasn't until after they had left the building that Kerrigan stopped. He lifted the sleeve of her kirtle to his face so that he could inhale the scent of Seren mixed with the cedar of the box.

He missed her already.

Oh how he wished that things were different. That

he was different. But wishing was good for naught. This was the way of it.

His resolve set, he handed the bundle off to Blaise. As he did so a small copper thimble fell free of the cloth. Kerrigan bent down to retrieve it.

How paltry it was. How worthless.

But it was Seren's.

'You're not planning to go to Avalon, are you?' Blaise asked.

'Nay,' he said as he clutched the tiny thimble in his hand. 'We both know that the Lords of Avalon would never allow me to their shores. Not that I blame them. We've been at war far too long for them to welcome or tolerate me. I made my choice centuries ago. I'm man enough to live with it.'

Blaise arched a brow. 'Honestly, I don't want to go there, either. You know how I feel about good guys. They're boring.'

Kerrigan gave a short laugh at his words. 'Morgen will kill you if you stay with me. Besides, Seren will be lonely and afraid at Avalon. She needs a friend.'

'She would rather have you.'

Kerrigan handed both of Seren's necklaces to the mandrake. As he started to hand over the thimble, he paused.

It was a part of her he couldn't let go. Closing his fist over it, he lowered his hand.

Blaise gave him a hard stare. 'Do you have anything you wish me to tell her for you?'

'Just convey Wendlyn's words to her.'

'But none from you?'

Kerrigan shook his head. 'Words are ever deceitful. There's nothing more to be said between us.'

By the expression on Blaise's face, he could tell the mandrake wanted to argue, but he didn't. 'You know that when I leave here, you're stranded in this time.'

'Nay, I still have *my* Merlin's magic to sustain me.' With that he could still evade them.

'But nothing else.'

Not true. He had a copper thimble and the memory of a fair-haired lady who'd given him the only sense of peace he'd ever known.

It was more than he'd ever had before.

'I shall battle onward. 'Tis what I excel at.'

Blaise let out a long, weary breath. 'It's been an honor to be with you all these centuries, Kerrigan. I've always considered you a friend.'

'I know. It's why I never killed you for your insubordination.'

Blaise laughed.

'But,' Kerrigan said, interrupting his amusement. 'I would ask one thing of you.'

'And that is?'

'Find someone to marry Seren before she shows her pregnancy. Her worst fear is to have the baby bastard born.'

'If she's unwilling?'

'She won't be. She knows that the child needs a father to claim it.' But inside he was aching at the thought of that father being someone other than he.

She was his . . .

He clenched his teeth as the pain of it overwhelmed him. Damn it, no wonder he'd always profaned altruism. What good was it? All it did was hurt.

Yet for her, he was willing to suffer, and that was the most amazing part of all.

'I'll find her a husband.'

'Thank you.'

Blaise inclined his head to him. 'God speed you, Kerrigan.'

He snorted at that. 'God speed you, my friend. He was never with the likes of me.'

And then he watched as the mandrake faded out of this existence, to manifest himself on the shores of Avalon.

Kerrigan tightened his grip around the thimble as he imagined the look of hurt on Seren's precious face when Blaise appeared without him.

But what was done, was done. It was for the best.

Shaking his head, he listened to his internal voice scream at him that he was an idiot. He had traded his kingship so that Seren could live as a queen. And for what?

'For the woman I love,' he whispered. The truth seared him. He wasn't sure how she'd managed to wiggle into his diseased heart, but she had.

He had given her his worst and she had brought out a best in him that he'd never even known he possessed.

Now it was time to finish this. Even without the sword or Seren's necklace, his magic was enough that he could still time-travel to escape Morgen's army, but to what purpose?

He'd never once in his life been craven and he wasn't about to start now. There was only one way to make sure that none of his kind ever hunted Seren again.

'Morgen!' he shouted in the alleyway. 'If you want me, I'm here.'

Within a few seconds, four Adoni appeared. They flashed into the alley, then looked about nervously as if expecting a trap.

Kerrigan sneered at them and their fear. 'Oh, what's this, Morgen? When have you ever been a coward? Face me.'

Morgen appeared between the Adoni. Her arms

folded, she narrowed her gaze on him. 'Where is she?'

He kept his face completely blank. 'She's gone.'

'Gone where?'

'Avalon.'

She gaped before her face was contorted by her anger. 'Have you gone mad? Why would you let her go?'

He shrugged with a nonchalance he didn't feel. 'It's where she belongs.'

Morgen shrieked in outrage. 'Have you completely lost all reason? Why would you do such a thing?'

He offered her a taunting grin. 'I did it just to piss you off. Your face always turns such a becoming shade of red whenever you lose your temper.'

Hissing, she closed the distance between them. And as she drew nearer, he could see the moment she realized that he no longer had Caliburn.

The rage melted under a wave of disbelief. She raised her hand up as if she were sensing the air around him.

A slow, evil smile curled her lips. 'I may have lost my temper and my pawn, but you, dear boy . . . you're going to lose more than that. A *lot* more.'

Chapter Fifteen

Seren had to give Merlin credit; the woman certainly made her feel at home. She was brought into the castle and set up in a room that made the one she'd had in Joyous Gard seem like a hovel.

But no sooner had she stepped into her room than something strange happened to her. Everything began to spin. One minute she was on her feet listening to Merlin, and the next she was kneeling on the floor as an awful pain ripped through her.

It felt as if she were being torn asunder.

'Seren?'

She could hear Merlin, but she couldn't respond as she knelt on all fours, trying to fight off whatever held her in its grip. It was as if something volcanic was building up inside her, getting ready to erupt.

Suddenly, things were flying around the room, breaking, tumbling.

The entire world was out of control.

And then she felt . . . something even more foreign. It slithered through her body like poison, moving slowly, methodically.

It was Kerrigan's magic. That dark and frightening part of him that lacked all humanity. She could feel his

Merlin's powers taking root inside her, and with them came archaic knowledge. They were all-consuming and so incredibly painful.

Merlin backed up as she saw Seren open her eyes. No longer green, they were a frightening shade of yellow with streaks of red in them.

'Seren?'

'Do you fear me?' It wasn't Seren's gentle voice she heard, but rather a deep, demonic one.

'Nay.' But Merlin knew it for a lie. She was afraid of this. She could feel the evil that radiated from Seren. She didn't know what held possession of the woman, but it wasn't benevolent or kind.

And then a new maelstrom rushed through the room. It was blinding as cold winds whipped her around. Paintings and tapestries were torn from the walls as objects crashed to the floor. Objects flew at her so furiously that she couldn't even identify them.

Merlin tried to duck as best she could, but it wasn't enough. Things slammed into her body with a stinging resolve. Her hair streamed around her, snapping in the wind as her dress was plastered against her body. 'Seren!'

Demonic laughter answered her.

Merlin saw another flash by her side an instant before something rushed across the room to wrap itself around Seren.

Two seconds later, the winds stopped.

Merlin touched her hand to the place on her forehead that was throbbing most to find a cut there. She wiped away the blood as she realized what the flash had been.

It was Blaise who was now holding Seren as a mother might hold a screaming child.

'Seren,' the mandrake cooed to her. 'Let it go.'

Seren screamed out madly. 'I want the power. It nourishes me.'

'But it could kill your baby.'

The winds picked up for a heartbeat, only to settle down once more as those words reached Seren.

Merlin felt a jolt go through her as the power in the room evaporated.

Still Blaise held Seren to him, rocking her gently in his arms. 'It's Kerrigan's power to wield, Seren, not yours. He only gave it to you because he thought he'd be around to help you control it so that you could fight Morgen's army. You no longer need it. Now let it go.'

Seren clung to him as if he were her lifeline. 'Where is Kerrigan? You were supposed to bring him here.'

Merlin's heart clenched at the pain she heard in Seren's tone.

'I left him in London.'

Anger descended on her pale face before Seren shoved at Blaise's chest. 'Let go of me. You promised you'd bring him here.'

'I know, Seren. I know.'

Merlin crossed the room to kneel on the floor beside them. How she wished she could soothe Seren's pain, but she knew Seren was past that. 'It's for the best, Seren. Kerrigan doesn't belong here.'

Her eyes flashed back to yellow. 'Then neither do I.'

'Yes, you do.'

Seren paused as she heard another voice. This one wasn't Merlin's and it wasn't Blaise's.

More than that, it wasn't coming from outside her body. She could hear it only inside her head.

'Kerrigan?' she barely whispered his name.

'Aye, little mouse. I'm here with you. And I need you to do as Merlin says. Let her care for you and the baby.' The deep cadence of his voice was music to her, but it wasn't enough.

Closing her eyes, she used her thoughts to talk to him. *I would rather you were here.*

'I know. But trust me, this is for the best. You're safe there.'

What of you?

'I'm fine, little mouse. I've escaped Morgen's clutches and am forced to travel to keep her from finding me or you. There's no need to worry over me. You do as Merlin tells you, and I will be here whenever you need me.'

Where are you?

'I'm . . . I'm where I can be with you. But not at the moment. I need to go for a bit.'

She felt him pulling away from her.

'Kerrigan!' she cried, trying to pull away from Blaise.

But it was too late. He was gone.

She looked up at Blaise, who was still holding her. 'What is wrong with me? Why can't I control anything?'

It was Merlin who answered. 'Your body is trying to acclimate itself to the evil that Kerrigan gave you. I can bring you a purge that will remove his powers from you.'

'Nay,' she said, interrupting her. 'I don't want a purge. I want to keep Kerrigan within me.'

Merlin looked skeptical, but didn't argue.

As Blaise released her, Seren's gaze fell to her belongings, which were on the floor beside him. She'd never thought to see any of it again, and even though it was a worthless bunch of objects, those few things meant the world to her.

Picking up her loom, she held it to her as gratitude overwhelmed her.

She almost felt whole again as Blaise passed along Wendlyn's words.

How she wished she could see her friends again, but Morgen would never allow that, and she knew it. If she went to them, Morgen would find her.

Blaise hesitated before he held his hand out to her.

Seren frowned as he placed something cold in her palm. She opened her hand to see her mother's two necklaces. One brought relief to her, but the other . . .

It infuriated her.

'Kerrigan has no way to come here.'

Blaise shook his head. 'He wanted to make sure the doorway was closed. For your safety.'

'For *my* safety?'

'Aye, Seren. What he did, he did for you.'

Still it didn't make sense to her. 'But why? Why won't he come?'

'The Kerrigan is our enemy,' Merlin said quietly. 'And he knows this. The men who have fought him all these centuries past would never welcome him here.'

Stunned, she indicated Blaise with her hand. 'Is he not an enemy as well? He's Kerrigan's servant.'

Merlin's next words stunned her most of all. 'Blaise has been a friend of ours for many centuries, Seren. He's no enemy of Avalon.'

'What?'

Blaise nodded. 'I was taken in as a child by Emrys Penmerlin. I was there when Camelot fell to Morgen, and she captured me to be her servant as punishment after Emrys vanished. I was given to Kerrigan, but I've been in touch with Merlin many times over the years.'

'You spied for them?'

'Aye.'

Seren shook her head in disgust. 'You know the truth of Kerrigan. Tell her that he isn't evil. He belongs here, too.'

Blaise looked away.

Even angrier than before, she met Merlin's gaze. 'Is it the will of the Merlin that a man who sacrifices so much for the well-being of another person should be denied entrance to this place?'

Merlin sighed. 'There is much in our past that you don't know about or understand. Kerrigan—'

'I don't want to hear one word against him,' she snarled between clenched teeth.

Glancing down, Seren saw the medallion her mother had given her in her dream. Aye, with this she could go to Kerrigan. She didn't have to stay here.

That thought had barely completed itself before Blaise snatched the medallion from her hand. 'You can't leave Avalon, Seren. Ever.'

'Fetch me more wine, slave.'

Kerrigan hissed as he felt the bite of Morgen's whip against his back. He tried to send a sorcerer's ball at her, but she easily deflected it and sent another one straight into his chest. The blast of it knocked him off his feet and sent him skittering across the stone floor.

He tried to rise, but couldn't. His body ached too much. The pain of her abuse tore through him like shattered glass.

Morgen crossed the room to kick him over, onto his back. She glared down at him with open hatred. 'Poor worm. Look at you. Yesterday you were the Kerrigan, king of Camelot. Now you're nothing but a nameless slave. Worthless. Disgusting. And for what? For a peasant who cares nothing for you.' Curling her lip, she kicked him again and again.

Kerrigan couldn't even move. Without the magic of Caliburn to back him, his Merlin's magic was no match for Morgen's.

'Mistress?'

Morgen paused to look at a female Adoni who was in the doorway. 'What?'

'They are fighting in the hall over who is to be the next king.'

Morgen made a sound of disgust in the back of her throat. 'You,' she snarled at Kerrigan before she kicked him again, 'stay here.'

She stalked from the room.

Kerrigan lay there for several heartbeats as he struggled to breathe. Knowing he had to get off the floor, he drew a deep breath and tried to push himself up. The best he could manage was to sit up as a wave of pain assailed him.

'Here.'

He looked to find Brevalaer, naked as always, beside him, holding out a cup of water.

'What are you doing?' he growled at Morgen's Adoni lover.

There was no pity in Brevalaer's eyes, only sincere sympathy. 'You need it.'

Those words only made him suspicious. 'Why are *you* helping me?'

Brevalaer set the cup down beside him. 'Drink it or don't. You're not my concern.'

He watched as the Adoni courtesan backed away.

His bruised hand shaking, Kerrigan took the cup and greedily drank from it. Nothing had ever tasted better than that fresh water. Nothing . . .

Other than Seren's lips.

He forced that thought away.

Brevalaer took a seat on one of Morgen's red-cushioned chairs, then watched as Kerrigan drank. 'You played right into Morgen's hands, you know?'

'How so?' Kerrigan asked before he took another deep gulp of water.

'All she wanted was for you to take that chit to your bed and impregnate her. She even had Magda trying to convince the girl to seduce you from the beginning. You should never have touched the peasant.'

Growling, Kerrigan threw the empty cup at him, which Brevalaer easily ducked. 'That's no concern of yours.'

'You're right,' he said in a low tone. 'It's not. But I do have one question for you.'

Kerrigan rose to stand, but his legs were such that he half expected to fall again. He remained on his feet by nothing more than his sheer will not to fall. 'And that is?'

'Was it worth it?'

He frowned at Brevalaer's odd tone. It was as if the man needed to hear the answer to a question he didn't understand. 'Was what worth it?'

'The woman. Would you do this again for her?'

Kerrigan narrowed his eyes on Morgen's favorite toy. Born into the Adoni courtesan caste, Brevalaer had been trained from puberty to please others and to take nothing for himself.

Until now Kerrigan had never held any respect for the Adoni courtesan. But now . . . now he understood. The concept of love was as foreign to Brevalaer as it had been to him, and the Adoni was trying to comprehend why Kerrigan had done what he had.

'Aye. She's worth all this and more.'

Instead of seeing disdain, he saw respect in Brevalaer's eyes. 'I still say you were a fool to trade what you had for this existence.'

Kerrigan gave a weak half laugh. 'Believe me, I couldn't agree more.'

Days went by as Seren learned her new powers. With

Merlin's help and with Kerrigan's shared blood, she was able to master them in little time.

But because of Kerrigan's blood and because of the baby she carried, she had to be careful. The demon inside her had a nasty tendency to want out. It was a cruel beast who wanted to lash out and hurt anyone who came near her, even Merlin and Blaise. Living with that internal beast was hard, and as she grappled with that side of herself, it made her truly appreciate every kindness Kerrigan had shown her. Kindness was definitely not in his nature.

Day by day, she was slowly coming to terms with her inner demon.

What she couldn't come to terms with was the endless parade of the Lords of Avalon who kept offering for her hand so that her child would not be bastard born. They were handsome, to be sure. And as Kerrigan had predicted, they treated her with utmost kindness and deference.

They treated her like a queen.

But they weren't what she wanted. She no longer dreamed of a gentle-spoken man who sat quietly by her side. She dreamed of a dark, surly beast who groused and snapped.

'Kerrigan?' she whispered as she sat alone in her room, working on a small tapestry that she'd begun the night before when sleep had eluded her.

No answer came.

Seren held her breath. Any time she called for him and he failed to answer, the worst scenarios would play through her mind. The thought that he was lying injured somewhere, unable to get help. Or worse, the fear that Morgen had found him and killed him.

'Kerrigan?' she tried again.

'Aye, Lady Mouse. I am here.'

Relieved, she smiled at the sound of his voice in her head. During the day, he was oft silent. But at night ... at night he would speak softly to her and tell her of his travels through time as he eluded those who were after him.

'Where are you today, my lord?'

'I'm in Venice, during a carnival. It's beautiful here. There are minstrels and acrobats all around. Plenty of places to hide from Morgen and her spies.'

'You are safe?'

'Aye, Lady Mouse. I am always safe. But I've no wish to talk about me. How are *you* doing?'

'I miss you.'

She swore she could feel his pain as well as her own.

'I miss you as well and I think of you constantly.'

Seren moved toward his sword, which she kept on the wall beside her bed. She didn't know why, but she had yet to tell him that Brea had given it to her. In truth, she liked to keep it close by. It made her feel somehow closer to him.

She stroked the cool metal, wishing it were Kerrigan she touched.

'How is your tapestry coming?'

'Very well,' she said, her voice breaking. 'But I—'

'Shh ... I must go now. God keep you, my lady.'

A tear slid down her cheek as she felt him pulling away from her again. As always his absence tore through her. She hated to feel this emptiness. Hated to miss him so very much.

Perhaps Kerrigan and Blaise were right. The kindest thing would be to marry one of the others, but she couldn't quite make herself do it. She didn't want another man.

She wanted only one.

Sighing, she moved away from the sword to leave

her room so that she could wander through the hallways outside. The castle was enormous, filled with all sorts of marvels and delights.

None of them pleased her.

She was restless. Most of all, she was lonely even though she was seldom ever alone here.

Sighing, she paused in the gallery room where paintings of kings, knights, Merlins, and battles lined the room from floor to ceiling. There was one in particular that always seemed to draw her attention. It was the painting of her ancestor Emrys.

The painting itself was over ten feet tall and five feet wide. It hung in the center of the wall that was across from the conservatory where all manner of flowers bloomed amid the greenery.

The figure of Emrys was as commanding as it was eerie. He was a lot younger than she would have thought given the stories she'd heard of him. He didn't appear any older than his early thirties, even though his long hair was as white as Blaise's.

Standing near the edge of a dark cliff at night, he was dressed in a black robe and held a staff that had been fashioned to look like a snake, the eyes of which were encrusted with dark rubies that made them a sinister red. A deep glow radiated from them.

His eyes, like hers, were green and seemed to stare out from the painting as if he could see her. She reached to touch the heavy brush strokes that stood out from the canvas like waves from the ocean. The paint was as cold as her heart, but even so she felt an inner connection to the scene.

'He's lying to you, you know.'

She turned at the sound of a deep, gravelly voice behind her to find a tall, handsome man standing in the doorway that led to the hall. He appeared around the age of two score, and yet he was as lean and well muscled as a man half his age.

His wavy, dark brown hair brushed his shoulders, framing a face that was sharp and refined even with several days' worth of whiskers covering his cheeks. He was dressed as an archer in a dark green leather jerkin and breeches. His longbow was draped around him and leaned in the opposite direction from his quiver of arrows.

He had a sword strapped to his right hip as he leaned nonchalantly against the far wall with his arms crossed over his chest. Even from her distance, she could see a small lady's ring he wore about his neck on a thin gold chain.

Even though he was dressed as a peasant, there was something regal about him. Indeed, he was rife with an air of power and wisdom.

She lowered her hand from the painting. 'I beg your pardon, sir? Were you speaking to me?'

He nodded. 'My name is Faran, my lady.'

'Are you one of the Lords of Avalon?'

'Nay,' he said with a small twist to his mouth. 'I'm not worthy to be included in their esteemed company. I'm merely a friend to the Merlin and to you.'

'To me, sir? But I don't know you.'

He gave her a gentle smile. 'Sometimes the best friends to have are the ones you don't know about. They are the ones who help you without asking for anything in return.'

What an odd man.

He pushed himself away from the wall to move closer to her. 'I have to admit, Kerrigan has surprised me. I would never have thought him capable of such a sacrifice.'

'What sacrifice?'

272

Faran paused before her. His hazel eyes were troubled as he stroked the whiskers on his chin. 'To ensure your safety, he has enslaved himself to Morgen. He's so worried about you that he thinks Morgen won't kill him. Poor bastard. He's deluding himself as much as he's deluding you.'

Terror gripped her at his words. Was he serious? 'Kerrigan told me that he's safe. Morgen hasn't found him.'

'And he's a self-professed liar, Seren. He would tell you anything to keep you happy here in Avalon.'

'I don't believe you.'

'Then that's a pity. Because I know Morgen, and knowing her, I can guarantee you that his time is very limited. She has no more use for him now that Caliburn is safe inside the walls of this castle. Once she grows bored with torturing Kerrigan, she will kill him.'

Seren's head whirled at his prediction. 'Kerrigan.'

'He won't tell you the truth, Seren.'

'Kerrigan!'

He didn't answer.

'Why are you telling me this?' she asked Faran, her voice shaking from the weight of her fear that he was right and her anger at herself for allowing Kerrigan to deceive her.

'Because I've seen too many good men fall to Morgen. Not that Kerrigan is particularly good, but I would hate to see him die after he'd sacrificed so much to keep you here. Surely a man who is capable of this kind of nobility has something worth redeeming inside him.'

'Aye,' she breathed. But even as she said that, she still wasn't so sure that this wasn't a trap. For all she knew, Faran could be working for Morgen. He'd said that he knew her. It would stand to reason.

Leaving him in the gallery, she headed for the refectory. There were several knights there, but no sight of Blaise.

Seren closed her eyes and used her newfound magic to focus on the mandrake. He was outside in the garden, kissing one of the maids who worked in the hall. She knew she should leave him alone, but the demon in her refused.

Instead, it manifested itself beside the embracing couple, who had no idea she'd just appeared next to them. Seren rudely cleared her throat.

Frowning, Blaise pulled back. The woman he was holding blushed profusely.

'Can I help you?' Blaise asked in an irritated tone.

'Aye. Let go your maid and come with me.'

He arched a brow at her words. 'You know, there for a moment, you sounded so much like Kerrigan that it actually gave me a chill.'

'And if you don't do as I say, I'm going to give you a lot more than that.'

He released the woman immediately. The maid scurried off toward the castle as quickly as she could. 'What has gotten into you?'

'Anger. Fear,' Seren snapped. 'Take your pick. I've been told that Kerrigan is at Camelot and that he is suffering because of me. I need to know if it's true. When you left him, what exactly did he say to you?'

Blaise shrugged. 'He told me that he intended to battle onward.'

'How so?'

'He didn't say. I told him that he would be stuck in your time period and—'

'What?' she asked, growing cold at those words. She could feel the blood draining from her face.

'I told him he'd be stuck in your time period without the medallion to amplify his powers.'

Seren took his arm in her hand as her fear mounted. Inside, she was praying that Blaise was mistaken. 'Are you sure about that? He's been telling me that he was traveling all through time and all over the world.'

Blaise scowled at her. 'Telling you how?'

'In my thoughts. I can hear him. At least some of the time.'

Blaise's frown increased. 'He talks to you?'

'Aye.' Seren tightened her grip on his arm. 'Are you sure he would be marooned?'

'Without the medallion, aye. At least for the most part. He would have the ability to jump once or twice in a month or so, but not frequently.'

Seren actually cursed as she realized the Faran had been telling her the truth. Kerrigan was in danger.

'Damn you, Kerrigan,' she said under her breath. 'I'm not a child to be told bedtime stories while you do something so imbecilic.'

The demon in her snapped and told her to leave him in the hole he'd dug for himself.

But lucky for him, there was enough of the woman who loved him inside her that she couldn't do that.

She grabbed Blaise's hand and hauled him back toward the castle.

'What are you doing, Seren?'

'We're going to see Merlin about a rescue.'

Chapter Sixteen

Kerrigan lay on his pallet made of sharp rocks, staring up at the black ceiling. His entire body ached and burned as if it were on fire. Morgen had been beating him for days now. He could no longer even recall a time when his body hadn't hurt. And he would give anything to have one day without Morgen's relentless humiliation and torture.

But through the misery came an image of a tender face. Closing his eyes, he conjured the memory of Seren in his arms. The softness of her hand against his flesh. The smell of her hair . . .

Even now it was soothing.

'Kerrigan.'

Even though it hurt, he smiled at the sound of her voice. 'Aye, Lady Mouse?'

Suddenly, he felt the presence of someone beside him. He opened his eyes, expecting it to be Morgen. Instead he saw the plain, yet beautiful face of his little mouse. Happiness burned through him with such force that it brought tears to his eyes.

His bloodied and bruised hand trembling, he reached to touch the velvet softness of her cheek.

But there was no warmth there. It was cold, and in

that moment he knew.

'Morgen,' he snarled, dropping his hand away.

She laughed evilly at him. 'You didn't really think that your whore would come for you, did you?'

'She's not a whore.' But even as he moved against Morgen, she threw him back to the floor. She put her foot to his throat and pressed the whole of her weight against it.

Kerrigan gasped as his throat closed, choking off all the air from his lungs. He tried to push her foot away, but she kept it there, biting into his throat even more.

'You pathetic oaf. I can't believe I ever took something as worthless as you into my bed. I thought you had more strength than this. But no matter.' She stepped back. 'Maddor,' she called, summoning the mandrake leader to her.

Kerrigan coughed as he drew ragged, wheezing breaths through his bruised esophagus.

Maddor appeared instantly. With long dark hair and equally dark eyes, he was dressed in a black tunic and breeches. 'Aye, my queen?'

'Drag this wretch to the hall. I have something fun planned for him.'

Maddor inclined his head to Morgen before he reached for Kerrigan and pulled him up from the floor by his hair.

Kerrigan shoved the mandrake back, only to have him backhand him so hard that the blow loosened several teeth. Spitting his blood out on the floor, he glared at the beast.

Maddor seized him again and this time managed to subdue him. Kerrigan snarled as he was unceremoniously dragged from Morgen's chambers into the crowded hall where Morgen's court was busy with yet another orgy.

As he was kicked to the floor, Morgen appeared in the center of the hall, where a light shone on her, highlighting her red gown and fair skin. She stood with her hands on her hips and a nasty smirk on her deceptively angelic face.

'Good Adoni, mandrakes, and knights of my table,' she called, gaining the notice of the revelers who stopped their hedonism to give their queen their undivided attention. ' 'Tis time to crown the next king of Camelot. Tell me, who among you has the courage to battle Kerrigan now?'

Kerrigan sucked his breath in sharply as virtually every male there stepped forward. The taste of defeat choked him. There was no way in his current condition that he could win a sword fight with even a maid, never mind a man full-grown.

Morgen laughed at her soldiers. 'Good. For once there are many takers.' She looked at Kerrigan and smiled. 'The king will soon be dead. Long live the new one.'

Merlin's heart ached in sympathy as she faced Seren in her hall. She looked past the young woman to see Blaise, whose face showed his own sadness that there was nothing to be done for Kerrigan. 'I can't go after him, Seren.'

'Why not?'

'Because I am the Penmerlin. If I voluntarily enter Camelot, Morgen will have the power to destroy the entire world. It's the same reason why your child cannot be born there, and why once your child is born, we must make certain that she never ventures to Camelot.'

Instead of deterring her, that only seemed to strengthen Seren's resolve. 'Then give me some of your knights. We can—'

'Can do what?' Merlin asked in an exasperated tone. 'Storm the castle? Fight a thousand knights, demons, dragons, minions, and gargoyles? Morgen would kill all of them and take you prisoner until the baby is born, and then she'll kill you, too.'

'We could all sneak into—'

'Nay, you can't,' Merlin said, her voice filled with sympathy. 'If any more than four magical beings travel through the portal together, it'll alert her instantly to your presence. And she will be able to draw her army straight to you to fight. Why do you think Kerrigan took you into the future to begin with? He knew that Morgen would be limited to how many could open the portal at a time and step through it to fight. Not to mention, the future negates the dragons and gargoyles, who tend to set off military alarms.'

Seren raked her hands through her hair. Her frustration reached out to Merlin, but there really was nothing she could do to help either of them.

Her eyes burned as she met Merlin's gaze. 'Then what would you have me do?'

If Merlin had her way, she would save Kerrigan. However, that wasn't an option. 'Do as Kerrigan wanted. Stay here, marry one of our knights, and raise your child.'

Seren's eyes flashed bloodred. But it lasted only a heartbeat before they returned to green.

Before her eyes, Seren seemed to calm down and come to terms with her decision. 'Fine then. If that's they way it's to be ...'

'It is,' Merlin said sternly.

She watched as Seren turned her back and left with Blaise in tow, but even as the woman walked from the hall, Merlin knew that Seren hadn't given up.

'She's going to try and rescue him alone.'

Merlin glanced over to Elaine, who was standing just inside the back doorway in the shadows. Elaine's red hair was pulled back into a severe braid. True to form, she wore the armor of a knight, but instead of carrying a sword, Elaine carried a small bow.

'I know.'

Elaine stepped forward into the room. 'Are you not going to stop her?'

'I can't stop her,' Merlin said as she walked over to the table where she'd left her cup of wine after Seren had barged into the room. 'She has the power of two Merlins and the resolve of a woman who wants only to protect what she loves.'

Elaine scowled. 'If Morgen captures her—'

'Nothing in life comes without risk.'

Elaine's eyes snapped with inner fire. 'This is more than a risk. She gambles with the entire fate of us all.'

'Relax, Elaine. She might very well succeed. After all, Seren has already done the impossible. She's done what even I couldn't do.'

'And that is?'

Merlin smiled at the older woman. 'She's returned Caliburn to us. More than that, she's turned Kerrigan away from the blackness that has consumed him for all these centuries.'

Elaine sneered. 'It was his choice that he serve Morgen.'

Merlin swirled the wine in her golden cup. What Elaine didn't know was that she could see the future in the dark liquid. She saw it plainly. 'Yes and no. I made a mistake when I sent you and Galahad to him after he found the sword and activated it. I was young then. Too young perhaps to understand that I chose poorly.'

She looked up to meet Elaine's angry glare. 'Given the way his choices were presented to him, I can't really fault Kerrigan for his decision. I would have chosen Morgen myself.'

Elaine huffed at that. 'You're making excuses for him.'

'Perhaps. But if you're so concerned that I'm making a mistake now, then go with her.'

Elaine narrowed her eyes as she took the cup from Merlin's hand and returned it to the table. 'I will. But I'm only going for one reason.'

'And that is?'

'If Morgen goes to capture her, I'm going to kill Seren myself.'

While Blaise stood behind her with a disapproving scowl, Seren could feel the feral demon within as it clawed and demanded freedom. For once she didn't try to restrain it. She would need it if she were to succeed in this.

Dressed in the red tunic she'd made for Kerrigan, which was covered by a black jerkin and black leather breeches, she pulled Caliburn from the wall and strapped the sword to her hips.

'Garafyn!' she called, summoning the gargoyle to her side. 'If you can hear me, then I would ask you for a favor on Kerrigan's behalf.'

'He won't come,' Blaise said. 'We'll have to steal your medallion back from Merlin to summon him.'

She snarled at him. 'We wouldn't have to steal it back if *someone*' – she gave him a pointed look – 'hadn't given it over to her.' She moved away from him. 'Garafyn!'

She was just about to believe Blaise when the air around her stirred.

Two seconds later, Garafyn and Anir appeared before her.

'What is your damage?' Garafyn asked irritably. 'Did it not occur to you that we might be occupied? You know, it is possible for even masonry to have some fun from time to time. God forbid.'

Seren frowned at his odd clothing. He wore some type of red and black form-fitting material, the likes of which she'd never seen before. Cocking her head, she reached to touch the shiny cloth. 'What is that?'

Anir answered. '*Star Trek* costume. We've finally found our niche – twentieth-century science fiction conventions. We not only blend, but we keep winning the costume competitions. Talk about getting booty . . . and I mean that in more ways than one.'

Seren gave him an arch look. Was that even English he spoke? Unwilling to waste time asking about it, Seren chose to ignore it.

'Why did you call us?' Garafyn asked.

'I need you. Kerrigan is in trouble and I need to return to Camelot to—'

'Whoa!' they said in unison.

Garafyn shook his head. 'You can forget it. I'm not ever returning there again. Ever . . . ever . . . ever.'

'Please,' she begged. 'Kerrigan needs you. *I* need you.'

Garafyn narrowed his eyes. 'And I don't care.'

'Aye, you do.'

Seren turned at the new voice to see Elaine nearing them. She'd met the woman only a time or two, but she knew from experience that Elaine was standoffish. She had an intensity that was sometimes hard for the men to take. She also expected only the best from people and tended to be a bit unforgiving.

'Greetings, Garafyn,' Elaine said in a cool tone as she joined their small group. She looked him up and down. 'My how you've changed.'

Garafyn curled his lip. 'Don't start on me, Elaine. A lot more than my appearance has changed. I no longer feel any kinship with you or the others.'

'Really?' Her voice was thick with sarcasm. 'I would never have guessed it, given how all of you turned on us.'

Garafyn rolled his eyes as he sneered at her. 'Yeah, *we* turned on *you* ...' He narrowed his gaze menacingly. 'Use your head, woman ... and I use that term loosely. Who's the friggin' gargoyle here and who isn't? Don't you think that if we turned on you, Morgen would have rewarded us with something more than this damned curse?'

Elaine's expression didn't change. 'Given that it's Morgen ... No.'

Anir scratched his head with one claw. 'She has a point there.'

'Shut up, Anir,' Garafyn snapped.

'Sorry, but she does.'

'And I don't care,' Seren said between clenched teeth as she added her own glare to theirs. 'Right now, the only thing that matters to me is the fact that Kerrigan is suffering because he helped us. Now, who is decent and caring enough to help me rescue him?'

Garafyn let out a snide laugh. 'For the record, that's not particularly motivating to those of us who pride themselves on being indecent and indifferent. Just FYI.'

Seren clenched her fists and made a sound of disgust. 'I don't understand half of what you said, but I don't care. Give me your key to open a portal to Camelot and I'll go alone.'

'I don't—'

'Give me the key,' she said, letting her demon show.

'Wow,' Garafyn said at the sound of her demonic

voice. 'That's pretty damned scary. Good tone, and the red irises are a particularly nice effect.'

He held the medallion out to her.

Before she could take it, Blaise did.

Seren growled at him.

Blaise stared her down. 'Don't give that Kerrigan look to me, young lady. You don't know your way around Camelot. I do, and I'm not about to let you go alone.'

'I'm with you,' Elaine said, much to her surprise. Elaine didn't strike her as the type of woman to do something so foolish.

But in truth, Seren was glad not to be going alone.

They all looked at the gargoyles.

'Only four can go without warning Morgen,' Elaine reminded them.

Garafyn let out an agitated breath. 'I might as well be the idiot. This kind of noble stupidity is what got me cursed to begin with. Maybe I'll get lucky and Morgen will actually kill me this time.'

'I would argue,' Anir said, 'but I'm still young and that really attractive redhead at the *Star Trek* party was making eyes at me.' He clapped Garafyn on the back. 'I've too much to live for. Good luck.'

'I really hate gargoyles,' Garafyn growled. He turned toward Seren. 'All right, princess. Let's go die.'

'Let's not,' Elaine said. 'But if we do get into trouble, I say we sacrifice the gargoyle.'

Seren thought Garafyn might have made a face at her, but with a gargoyle one was never sure if it was a face or just his natural countenance.

Blaise held his hand out. The medallion was wrapped around it. Seren covered his hand with hers, then Elaine and finally Garafyn, who still looked as if he didn't really want to do this.

They faded from Avalon, then appeared in a small, empty room in Camelot.

Elaine grimaced at the black and gray color scheme of the spartan place. There were no chairs or bed. It looked like an empty storage room.

'First time back?' Garafyn asked Elaine.

She nodded. 'Can't say I like what Morgen's done to the place.'

'Can't say I like what Morgen did with my face, either . . .'

For the first time, Seren saw pity in Elaine's eyes as she looked at Garafyn. 'I don't know,' Elaine said charitably. 'You look pretty good as far as gargoyles go.'

'Yeah, right. I make a pass at you . . .'

'And I start chiseling off vital parts of your anatomy.'

'Exactly.'

Lifting the cowl of his black tunic, Blaise cracked open the door to look out into the hallway. 'All right, children,' he whispered over his shoulder. 'Let's stay together and try to remain inconspicious.'

Seren lifted the cowl to her cloak at the same time Elaine did. They made sure to keep their faces lowered and hidden by the hood.

They looked at Garafyn, who stared back unblinkingly. He'd dissolved his clothes so that now all he wore was a small gray loincloth. 'What?'

'Are you going to walk around like that?' Elaine asked.

'Oh yeah, like a gargoyle in a cloak wouldn't stand out in this place. Trust me, no one's going to look at me. Hell, Morgen can't even tell us apart.' As if to prove his point, he ambled out of the room first. 'Besides, I'm not walking around in an ensign's *Star*

Trek uniform. Those guys always get killed.'

Shaking her head at the surly beast, Seren followed with Elaine and Blaise just behind her.

The castle was eerily quiet. No one was about. It was as if the entire place had been deserted for some reason.

'Is this normal?' Elaine asked.

Garafyn snorted. 'The creepy factor, aye. The quiet part, no.' He glanced about nervously. 'Where is everyone?'

No sooner had he spoken than a loud roar went up at the end of the hallway.

'Something's happening in the great hall.' Blaise led them toward the noise. When they reached the end of the hallway, he opened the large oak door a tiny degree before he squeezed through it.

One by one, they followed suit until they were all inside the great hall where they could see a large crowd, staring at the center of the room.

Seren couldn't see much due to her short height and the fact that she didn't dare lift her head for fear of losing her cowl. But as they made their way through the crowd, she realized that she could probably be naked and no one would notice her. Everyone's attention was focused on whatever was happening in the center area.

'What's going on?' she whispered to Blaise.

'I'm not sure.' He continued to move through the mass that was busy shouting unintelligible words.

All of a sudden, Blaise stopped short. Seren collided with him. She looked up to see his face drained of color while he stared over the heads of the onlookers.

Standing up on her tiptoes, she turned to see what held him captivated and felt her own heart sink at what she saw.

At first she didn't recognize the body on the floor. Wearing only a pair of ragged and torn black breeches, the poor soul had been beaten and whipped until he barely appeared human. Swollen welts and bruises distorted every part of him. But as he lifted his head, she recognized Kerrigan even though both of his eyes appeared to be swollen shut.

Even Elaine cursed under her breath.

'Get up!' Morgen shouted at him before she kicked him in the ribs. 'Fight, you worthless dog.'

Seren saw red as her powers flowed through her. Infuriated, she pushed her way through the crowd, even though Blaise was trying to hold her back.

Unable to take it, she paused at the edge of the crowd with Blaise still attempting to pull her back out of sight. She shrugged off his grip and pushed him away.

Morgen shook her head at the sight of Kerrigan before she turned away from him and manifested a sword in her hand. 'Masden?' she said to one of her demon knights. 'Care to be the once and future king?'

With an evil laugh, he took the sword from Morgen's hand.

Kerrigan forced himself to his feet even though his arm was broken from Maddor's 'gentle' touch. Every part of his body ached, but he refused to die on the ground like a beggar. Morgen might have returned him to the life of a slave, but he wasn't going to die like one.

He held his broken arm to his side as he faced the knight who'd once been human. Now there was no humanity to be found in the beast that faced him. Masden was all too eager to end his life.

Morgen sneered at Kerrigan. 'Look, the slave is

trying to be kingly.' She moved to stand before him. 'But once rubbish, always rubbish.'

Kerrigan snarled at her. 'Fuck you.'

She backhanded him.

Kerrigan laughed at the blow he couldn't even feel over the rest of the pain of his body.

Hissing, Morgen drew back and turned to face Masden. 'Kill him.'

Kerrigan held his ground as the man came forward with his sword raised. If he had a sword, he'd at least make the bastard pay somewhat for his death. As it was, there was nothing he could do except run, and he wasn't about to give Morgen and the others the satisfaction of laughing at his cowardice.

There for a time he had been a king. He would die with his honor intact.

He braced himself for the fatal sword strike.

Just as Masden reached him, Kerrigan saw a flash an instant before the killing blow was deflected from his body. Out of nowhere, another figure wrapped in a black cloak appeared with a sword.

With the skill of a trained knight, the small form twisted around and forced Masden back with attack after attack.

Who would dare defend him?

Stunned, Kerrigan couldn't understand what was happening until the cowl fell back from the combatant and he saw the long blond braid. Saw the determined face of what to him was the most beautiful woman in the world. Love and joy welled up inside him as he looked upon the impossible.

'Seren?'

She didn't respond as she drove the knight back toward Morgen, who was now laughing.

'Oh, this is rich,' Morgen snarled. 'Look what has

returned of her own free will to our company.' Her eyes were light with triumph. 'Big mistake, little girl. *Big* mistake.'

With one fell swing, Seren killed her challenger, then turned on Morgen with a glare. 'Shut up, bitch. I've had enough of you.'

Morgen gaped an instant before she shrieked. Throwing her hands out, she shot a blast at Seren, which his little mouse deflected without effort. The blast headed into the wall, above the hearth, where it left a large, black, smoldering hole.

That only increased Morgen's anger.

One minute she was before Seren and in the next, she was directly behind Kerrigan.

Seren turned about to see where Morgen had gone. Her breath caught in her throat as she saw the dagger in Morgen's hand.

'You want him, whore? You can have him . . . dead.' Quicker than anyone could move, Morgen cut his throat and shoved him away from her.

Kerrigan fell straight to the floor.

Everything seemed to slow down as Seren flashed herself to Kerrigan's side. He lay on the floor with one hand against the vicious cut on his neck that had come close to decapitating him as blood rushed from the wound, over his hand.

'God's mercy,' she whispered as tears filled her eyes. 'Nay!'

Morgen reached for her. The instant she did, Seren threw the evil queen back against the wall as the demon took over her body entirely. There was nothing human left inside. Nothing even humane.

A wave burst through the room, knocking everyone, even Morgen, off their feet.

Her heart breaking, Seren fell to her knees beside

Kerrigan, whose face was pale.

'Kerrigan,' she whispered, her voice its normal tone.

He couldn't speak from the damage done to his throat. He reached his bloodied hand toward her face, then fell back as his eyes turned dull.

Kerrigan was dead.

Seren screamed out in pain as her grief shook her to the core of her soul. The demon cried out in anger, demanding vengeance. And the two coalesced into a swirling maelstrom reminiscent of a tornado as it ripped through the room. Demons, gargoyles, and Adoni went flying.

'Seren! Stop!' She recognized Blaise's voice, but it did nothing to lessen her pain or her resolve.

Throwing her head back, Seren called out to the darkest powers for something she knew she had no right to ask.

Yet it was something she had to do.

She would not let Morgen win. Not this time. The bitch had done enough harm in her lifetime. For once the good side would win.

Her eyes rolled back in her head as ancient, forbidden power roiled through her. Primordial and cold, it chilled her through and through as she gathered Kerrigan into her arms and placed Caliburn over him.

'*Atiera gara tuawaha ethra verus tiera.*' She didn't know where the words or power came from, but she whispered them over and over again as dragon's breath swept through the room and covered them all.

She cupped Kerrigan's cold cheek in her hand. 'In the whisper of the ancient stone and in the mist that belongs to the dragons, my breath is your breath. My heart is your heart and my life is your life.'

With those words spoken, she leaned over him and

gently placed her lips to his. As soon as they touched, she felt the tremor of power pass from her to Kerrigan's lifeless body.

With her tears falling down her cheeks, she pulled back expectantly.

Only to be disappointed as nothing happened.

'Nay!' she screamed as more power surged through her. She wanted him back.

Then slowly ... painfully slowly, she watched as Kerrigan's lips returned to their normal hue. The color continued on from his mouth, over the rest of him, healing each injury as it passed until he was once again the handsome man who had given her his life.

Still, he didn't move.

'Kerrigan?' she choked, cupping his face in both of her hands. 'Come back to me.'

Suddenly, he drew a deep breath before he opened his eyes to look up at her. Instead of their normal black hue, they were a bright, crystal blue – the same color they had been when he was human.

Seren choked on her happiness as she let out a small cry. Thunder and lightning crackled and boomed through the room. Thrilled that he was alive, she threw herself over him and held him tight.

Kerrigan was dazed. He couldn't move for several heartbeats as he held Seren in his arms. Over and over he saw in his mind Morgen killing him.

He felt the stinging bite of the knife. ...

But there was no pain in him now. He could feel nothing more than Seren holding him close. Feel her hot tears on his skin as his love for her coursed through him.

Stunned, he looked about the hall that was no longer in black and gray. There was color now, along with lightning.

'Little mouse?'

She pulled back to kiss him soundly. He'd never tasted anything better than her lips. Her passion set fire to him as she pulled back with a delighted laugh.

And it was then he knew he wasn't what he'd been before. He felt hungry, and not just for the woman who'd saved him. He wanted food. Real food.

He was human again . . .

But he could still feel his Merlin's powers. They hadn't been taken from him.

'You're warm,' Seren said as she laid her hand to his lips. A slow smile spread across her face.

Before he could respond, the color faded from the room as a shriek rang out.

Morgen came to her feet, her eyes glowing red. 'Do you think you can compete with me?'

Manifesting his armor back onto his body, Kerrigan came to his feet barely before Morgen began raining lightning on top of them. He deflected her blows.

To his complete shock, Elaine jumped out of the crowd to fire two arrows at Morgen, who caught them in her hand before she tossed them back at Elaine. Elaine dodged one, but just as the other was about to embed itself in her heart, a blast averted it harmlessly away.

Her features startled, Elaine looked to see Kerrigan holding the arrow. She inclined her head to him in gratitude.

Kerrigan dropped the arrow to the floor as he faced the queen of the fey. 'You can't defeat us, Morgen,' he said between clenched teeth.

'Oh, but I can. The minute the three of you try to leave here . . . you're mine. I'll be able to kill you.'

Seren sent a blast toward Morgen. She deflected it.

'How do we end this?' Seren asked him.

It was Morgen who answered. 'We end this when you drop that brat, then I will have the power I need to kill you both.'

'She's right,' Kerrigan said under his breath.

Seren looked up at Kerrigan. 'Is there really nothing we can do?'

'I'm working on it, but I haven't any unique ideas at the moment.'

Suddenly a loud, thunderous clap started. It sounded like a thousand wings flapping. The shutters flew open as gargoyle after gargoyle flew into the room to circle it.

Kerrigan and Seren braced themselves to fight as Blaise and Elaine joined them. Back to back they stood, prepared to defend against the stone invaders.

However, they didn't attack. Instead the gargoyles surrounded Morgen, who blasted three of them to gravel before she was overwhelmed by them.

'What are you doing?' she screamed.

'We are protecting you, my queen.'

Seren gaped at the sound of Garafyn's voice. He flew away from Morgen to land beside them. Winking at her, he looked back at his men. 'Whatever you do, legion, don't let anyone blast Morgen. You must protect our queen from the evil Lords of Avalon. Help her.'

Morgen cursed. 'Get away from me. Damn you! Off,' she screamed out. 'Adoni, get the gargoyles off me.'

Her court ran to help their queen.

Garafyn gathered their group together. 'Okay, Blaise, now would be a damned good time to get us out of here before the Adoni attack us, too.'

'What about the other gargoyles?' Elaine asked.

'Those are the real gargoyles. My legion isn't here.

I'm not that vicious. Let her destroy the boxes of rocks. But we gotta go. C'mon, there's only two more weeks left on my Greyhound pass. I gots to get out of here.'

The Adoni and Morgen were blasting through the gargoyles.

'Maddor!' Morgen screamed. 'Grab the Merlin.'

Seren looked up as the mandrake moved toward them with determined strides.

She felt his hand on her arm, pulling at her . . .

Blaise held his hand out and again they laid theirs over his before they vanished.

For a second, Seren was relieved, until she realized that Maddor had traveled through the portal with them. He grabbed her about the waist and pulled her away from the others.

Kerrigan launched himself at the mandrake, knocking him away from her.

Maddor crouched low as if he were about to attack.

Before he had the chance, Kerrigan blasted him. Maddor turned with a hiss as if to attack, but before he could, Kerrigan blasted him again.

Seren gaped as the mandrake vanished. 'Did you kill him?'

'Nay. I gave him something much worse than that. I sent him back to Camelot.'

Elaine rubbed her neck as if she had an ache in it. 'That is truly the worst punishment I can think of.'

'You are so unimaginative,' Garafyn said snidely.

Elaine curled her lip at him. 'Shut up before I send *you* back there.'

Garafyn snatched his medallion from Blaise's hand. 'G'head. I gots a key, babe.'

While the two of them fought, Seren walked into Kerrigan's arms and threw her arms around his neck.

Kerrigan couldn't breathe as the scent of her hair filled his head and he finally held her again. Closing his eyes, he reveled in the sensation of her body nestled against his.

But before he could get too comfortable, a battalion of knights on horseback came riding up in front of them. The standard of Avalon rippled in the breeze as the horses snorted and pranced in expectation of battle.

Kerrigan let go of Seren. He put himself between her and the others as he prepared himself for the coming fight.

'What is the meaning of this?' Seren asked from behind him.

Agravain rode his horse forward. 'Kerrigan is a threat to all of us.'

Seren opened her mouth to refute him, but before she could speak, Elaine moved to stand beside Agravain. 'And so's your incompetent brother. Yet we let him live ... and in the castle, no less.'

Agravain grimaced at her. 'You would side with our enemy?'

Elaine looked at Kerrigan before she turned back toward Agravain. 'He saved my life from Morgen and I saw how much he suffered to protect Seren. You throw him out and I go with him.'

'As do I,' Seren said.

Blaise moved to stand by their side. 'And I.'

Garafyn snorted. 'Like I have any choice, huh?'

Agravain looked disgusted, but before he could argue, Merlin appeared between their two groups. Without paying any attention to the Lords of Avalon, she turned toward Seren and Kerrigan.

Kerrigan was prepared to battle as the Penmerlin approached him. But her face remained open and friendly.

She extended her hand out to him. 'Welcome home, Kerrigan.'

He looked about suspiciously, unable to believe that they would let bygones be bygones. There was too much history between them. 'Is this a trick?'

'Nay. I would never play with anyone so cruelly. I'm not Morgen.'

Agravain made a sound of detestation. 'You're not just going to forgive him for all he's done to us over the centuries, are you, Merlin?'

Merlin gave Agravain a pointed stare over her shoulder. 'We've all made mistakes, haven't we?'

Agravain looked away shamefaced, making Seren wonder what he'd done in the past.

Merlin offered Kerrigan a kind smile. 'I somehow think that Kerrigan has had enough of Morgen's rule.'

Kerrigan finally took her hand. 'You've no idea.'

She clasped his hand in both of hers. 'Then welcome to Avalon. I'm sure Seren will be most delighted to show you to your rooms.'

Seren grinned wickedly at the prospect. 'Absolutely.'

Merlin inclined her head to them, before she turned toward the castle. She paused beside the army and shook her head. 'Go home, guys.'

Elaine stepped forward and offered her hand to Kerrigan. 'Thank you for what you did.'

'Anytime.'

Smiling, Elaine left them and hurried after Merlin while the rest of the knights broke rank and followed suit. All but Agravain, who continued to glare at Kerrigan as he sat on the back of his white horse.

'I still don't trust you, demon. I'll be keeping my eye out for you.'

As he turned to join the others, Kerrigan let fly a bolt from his hand to knock Agravain off his horse.

Agravain shot up and pulled his sword out.

'What?' Kerrigan asked in feigned innocence.

'You attacked me,' Agravain sputtered as he rose from the beach with sand coating his entire body and face.

'I didn't do anything. You said you were going to watch me. I can't be held accountable for what nature does.'

'You lying—'

'Vain!' Elaine shouted. 'Get over here with the rest of us, or I'm going to embarrass you by beating you before your friends.'

If looks could kill, Kerrigan would have been sliced in twain by Agravain's glare.

For an instant, Seren thought he'd attack anyway. But after three heartbeats, he sheathed his sword, dusted the sand from his body, then remounted his horse.

Seren shook her head at Kerrigan. 'I can't believe you did that.'

'Me? I can't believe the lot of you came back for me.'

'Why not?' Blaise asked. 'After all, we're family.'

Kerrigan couldn't speak as unnamed emotions tore through him.

Family. It was something he'd never thought to have.

'Yeah, well, while this is getting really mushy, the stone feels the deep need to cut out. I'm going to find Anir and return to our con. There's a full moon tonight, which means Mr. Rock here gets to be human for a couple of hours, and I've got a date with the newly crowned Miss Klingon Empire.' He wagged his eyebrows at them.

Seren shook her head as Garafyn took flight. 'I only understand about ten percent of what he says.'

'You're not the only one,' Kerrigan said as he offered her a charming grin.

Blaise held his arm out to Kerrigan. 'Welcome back, my friend.'

Kerrigan shook his arm. 'Thank you, Blaise.'

He inclined his head. 'You two have some catching up to do. I'll see you later.'

Seren watched as he faded away and left them alone.

Kerrigan kissed her gently. 'I can't believe this is real. I keep expecting to wake up and find Morgen over me again.'

'There's no Morgen here. But I . . . I have my own torture for you, my lord.'

He looked baffled by her words. 'What?'

'You, evil man, made me a promise that you have yet to fulfill.'

He actually looked worried by that. 'And that is?'

'To give my baby a name.'

Relief spread across his face as Kerrigan took her hand into his and placed a gentle kiss to her palm. 'That is one promise I fully intend to keep.'

'Good, because I want to make an honest man of you.'

He laughed at that. 'I wouldn't go quite that far, Lady Mouse. There's only so much changing a man can do.'

'We shall see, my lord. We shall see.'

Epilogue

Four years later

Seren sat quietly in her room in front of her loom, nursing her infant son as he cooed and suckled. Her heart pounding with love for him, she gently brushed at his mop of dark hair. She so loved the quiet times alone with the baby. She treasured those as much as she treasured the quiet times alone with her husband.

A smile curled her lips as she thought about Kerrigan, and a thick warmness consumed her. Even after four years, she still loved him more than her own life.

'You look just like your father,' she whispered as her baby suckled her. At two months in age, Liam held the same dark hair and light blue eyes. Aye, he would be a strong knight one day. She could just imagine how handsome he would be . . .

Suddenly, there was a flash in front of her.

Frowning, she looked up to see Kerrigan sitting on the floor with Alethea held in his lap. The two of them looked as if they were up to some great mischief. As was typical, Kerrigan had their daughter dressed as a squire in tunic and hose, while tendrils of her dark hair had come free of their braids.

Aggravation filled her as they laughed together. 'What have you two done now?'

Sobering, they both gave her an innocent stare that she knew belied their actions.

Her daughter actually managed to look a tiny bit contrite. 'Alethea did nothing, Mommy.'

But by the gleam in Kerrigan's eyes, she knew he couldn't say the same.

And then she heard it. The heavy footfalls in the hallway. Seren had barely managed to cover herself and her son before the door was thrown open.

Looking toward the disturbance, she burst into laughter.

Agravain stood in the doorway with a furious glower on his face. That wasn't so bad. It was the horns on his head and green hair and beard that made him look so fearsome.

'This is not funny,' he snarled. 'Fix me back.'

Seren forced herself to sober. 'Alethea, what has mommy told you about practicing your magic on Uncle Agravain?'

She gave her a sweet, innocent stare. 'But Daddy said it would make Uncle Aggie look better. Doesn't he look even more handsome now?'

Agravain let out a deep, guttural growl.

Seren cleared her throat to keep from laughing again. 'I think Uncle Aggie would appreciate it if you would turn him back into the way he was.'

'Oh,' Alethea said innocently. 'Very well.' She pointed her tiny finger at him. The horns quickly melted back into his hair which then returned to blond.

'Thank you,' Agravain said to Seren. He cast a feral glare at Kerrigan before he turned to leave.

And as he was walking out the door, she saw

Kerrigan gesture toward him.

Two seconds later, just as Agravain was closing the door, a long, forked tail sprouted from his rear.

Alethea burst out laughing as she jumped up and down in Kerrigan's lap and clapped.

Seren shook her head at them. 'What am I to do with the two of you? 'Tis a wonder Agravain hasn't killed you.'

Kerrigan's warm laughter filled her ears. 'I told you long ago, my love, that there was only so much changing I could do.'

Aye, and he'd been right. The man was still evil to the marrow of his bones, and both she and Merlin had their hands full trying to curb his demon form.

Kerrigan lifted Alethea off his lap before he came over to her. He pulled the blanket back so that he could lean over and kiss Liam on the head. Liam let go of her to coo at his father, and she saw the heat that came into Kerrigan's eyes as he saw her bared breast.

Embarrassed, Seren covered herself while her daughter crawled under the bed to fetch her box of dolls.

Kerrigan gently nuzzled her cheek with his face. 'You are ever beautiful, my mouse.'

'And you are ever evil.'

He winked playfully. 'Aye, I am and I enjoy it so.' Then his face turned darkly earnest. 'But not nearly as much as I enjoy *you*. I love you, my Seren.'

'And I love you.'

Overwhelmed by her emotions, she leaned forward to kiss him, only to have their embrace broken by a shrill shout.

'Kerrigan, you evil bastard!'

Seren pulled back with a laugh. 'I think Agravain found his tail.'

His eyes turned devilish before they flashed to black. 'That's all right. It's what he won't be finding next that'll have him even more furious.'

Seren cringed for the poor unsuspecting knight. But at least her life was never boring. Grateful for that, she kissed him again and knew that no matter what, they would always be together.

The Stone of Taranis

Cornwall, 1114

Arador leaned against the back thatched wall of the old church with a smug smile on his face, as he and his brethren of thieves compared their daily spoils. It was an evening ritual they'd been practicing for the last two years. Every night, the four of them would meet here to see which of them had stolen the most money.

So far no one had ever beaten him.

And they never would. When it came to taking from others, he was the best.

Simeon scowled as he counted the last of Martin's stolen coins. His lip curling, he tossed the purse back at Martin. 'Arador wins ... again.'

They all cursed. All except Arador, who laughed. 'Pay up, good lads. I've no time to waste with you.'

Simeon's disgusted look intensified as he slapped two silver marks into Arador's hand. 'How do you do it?'

Arador held his arms out to show them his elegant clothes. 'I look noble so they let me near them. You dress as a peasant, and the instant you draw close, the nobles clutch their purses.'

Martin spat on the ground before he handed his

money over. 'Bah! You ever let them nobles catch you masquerading as one of them and you'll be whipped like the dog you are. Then they'll slit your nostrils and ruin that pretty face of yours for good.'

Unperturbed, he tucked Martin's coins into his purse. 'They have to catch me first, and Lucifer will return to grace before that day comes.'

'You are a demon bastard,' Martin muttered as he moved away.

Arador hid the anger and pain those words evoked. What Martin didn't know was just how right he was. He was the son of a demon. Hell-spawned and cast out into this world to make his own way.

Hamm was the last to draw near. 'You have an unholy gift,' he whispered before he handed over his bet.

As soon as the coins touched his hand, Arador felt something hot singe his palm. Hissing in pain, he looked down to see not a silver mark, but rather a palm-sized stone. He wanted to let it go and yet he couldn't bring himself to do so.

The stone glowed red, illuminating them all. Simeon crossed himself an instant before he and Martin ran off. Hamm stayed and stared at him in disbelief.

'What the devil is this?' Arador asked, holding his burned palm out toward him.

'The stone I use to sharpen me dagger. I didn't mean to give it to you.'

Arador barely heard those words as a red haze descended over his eyesight. He felt a foreign power sweep through him. Wicked. Scalding. Consuming.

Hamm's face turned deadly pale. 'Jesus, Mary, and Joseph!' He stumbled away from him, then turned and ran as if the devil himself had materialized in the old churchyard.

Arador could barely breathe as he felt an unholy power surge through his body. From both his mother and his father, he'd been gifted with the power of sorcery, but whatever this was, it made a mockery of his paltry abilities. This was unlike anything he'd ever known.

Suddenly, he heard a light, feminine laugh echoing around him. Arador turned around, trying to find the source of it.

He found nothing.

At least not until a bright flash of light almost blinded him. A heartbeat later, a beautiful blond goddess appeared to his right. Dressed in red, she was stunning, and she gifted him with a lascivious smile as she approached him.

'What have we here?' she asked, covering the stone in his hand with hers. She lifted his hand up to kiss his fingers as she continued to smile at him. 'My, my, you are a handsome one, aren't you? More so than even the last Kerrigan was . . .'

'Kerrigan?'

Before she could answer, a knight appeared at the corner of the church.

'Back away from him, Morgen.'

The woman let out a heavy sigh. 'Must we always go through this, Agravain?' She looked at the knight with a droll stare. 'I promise you, this one is mine.'

'And how do you know that?'

Her smile returned. 'Tell the good knight, Arador, who fathered you.'

'How do you know my name?'

She laughed again. 'I know all about you, my boy. I've been waiting a lifetime for you to find that stone in your hand. Now be a good lad and give us the name of your father.'

'Taraka.'

The knight's face paled even more than Hamm's had. 'The demon lord?'

'Aye,' Morgen said as she wrapped her arms around Arador. 'You took Kerrigan from my side. So be it. Now Damé Fortune has sent me a far better replacement. Meet the new king of Camelot, and may your God have mercy on you, Agravain. I can assure you that we won't.'

The Legend

In a world of magic and betrayal, one king rose to unite a land divided and to bring unto his people a time of unprecedented peace. A time when might no longer made right. When one man with a dream created a world of chivalry and honor.

Guided by his Merlin, this man's destiny was to be the Pendragon – High King of Power. But Arthur was a man who had many enemies, and none of them greater than his own sister, Morgen. Queen of the fey, she was ruled by her own jealousies and by her desire to rule as Pendragon in her brother's stead.

It is a story that has been told for centuries. The rise and fall of the great King Arthur, the betrayal that led to the destruction of the Round Table.

But what happened the day after the battle of Camlann? Arthur is mortally wounded and taken to the isle of Avalon. The sacred objects of Camelot that gave him his power have been scattered to protect them from evil. The Round Table is fractured. The good guys have retreated to Avalon to serve their fallen king and the surviving Penmerlin, who came forward after Arthur's Merlin mysteriously vanished.

Camelot has now fallen into the hands of Morgen

and her comrades. No longer the place of peace and prosperity, it is now the land of the unholy. Demons, mandrakes, and darklings make up the brotherhood of the new table, and another Pendragon has stepped forward to take Arthur's place.

Once human, he is now something else entirely. A demon with one single mission: to reunite the Round Table and to claim the sacred objects. With those under his control, there will be nothing to stop him from making the world into whatever he chooses.

The only hope mankind has is those who still remain from Arthur's company. No longer the knights of the Round Table, they are now the Lords of Avalon. And they will do whatever is necessary to stop the Pendragon from succeeding.

The line between good and evil has become blurred. It is a realm of chaos and of champions. Of wizards and warriors who struggle to right the balance that was upset when one man put his trust into the wrong person.

Welcome to a realm that exists out of time. Welcome to a world where nothing is ever as it seems. It's a battle that ranges from the Dark Age moors of Arthur well into the future, where the one true king and Mordred may one day fight again.

Theirs is a world without boundary. A place without borders. But in this power struggle, there can only be one winner . . .

And winning has never been more fun.

The Thirteen Sacred Objects

These were the sacred objects that the Penmerlin Emrys, entrusted to Arthur Pendragon so that he could rule the land peacefully without contestation. But once Camelot fell to evil and the king vanished, the new Penmerlin entrusted the sacred objects into the hands of their Waremerlins. They were scattered and hidden in the realm of man and of fey so that they would never fall into the hands of evil.

It is now a race to reclaim and reunite the lost objects.

1. **Excalibur**
   Sword created by the fey for good. The one who wields it cannot be killed, nor can he bleed so long as he holds the scabbard that sheaths it.

2. **Hamper of Garanhir**
   Created in order to feed the Pendragon's army while at war. Put in food for one, and out will appear food for one hundred.

3. **Horn of Bran**
   Given as a companion for the hamper, this horn is

a never–ending cup that will provide wine and water for any to drink from it.

4. **Saddle of Morrigan**
A gift to the Penmerlin from the goddess Morrigan, this will enable a person to go instantly wherever he desires. It was created so that the Pendragon would be able to oversee his kingdom with ease. No distance or time is too great. It can move a person from one continent to another or from one time period to another.

5. **Halter of Epona**
Given by the goddess Epona, the halter, if hung on a bedpost at night, will grant the one who possesses it whatever horse he desires in the morning.

6. **Loom of Caswallan**
A gift from the war god. Any cloth produced from this loom will be stronger than any armor forged by a mortal's hand. No mortal weapon will ever be able to penetrate the cloth.

7. **Round Table**
Table of power that was created by the Penmerlin. When all people are seated and the objects are in place, it is the ultimate in power. Whoever rules the table rules the earth.

8. **Stone of Taranis**
A gift from the god of thunder. Should a knight sharpen his sword with this stone, it will coat the blade with a poison so potent that even a tiny scratch from the blade will bring instant death.

9. **Mantle of Arthur**
A gift from the Penmerlin, this will enable the wearer to become invisible to everyone around him.

10. **Orb of Sirona**
Created by the goddess of astronomy, this will enable the person who holds it in his hand to see clearly on even the darkest night.

11. **Shield of Dagda**
Whoever holds the shield of Dagda will be possessed of superhuman strength, and so long as the shield is held in place, he cannot be wounded.

12. **Caliburn**
A sword of the fey, this is the evil sword that balances out Excalibur. It is said that this one sword carries even more power and that it can destroy the other sacred objects.

13. **Holy Grail**
No one is quite sure what it is or where it came from. It is the greatest object of all for it can bring the dead back to life.

Vocabulary

Adoni—a beautiful race of elflike creatures. They are tall and slender and capable of complete cruelty.

Grayling—as ugly as the Adoni are beautiful, they are essentially servants in Camelot.

Mandrake—a race of beings who have the ability to become dragons or human. They have magical abilities, but are currently enslaved as a race to Morgen.

Merlin—magical advisor.

Miren—a magical being who can sing a song so beautiful that it will kill whoever hears it.

Mods—minions of death. Interesting creatures who will be around in many future tales.

Pendragon—the High King of Camelot.

Penmerlin—the High Merlin of Camelot.

Sharoc—shadow fey.

Stone Legion—cursed race, the Stone Legion is under the command of Garafyn. By daylight, they are ugly gargoyles who are forced to sit as stone (they can only move if they are commanded by the one who bears their emblem), but at night, they can move about freely, and under the light of a full moon, they can again take the form of handsome warriors and knights – but only so long as the full moon touches them. Should they leave its light, they will immediately return to their gargoyle state. There are those who say there may be a way yet to lift their curse, but so far all those who have tried have met with failure and death.

Terre derrière le voile—land behind the veil. A term for both Avalon and Camelot since they exist outside of time and place.

Val Sans Retour—Valley of no return. An area outside Camelot where the damned wander in eternal misery.

Waremerlin—term for any Merlin.

Also available in the thrilling Lords of Avalon *series, available now from Piatkus Books:*

KNIGHTS OF DARKNESS

In a world of magic and betrayal, one king rose to unite a land divided and to bring unto his people a time of unprecedented peace. But the new king of Camelot wears no shining armour: Arthur and his knights have fallen and a new king rules . . .

For countless centuries Varian du Fey has been the assassin for the infamous Merlin. However, because of his heritage, Varian has never been truly accepted as one of the Knights of Avalon. Lancelot may have been his father, but his mother is one of Morgen le Fey's closest allies, and both she and Morgen are keen for Varian to take his rightful place in the conflict between good and evil . . .

Merewyn's beauty has brought her heartache so she has traded her loveliness and ended up an old hag doomed to be a servant at Camelot for eternity. Varian's devious mother promises Merewyn her beauty and her freedom back if she seduces Varian to the dark side and forces him to join her Circle of the Damned . . .

Praise for Sherrilyn Kenyon:

'Kenyon gives readers scrumptious heroes . . . [and] creates a world full of depth and intelligent details . . . and gives her stories an underpinning and a foundation in authenticity without sacrificing the breathless pace of her plots – no small feat!' *Romantic Times*